The Golden Door

Also by Tom Milton
Sara's Laughter
A Shower of Roses
Infamy
All the Flowers
The Admiral's Daughter
No Way to Peace

The Golden Door

Tom Milton

NEPPERHAN PRESS, LLC
YONKERS, NY

Copyright © Tom Milton, 2012

All rights reserved. No part of this book may be reproduced or transmitted in any form or by any means, electronic or mechanical, including photocopying, recording, or by any information storage and retrieval system, without written permission from the author, except for the inclusion of brief quotations in a review.

Published by Nepperhan Press, LLC
P.O. Box 1448, Yonkers, NY 10702
nepperhan@optonline.net
nepperhan.com

PUBLISHER'S NOTE

This is a work of fiction. Names, characters, places, and incidents are the product of the author's imagination or are used fictitiously, and any resemblance to actual persons, living or dead, events, or locales is entirely coincidental.

Printed in the United States of America

Library of Congress Control Number: 2012910562

ISBN 978-0-9839412-1-7

Cover art was licensed from Publitek, Inc.

For Marie

Give me your tired, your poor,
Your huddled masses yearning to breathe free,
The wretched refuse of your teeming shore.
Send these, the homeless, tempest-tost to me,
I lift my lamp beside the golden door!

From the poem by Emma Lazarus on a plaque at the entrance to the pedestal of the Statue of Liberty

Do not mistreat or oppress aliens,
for you yourselves were once aliens in Egypt.

Exodus 22: 21

Harperville, 2011

ONE

"THIS LAW WILL protect the jobs of Americans in Alabama, in Maynard County, and in Harperville," their state representative, Douglas Fraser, declared with political flourish. He was talking about the immigration law that the state legislature had passed yesterday. "It'll also reduce government spending on services for illegal aliens, and that'll reduce your taxes."

Maya listened, sitting next to her father in the back row of the town hall meeting room. Since they were illegal aliens they kept a low profile and let others do the talking.

"Sir," Judson McBride said, rising from his chair. Judson had been her family's sponsor since her father came here from Mexico to pick peaches in his orchards. That was fifteen years ago, and Maya was three at the time. "I have a question."

"Go ahead," Fraser said, tilting up his chin.

Judson was a wiry man in his mid-sixties who kept in shape doing physical labor and teaching karate. He was wearing the usual black polo shirt and jeans, which looked better on him than they did on most guys Maya's age.

"As you know," Judson said in a relaxed voice, "I grow peaches, and so do a lot of other farmers in this county. In fact, Maynard County is known for its peaches."

"I always promote them," Fraser said.

"Well, you can promote them till the cows come home, but if we don't have anyone to pick them, our peaches are going to rot on the ground."

Fraser frowned and leaned forward on the table from which he was speaking. "Where did you get the idea that you won't have anyone to pick your peaches?"

"I got it from this law, which will make it a crime for illegal immigrants to work."

"It's already a crime under federal law for you to employ illegal aliens, so how will our law change things?"

"It'll change things by driving immigrants out of Alabama."

"If it does, then you can employ other people."

"What other people?" Judson asked. "Until these good people came along, it was hard to find people who were willing and able to pick peaches."

"The economy was strong then," Fraser argued. "It's weak now, and a lot of people are looking for work."

"They're not looking for work in peach orchards."

"If unemployed Americans don't have to compete with illegal aliens who'll work for nothing, they'll look for work in peach orchards."

"These good people don't work for nothing. We pay them well. That's not the problem."

"Then I don't rightly know what the problem is," Fraser said, looking for a person to support him. "Mr. Jennings, would you like to comment?"

"Yes, sir," a man said, rising. He was a big man, and the back of his neck was flaming red. "I want to commend you for passing this law. It's about time we did something about the people who come here illegally and live on welfare at our expense. They don't belong here."

"They weren't born here," another man said.

"And they don't speak English," another man said.

Maya had learned from street encounters not to respond to this kind of talk, but it still made her angry. She would have liked to stand up and say: "We belong here as much as you do. Your ancestors weren't born here. They came here from Europe and stole the land from the people who lived here. And some of us speak English better than you do."

Before Fraser could call on anyone else a young man whom she recognized as a policeman though he wasn't in uniform rose and said: "According to this law, if I stop a person for a traffic violation I'm supposed to determine his immigration status."

"That's what the law says," Fraser said carefully.

"Would I always have to do that?"

"No. Only if you had a reasonable suspicion that the person was an illegal alien."

"And what would be the basis for my suspicion?" the policeman asked in a way that suggested he knew the answer and wanted to get Fraser to say it.

"Your instinct as a cop," Fraser said, refusing to say it.

"Yeah. Sure," the policeman muttered, sitting down.

"I'm a landlord," a stout man said, rising. "As I understand it, this law will make it a crime for me to rent an apartment or a house to an illegal immigrant."

"It will if you *knowingly* rent to an illegal alien."

"But how would I know if the person was illegal?"

"You'd ask for his papers."

"If I did that," the stout man said, "I'd be doing the job of the immigration department."

"They need all the help they can get."

"If they didn't waste so much time harassing people who are hard working and law abiding, they'd have more time to catch the criminals."

"People who are living here illegally are criminals."

"They're not criminals. You politicians are criminals, and if we deported all of you, our country would be a better place."

"That's the best idea I've heard in a long time," a man in front said enthusiastically.

At that point Trevor Wilcox, the lawyer who did pro bono work for the Latino community, rose and said: "I've read this law, and in my opinion it not only violates the moral principles on which our country was founded, it also violates the Constitution. In both respects it's even worse than the Arizona law."

"You're entitled to your opinion," Fraser said. "But we're confident that the Supreme Court will uphold this law."

"If they do, it'll be like the Dred Scott decision."

Fraser shook his head. "That's a bad analogy. This law has nothing to do with those issues."

"It has everything to do with them."

"It does indeed," Father Philip said, rising. "Like the laws that institutionalized slavery and racial discrimination, this law goes against the teachings of Jesus. And I don't see how you as a professed Christian could have voted for it."

"With all due respect," Fraser said, "I don't remember Jesus making any pronouncements on the subject of illegal aliens."

"He didn't have to. He included them when He commanded us to love our neighbors."

"I love those people—when they're in Mexico."

"I do too," the man with the red neck said. "I love tequila and mariachis."

"That's not what loving your neighbors is about," Father Philip said. "It's about treating them as you would want to be treated."

"I treat them well in Mexico," the man said. "I even tip them, though they don't deserve it."

As if he realized that the benefits of the man's support had reached their limits, Fraser called on the high school principal. "Mr. Baldwin, do you have a comment?"

"I have a question," Baldwin said, rising. "As I understand it, this law will require schools to report the immigration status of students."

"That's correct," Fraser said. "But the law doesn't require the schools to report names, only the number of illegal aliens. The purpose is to collect data."

"That may be the ostensible purpose, but I suspect that the real purpose is to make illegal immigrants afraid to send their kids to school."

"I don't understand why they'd be afraid. The schools won't be reporting names."

"The parents won't know how the information is used, and they won't trust the process."

"If illegal aliens take their kids out of your school," Fraser said, "you won't have to spend money on them, and you'll have more money to spend on American kids."

"You expect me to believe that if we don't spend money on those kids we'll have it to spend on other kids?"

"Of course you will."

"I don't believe it. Last year we eliminated an administrative position in our district, and our budget was cut by the exact amount of the money we saved."

"Well, things were tight last year."

"I still don't believe it," Baldwin said. "And I don't accept the premise on which this law was based. It assumes that immigrants are bad for our economy. But according to a recent study, the benefits of immigrants outweigh the costs."

"What are the benefits?"

"Labor and taxes and consumer spending. The costs are services like schools and hospitals."

"It must have been a study of New York."

"It was a nationwide study."

"Then it came from one of those liberal think tanks," Fraser said. "I can tell you on good authority that in Alabama the costs of immigrants outweigh the benefits."

"Would you tell me your source of information?"

"I'll tell you after the meeting. These people don't want to get bogged down in details."

"The devil is in the details," Trevor said.

Looking as if he had had enough, Fraser asked: "Are there any more questions?"

"I have another question," Baldwin said. "This law prohibits illegal immigrants from attending public universities. Would you explain the purpose of that?"

"It's to save money for taxpayers."

On top of all the other ways that the law could affect Maya and her family, this provision could affect her future since she was planning to attend the University of Alabama in the fall. She had a full scholarship, awarded not only for her academic record but also for her athletic prowess. She had been the top scorer on the high school girls' soccer team, which had made it to the semifinals of the state tournament in Huntsville, and she was on the roster of the university women's soccer team that was going to start practice early in August.

"But what if they have their own money to pay the tuition?" Baldwin asked.

"That's not likely," Fraser said, "unless they're drug dealers."

"I object to that," Judson said, rising.

"I do too," Trevor and Father Philip said, rising together.

"Well, how else would those people get that kind of money?" Fraser asked lamely.

"By working," Judson told him point blank. "You should try it sometime."

While Fraser was caught at a loss for words, Judson and Trevor and Father Philip headed for the aisle, effectively adjourning the meeting.

As they left the town hall Maya and her father tried to blend in with the crowd, which wasn't easy since except for a few black people everyone else was white. Not wanting to be overheard, they walked in silence until they came to where Judson, Trevor, and Father Philip had stopped on the sidewalk.

"We were trying to figure out," Judson told them, "how the politicians could have passed this law when most people don't support it."

"Most of the people who attended that meeting don't support it," Trevor said, "but what about the other people?"

"You mean the people who support this law had a reason not to attend the meeting?"

"Yes. They did. They don't want to be seen as racists."

"So are we the minority?"

"It looks like we are."

"The churches are against this law," Father Philip told them.

"The leaders of the churches are against it," Trevor said, "but what about the congregations?"

"I believe our congregations will follow us."

"I was in high school," Judson said, "when they put Martin

Luther King in the Birmingham jail. If you recall, his letter from jail was addressed to the clergy, who thought he'd gone too far in taking direct action. I hope the church leaders are mindful of the clergy's failure to join him."

"They're mindful of it," Father Philip said. "I have letters from more than a thousand churches that I'm going to send to the governor. I'd like to mail them on Monday, and I could use some help tomorrow stuffing envelopes."

"I'll help you, father," Maya said.

"Bless you. Could you come to the church around noon?"

"Sure." She was going to Judson's farm in the morning for a lesson in karate.

"If you need more help," Judson offered, "I could join y'all later. I have some errands to do in town."

"Thanks. I'll have enough help with Maya."

Maya and her father said goodnight and continued walking on Main Street. The meeting had started at seven, and it was now after nine, so the town was quiet. The only two businesses still open were the diner and the laundromat.

"Cómo te sientes?" her father asked, reverting to the language they used in the family.

"Me siento mal," Maya said glumly. "Those men said we don't belong here."

"They weren't speaking for most people."

"Was the state representative speaking for most people?"

"I don't believe he was. I believe he was speaking for people like those men."

"Then why did the legislature pass this law?"

"I think it was influenced by people like those men."

"But it's supposed to do what most people want."

"It's supposed to, but I don't believe it did. You heard what most people at that meeting said about the law."

"I did. But I also heard what Trevor said about the people who didn't attend."

"Well, he's a lawyer. He always sees the negative side."

Her father always saw the positive side, to a point where it became a matter of conflict between him and her mother. Maya wanted to share her father's optimism, but at times she had trouble seeing the world as he saw it. Based on her experience, she said: "There could be a lot of people like those men who want this law."

"There could be," her father said. "But I don't believe it."

At the next corner they headed down a side street into a residential neighborhood. The farther you walked from Main Street, the smaller the houses and the darker the people. About eighty-five percent of the people who lived in Maynard County were white, with the remainder divided about equally between black and Latino. The Latinos were the most recent arrivals, having started coming to the area during the 1990s as migrant workers to pick peaches and other crops. And those who settled there moved into what had been a neighborhood of blacks and poor whites, displacing the latter.

Their house, built of wood and painted gray, was more than a hundred years old, and it had been a handyman special when they moved into it. Her father had spent the last fifteen years fixing it up. He had not only invested his sweat in the house, he had also invested his dream in it. He had an agreement with the landlord that gave him an option to buy the house at its market value minus the value of the improvements he made, so even though he rented the house he had an equity interest in it.

Her mother was sitting on the porch, which extended across the front of the house and was two steps up from the sidewalk. The chairs, which her father had restored from castoffs, were away from the light above the front door, which attracted insects. Her mother and father usually sat there after supper during the summer since it was a little cooler outside. Like virtually all their neighbors, they didn't have air conditioning.

As they approached the sitting area her father asked: *"Dónde están los niños?"*

"They're supposed to be in bed," her mother said. They were referring to Maya's younger sister Selina, who was fourteen, and her brother Victor, who was twelve. They had both been born in America.

Her father sat down in the chair next to her mother, and Maya took another chair. He said to her mother: "They passed the immigration law."

"I heard," her mother said as if she had her own sources of information.

"Well, don't worry. It might not affect us."

"We're illegal immigrants. Why wouldn't it affect us?"

"We've lived in this country for fifteen years. We work and pay taxes, and we're raising three wonderful children."

"We're still illegal," her mother said.

"When they reform the federal immigration law we'll have a way of becoming legal."

"By the time they reform that law, if they ever do, it'll be too late for us."

"I believe that in his next term Obama will put a high priority on immigration."

"Maybe he will, but meanwhile we have a law in Alabama that makes it a crime for us to work."

"I believe we can find a way around it."

"How can we find a way around it?"

"I don't know," her father said. "That's one of the questions I have for Trevor."

After a pause her mother said: "The law will also make it a crime for our landlord to rent this house to us."

"I believe it won't affect us because of the deal we have with him. But that's another question I have for Trevor."

"And I'm sure you realize that the law will prohibit Maya from attending the university."

"Maya has already been admitted to the university. They can't apply the law to something that happened before it was passed."

"Why can't they?" her mother asked. "They're applying the law to people who came here before it was passed."

"I believe it won't apply to Maya."

Her mother stared out into the night. "The law will require

schools to report the immigration status of students. They'll use that information to deport people."

"The schools won't report names," her father said, "only numbers. And even if they did report names, Selina and Victor wouldn't have a problem. They were born in this country, which makes them U.S. citizens."

"Who said the schools won't report names?"

"Our state representative said that at the meeting."

"Well, I don't care what he said. They'll find a way to use that information against us."

"I don't believe they will," her father said, holding his ground.

"I know you don't," her mother said. "You believe this country lives by its principles."

"If I didn't believe that, I wouldn't have come here."

"Well, maybe we shouldn't have come here. And maybe we should listen to what this law is telling us."

"What's it telling us?"

"It's telling us to go home."

"This is our home," her father said. "We haven't lived in Mexico for fifteen years."

"If we went back to Mexico," her mother said, "we'd have the advantage of speaking English. And we'd have money."

"What money?"

"The money we invested in this house."

"We'd have to buy and sell the house to get that money, and I don't know how we could do it."

"Ask Trevor how we could do it."

"I will," her father said as if he hoped it wouldn't be necessary.

"If we had that money," her mother said, "we could buy a farm or a business in Mexico."

"I don't want to go back to Mexico. Our future is here."

"If the governor signs this immigration law, we won't have any future here."

"Well, maybe he won't sign it."

"Why wouldn't he sign it?"

"Maybe people like Judson and Trevor will convince him not to sign it."

Her mother shook her head doubtfully. "I don't believe there are enough people like Judson and Trevor to convince the governor not to sign it."

"Maybe there aren't," her father admitted. "Maya and I have a meeting with Trevor on Monday morning. Before we make any decisions we should hear what he says."

"Whatever he says," her mother said, "we have to be realistic about the situation."

"What does that mean?"

"It means we can't depend on people to do the right thing."

"I believe we can. Eventually, they will."

"Eventually, they might. But it took a hundred years from the time they abolished slavery for them to give equal rights to blacks. And I don't want to wait that long for them to give us equal rights. I don't want our children to wait that long."

"I don't either," her father agreed. He looked sad, but Maya could tell he still hadn't given up his dream of living in America. And while her head sided with her mother, her heart sided with her father.

A half hour later Maya left her parents and went upstairs. In the bedroom she shared with Selina the lights were out, so in order not to wake her sister she undressed in the dark and pulled on the long tee-shirt she slept in during the summer. She took her phone into the bathroom and checked for text messages. There was one from her boyfriend Shelby that asked: "How did it go?"

To show his solidarity with the Latino community, Shelby had wanted to go to the meeting with her, but she had asked him not to. She knew that if he had been seen with her at the meeting, his father wouldn't have been happy about it. And she didn't want to cause problems for him.

Of course over the fourteen months that they had been going together Shelby had been seen with her at school, at parties, and at athletic events, but a town hall meeting was different. It was a political event, where people took sides on issues, and by sitting with her at the meeting Shelby would be seen as taking the wrong side on the immigration issue, at least in the eyes of people like his father. Shelby's father, whose family the town was named for, was the most important person in Harperville. He owned the major bank, a real estate firm, an insurance agency, and a lot of property in the area. His house, which had been in the family for several generations, was a typical Southern mansion with columns that stood on a hill overlooking the town. Politically he was conservative, and though he never showed it, Maya could tell he wasn't pleased that his only son had a nonwhite girlfriend. She assumed that he supported the new immigration law, not only because it embodied his values but also because it provided a way to get rid of her. But he hadn't attended the meeting, maybe for the reason that Trevor had suggested: he didn't want to be seen as a racist.

Maya hadn't been attracted to Shelby because of his family wealth or position, but rather because he was cute and nice, a rare combination in boys—too often they were one or the other. When she first saw him passing in the hall at school she wanted to run her fingers through his soft brown hair and cuddle him. When they were in public together he held his head high as if he was proud of their relationship, and even when they parked by the river with no one else around he treated her with courtesy and respect.

Though they were from different backgrounds, they had two important things in common: they were both good students, and they both played sports. Shelby played on the high school golf team, and he expected to make the team at the university. They were both going to Tuscaloosa, and they would be living in dormitories that weren't too far apart.

Responding to his message, Maya said: "It didn't go well."

Within a few minutes Shelby asked: "What happened?"

"I can't tell you in a text message," she replied.

"You can tell me tomorrow," he texted back.

"Okay," she said. "I'll see you after work."

As she lay in bed she didn't think about Shelby, she thought about the law that threatened her family, and she prayed that people like Judson and Trevor and Father Philip would convince the governor not to sign it.

Her sister and brother were still asleep the next morning when Maya and her father left the house. Her family didn't own a car since even if they could have afforded one an illegal immigrant couldn't get a driver's license. The county bus service enabled her mother to get to the houses of her clients, but it didn't run anywhere near Judson's farm, which was about ten miles north east of town. Luckily, a man who owned a car and drove every day to a nearby farm lived in their neighborhood, and six days a week he gave her father a ride to work. Like her father he was from Puebla, and they had figured out how their families were related, which helped to cement the relationship. The man was a legal resident because after coming here as a migrant worker he had married a local girl.

Maya's father had a full-time job with Judson supervising the temporary workers who tended the orchards and picked the fruit as well as doing maintenance on the house, the vehicles, and the equipment. Her father was paid well enough so that her mother only had to work part time cleaning houses. Her mother had five or six regular clients, some of whom had been referred by Judson and others by word of mouth. She could have gotten more work since she had the two qualities that her clients valued most, reliability and honesty, but she needed time for raising her children, who came before everything else in her life.

Judson lived with a dog and two cats in an old country house that was big enough for a large family. He was born and raised in that house, and he attended the same schools as Maya. At the age of eighteen, not feeling ready for college, he enlisted in the army, and he did a tour of duty in Vietnam. He served his last year of the army in Germany, and he lived for a while in New York, where he made a living as a carpenter, got involved in issues of peace and social injustice, and earned a black belt in karate. On a trip home to visit his family he met the woman he described as "the love of my life." He married her and took over the farm from his father. He and his wife were planning to have a lot of children, but before they could have even one child she died of cancer, and he hadn't remarried.

Deprived of having children, Judson had started a karate school, which was on the second story of a building on Main Street. The school had been going for almost thirty years, and a number of the town's present businessmen and professionals had been students there. In fact, there were students in class with Maya whose parents had gone there. She was old enough now to understand that Judson's purpose wasn't to teach the kids karate but to mentor them, and having been categorized by teachers as "too aggressive" when she was younger, she could appreciate how karate had helped her channel her violent feelings into a disciplined activity. Playing soccer had done that too, and the two activities reinforced each other, not only in her social development but also in her ability to deliver a kick, whether it was a shot on goal or a *mae geri* (front kick).

Maya was going to Judson's house this morning because he had found some suitable boards for her to practice on. She was hoping to earn her brown belt at the *shiai* (belt-awarding ceremony) that was going to be held on Wednesday evening, and one of the requirements was to break boards with her hand. A boy her age had successfully done this at the last *shiai*, back in January, and he had told her there was nothing to it. But he was a boy, and he had probably been breaking things all his life.

Their neighbor stopped at Judson's driveway and let them out. They thanked him and headed for the back door, which led into the kitchen.

"Hey," Judson said, opening the door before they got there. "Come on in."

They went into the kitchen, where Kuro greeted them. Kuro was a black Labrador, and his name meant "black" in Japanese.

The two cats were in the corner eating out of separate dishes. If you used one dish, the yellow cat took all the food.

"Would you like some coffee?" Judson asked her father.

"No, thanks. I think I had enough for today." As always her father spoke English with Judson, and as always Maya was impressed by how well he spoke it. He had an accent, but otherwise he spoke it better than those men at the meeting, as she had wanted to point out.

"I tried to give up coffee," Judson said. "It's a powerful drug, and I'm addicted to it."

"So are a lot of kids," Maya said. "They drink Red Bull and Mountain Dew, which have more caffeine than coffee."

"No wonder they're so jittery," Judson said.

"You want me to look at the pickup now?" her father asked.

"That's the top priority. But there's no rush. How do you feel about last night?"

"I lay awake most of the night thinking about it."

"I did too. I'm driving down to Montgomery on Monday to join some people who have an appointment to talk with the governor."

"Do you think he'll listen?"

"I know he'll listen, but I don't know if we can convince him not to sign this law."

"Do you think the letters from churches will influence him?" Maya asked.

"They should," Judson said. "He claims to be a Christian."

"Whatever happens," her father said with determination, "we're not going to let this law stop Maya from attending the university."

"We're not going to let that happen," Judson agreed.

"Well, I better get to work now."

"We'll go with you. The boards for Maya are in the garage."

They went out, following her father. The pickup was in the driveway, and her father went directly to it. Judson led her into the garage.

"I have a good supply of boards," he told her. "So you can practice all you want."

"Could you show me again how to do it?"

"Yeah. Sure." He went over to a work table, on top of which there was a pile of boards. They were about nine inches wide and about eighteen inches long. There were also strips of wood about a half inch square. He took three boards and four strips from the table, and he got two trestles and set them up on the floor far enough apart to hold the boards with a little overlap. He carefully set a board on the trestle, and put a strip at each end, and set another board on the strips, then two more strips, and finally the third board.

"How far away do you stand?" Maya asked.

"Just far enough so that your hand comes down on the top board without your having to move your body." He showed her, measuring with his hand. "And you want to keep your fingers closed, as you do with a *shuto uchi*. You strike the board with the part of the hand between your little finger and your wrist. Don't let your little finger or your wrist hit it. Focus the blow on this part of your hand."

"*Osu!*" she said, inclining her head.

"Now, the most important thing is not to stop your hand when it hits the top board but to drive it through the three boards. So think about striking *through* the boards, not at them."

"*Osu!*"

"Get into a comfortable stance," Judson said, demonstrating, "and raise your hand and bring it down almost to the top board. You want to do that three times, and on the third time you strike through the boards."

"Do you *kiai* when you strike?"

"Oh, yeah. So here we go," Judson said, raising his hand. He brought it down twice to the top board, and then with a loud *kiai* (yell) he struck through the boards, breaking them into pieces.

It gave her a thrill.

"Now, you try it," Judson said, going to the table to get more wood. "And I want the governor to hear your *kiai*."

Maya understood, and she appreciated how Judson was enabling her to channel her feelings about the immigration law into a symbolic action.

When he had set up the boards for her she measured the distance and got into a comfortable stance. She raised her hand and brought it down almost to the top board, as Judson had shown her. She did that twice, and then with a *kiai* she hoped the governor could hear in Montgomery she struck through the boards, making the pieces fly into the air.

"That's the way," Judson said, applauding.

"Bien hecho," said her father, who was standing in the garage doorway.

Maya had done more than break the boards. She had shown the two men who mattered most to her that she had the courage and the force to prevail in a world where for all of God's glory there weren't enough men of good will.

TWO

JUDSON HAD ERRANDS to do in town, so when they had finished with the karate he drove her home, giving her some boards to practice on. She stored the wood in the shed and then went into the kitchen to check with her mother before she left for her appointment with Father Philip. Selina and Victor were in the kitchen, sitting at the table and eating Cheerios for breakfast. They both looked half asleep.

"We're going to the pool this afternoon," her mother told her. "If you finish in time you could go with us."

"I don't know when I'll finish, so don't wait for me."

"Okay. I'll see you later. Give my regards to Father Philip."

"I will," Maya said, heading back out.

The church, Immaculate Conception, was a twenty-minute walk from their house at the other end of Main Street. The Baptist and Methodist churches were closer to the center of town, and the Episcopal and Presbyterian churches were in the center. Shelby's family belonged to the Episcopal church, as did many of the influential families. Until the influx of Latinos, the congregation of Immaculate Conception had been declining, but now it was growing. It now had more members than the Episcopal church, though few of them had any influence.

Maya liked walking, and she didn't envy her classmates who had cars, which they pointlessly drove up and down Main Street. She could walk anywhere in town, and she had always been bused to school, so she really didn't need a car.

She passed the diner, where people were lingering over coffee and enjoying some temporary relief from the heat, and then the pharmacy, where she worked part time. As she walked by the town hall she felt a surge of anger, remembering what the big man with the red neck and his buddies had said. She wished she had stood up and said what she wanted to say. But she knew it only would have made things worse.

She was conscious of how far her spirits had fallen in less than a week from the euphoria she had felt at the graduation ceremony on receiving the award for the best all-around student in the senior class. It had made her parents so proud of her. But now, with those words of hatred echoing in her mind, she wondered if the people who acknowledged her with friendly smiles as they passed her on the sidewalk were saying in their hearts: "You don't belong here."

By the time she got to Immaculate Conception she needed the refuge it offered her. It was the only place other than her home where she felt safe and secure. She knew that the front door would be locked since the church couldn't afford to employ a full-time custodian, so she walked around to a side door and went into the corridor that led to Father Philip's office.

She found him there talking with Mrs. Gallagher, the parish administrator. He was sitting at his desk, and Mrs. Gallagher was standing in front of it. They were discussing the work being done to maintain the air conditioning system, for which there had been a special collection last Sunday. Evidently, the work was costing more than the initial estimate.

"He should give us more of a discount," Mrs. Gallagher said, referring to the contractor.

"He's giving us fifteen percent off," Father Philip said.

"If he gave us twenty, we could manage."

"Then I'll ask him to give us twenty."

"Hey, Maya," Mrs. Gallagher said, seeing her in the doorway. "How're you?"

"I'm fine. How're you?"

"I'd feel better if we had more money, but otherwise I can't complain."

Maya stepped aside to let Mrs. Gallagher leave the office, and then she advanced.

"Please sit down," Father Philip told her. He was in his mid-seventies, with silver hair and wire-rimmed glasses. Having been the pastor at this church for her First Holy Communion and her Confirmation, he had seen her through the major passages of her life. "How do you feel?"

She knew he meant about the meeting. "I feel angry."

"I know," he said with empathy. "I feel angry too. But we shouldn't act on our anger."

"I'm only going to break boards."

"Boards?" He looked puzzled.

"I'm going for my brown belt in karate, and one of the requirements is to break boards with your hand."

"Oh, I see. You mean instead of breaking heads."

"I would have liked to break the head of our representative."

"If there's one thing I can't stand," Father Philip said, "it's a hypocrite. The man professes to be a Christian, and he voted for a law that will hurt a lot of vulnerable people."

"Why did he do it?"

"He claims he did it to help people, but there are other ways to do that, so I don't accept his arguments. I've heard those arguments before."

"When?" she asked, wanting to learn.

"About fifty years ago. They claimed that segregation was better for both races."

"Were you involved in the movement to end segregation?"

"As much as I could be," Father Philip said reminiscently. "I was a young priest at the time, an assistant pastor at a church in Montgomery, and I wanted more than anything to join the civil rights activists in their demonstrations."

"So did you join them?"

"I finally did, but only after I had some words with people at a higher level. They supported the cause of civil rights, but they didn't want to get involved in the action."

"Is that what Judson meant last night about the letter from Birmingham jail?"

"Yes. Martin Luther King was criticizing the clergy for standing on the sidelines and cheering him but not joining him in the action."

"When you joined the action, what did you do?"

"We marched from Selma to Montgomery. It took us five days to get there, and Reverend King delivered one of his finest speeches from the steps of the state capitol. 'The end we seek,' he said, 'is a society at peace with itself, a society that can live with its conscience.'"

"Do we have that kind of society now?"

"I thought we were going in the right direction, but now I wonder. It's beginning to feel like Jim Crow is back in town."

"Do we have a chance of stopping this law?"

"We have three chances of stopping it," Father Philip said positively. "We can stop it from being signed, we can stop it from being implemented, and we can have it overturned. So first we want to try to stop it from being signed."

"That's what I came to help you do."

"The letters to the governor are in boxes on the table behind you. They've been signed by ministers, priests, and rabbis. If you stuff them into the envelopes, it'll be a big help. I can mail them on Monday."

"Okay," she said, rising from her chair. "Could I ask you something, father?"

"You can ask me anything," he said openly. "I may not have the answer, but go ahead."

"What made you come to Harperville?"

Father Philip smiled. "They sent me here as a punishment for joining that march. But you know what? It turned out to be a blessing for me."

"I'm glad it did. And it turned out to be a blessing for *us*."

"Thank you, Maya. Even priests need a kind word now and then."

It was after two when she finished stuffing the envelopes, and by then she was hungry, so she headed home. The back door was locked, and in the kitchen she found a note from her mother saying they had gone to the pool and inviting her to join them. They would have gone to the old public pool, which was within walking distance. Maya didn't feel like going there since it would be overrun with children splashing and screaming. Instead, she made herself a peanut butter sandwich and sat down at the table, where she checked her text messages.

There was one from her friend Courtney, a teammate from soccer who was going to the University of Maryland. It said: "Wow, is it hot. I wish there was a mountain where I could go and roll in the snow." There were three from Shelby: "My father wants me to play golf with him," "Whatever happens, I'm on your side," and "I love you."

"I love you too," she responded to his last message. "I'll see you at eight."

She worked from four to eight at Otis Pharmacy, which was on Main Street. By eight she would be hungry again, and Shelby would take her to Sonic for a burger and fries. On their second date he had offered to take her to a Taco Bell, and the look she gave him prevented him from ever again suggesting that they eat in a Mexican restaurant. Later, she explained to him that the so-called Mexican restaurants in America had nothing to do with Mexican food, and that she ate real Mexican food every day at home, so when she went out she wanted something different. From then on he usually took her to Sonic.

She was still eating her sandwich when she got a message from Selina who asked if there was any ice cream in the refrigerator. She got up and opened the freezer compartment and didn't see any ice cream, so she texted back that there wasn't any. Then she turned off her phone so it wouldn't even vibrate.

Though it could be useful, most of the time her phone was a nuisance, and she didn't understand how some people could send hundreds of text messages per day. As much as she loved him, she wished Shelby would text her only things she needed to know. If it was anything else she preferred to communicate face to face, so she could see the expressions of his eyes and his mouth. Her sister and her brother couldn't live without their phones, but her father had resisted their entreaties for a family plan with unlimited messages. Instead, they had a plan that rationed the messages among them, which in theory would help them learn discipline. When they got the first phone bill and found that Selina had exceeded her limit, her father took away her phone for a week, and after that she controlled herself.

Maya reached for the newspaper that her mother had left on the table. It was a regional daily that they had subscribed to as long as she could remember. Her parents claimed that reading the newspaper had been instrumental in helping them learn English, and they both still marked words they didn't completely understand—her father underlined them, and her mother circled them. The lead story was about the immigration law, and it quoted the governor as well as senators and representatives who supported the law. The story didn't tell Maya anything she hadn't learned at the meeting, but it did make her feel that there was more public support for the law than she might have guessed from the comments last night.

She was most upset by a statement from one of the law's authors, who said it attacked every aspect of the lives of illegal immigrants. "They will not stay in Alabama," he said. "This bill is designed to make it difficult for them to live here so they will deport themselves."

Out of curiosity she turned to the editorial page, and she read the paper's position on the law. While it opposed a few of the law's harsh measures, it generally supported the purpose of reversing the flow of immigration, and while it didn't mention Latinos, it certainly wasn't talking about Russians.

She read the letters. One said the law was necessary but shouldn't be enforced strictly. The other four were against the law, which gave Maya hope.

She finished the sandwich and folded the paper and washed the plate. Since she still had some time to kill before going to work, she went upstairs and straightened up the mess her sister had left in their room. Of course she did it to please her mother, who kept an impeccably neat house, maybe because she cleaned houses as a profession, and in this respect as in others Maya wanted to live up to her mother's standards.

At quarter to four she left for work, locking the back door, and she arrived at the pharmacy five minutes early, as she always did. It was good to have a overlap between her and Patsy, the woman who worked from nine to four. Patsy was old enough to be her mother, and from the beginning she had taken Maya under her wing.

"It's nice and cool here," Maya said, pulling the waist of her top away from her sticky skin.

"We haven't had many customers today," Patsy said. "It's too hot for people to be out doing errands. But their doctors have been phoning in prescriptions, so they'll come in this evening to pick them up."

Mr. Otis was standing behind the half wall that separated the pharmacist's area from the rest of the store, and his head was bowed in concentration over a task. The store had been founded by his grandfather in the 1920s. Back then it had a soda fountain and a lunch counter, which became an issue during the early 1960s when blacks claimed the right to be served. Mr. Otis's father was running the store at that time, and he got into trouble by defying the segregation law and welcoming blacks at the counter. The store was boycotted by diehard whites and closed down for legal infractions, but it reopened with support from the kind of people who spoke out against the immigration law at the town meeting. It had also helped that there were no other pharmacies in town then, and people needed their prescriptions.

The soda fountain and lunch counter were gone now, replaced by shelves of products for headaches and allergies and dry eyes and other ailments as well as products for hair and skin. And now the store had a lot of competition, not only from the Winn-Dixie in town and the Walmart outside of town but also from the CVS at the shopping mall. But many people preferred having their prescriptions filled by someone they knew and trusted, and Mr. Otis always took time to explain to people the effects of the drug they would be taking.

He had three children and seven grandchildren. Both of his sons were engineers: one lived in Birmingham and the other in

Houston. His daughter, a licensed pharmacist, lived in Harperville and had worked with him at the store for a while but was now busy raising three children. Mr. Otis hoped that when her children were grown up she would take over from him and keep the store in the family.

"Enjoy the air conditioning," Patsy said, heading out.

"I will," Maya said, taking her place behind the counter.

"Hey, Maya," Mr. Otis said, looking up from his task. "I reckon you don't mind being here on a day like this."

"I don't mind at all," Maya said. "Our house is like a furnace."

"We don't have air conditioning either. My wife says it gives her a stiff neck. We sit out on the porch in the evening and wait for a breeze."

"We do too. And sometimes we get one."

Mr. Otis laughed. "If my wife only imagines a breeze, it makes her feel cooler."

"How long have people had air conditioning?"

"Let's see. We put it in this store in the late sixties. My father didn't want it, but he felt it would make the customers happy."

"Were you in favor of it?"

"I didn't have a vote on it. I was still at Auburn learning the trade."

"I think your father was right about making the customers happy," Maya said, surveying the counter and making sure there was a pen handy. "I think people come in to cool off."

"I'm sure they do." Mr. Otis paused, and then he said: "I heard that people asked our state representative some tough questions at the meeting last night."

"They did. But he had supporters."

"I can guess who they were—the same people who fought integration tooth and nail."

"He must have other supporters, or he wouldn't have voted for that law."

"Unfortunately, he does."

"Well, most of the people at the meeting were against it."

"I would have liked to be there, but yesterday was my wife's birthday, and she didn't want to spend it at a town meeting."

"I don't blame her."

While Mr. Otis resumed his task, Maya checked her side of the half wall, which had open boxes for the prescriptions with a letter of the alphabet at the top of each one. As usual the boxes with "C" and "M" and "S" had the most prescriptions, but there was one in the "X" box, which belonged to the only family in town whose name began with that letter.

Since there were no customers in the store now, Maya started looking through each box to see the names on the prescription bags, so when someone came in for a prescription she would know it was ready.

She was on the "G" box when an elderly woman she knew came in. It was Mrs. Sánchez, who lived across the street from Maya. Her son, who had served in the Gulf War, was a legal resident, and he had brought his mother here after his father had died in Mexico.

Knowing that the woman spoke almost no English, Maya greeted her in Spanish, saying: *"Hola, señora. Cómo está?"*

"Bien, gracias. Y tú?"

"Bien. How can I help you?"

"I came to pick up a prescription."

"It's ready," Mr. Otis said from his side of the half wall.

Maya reached into the "S" box and took out the prescription bags. She quickly found the bag for Mrs. Sánchez.

"It's an antibiotic," Mr. Otis told Maya. "Could you explain to Mrs. Sánchez that she should take one pill three times a day with meals, not between meals but *with* meals?"

"Okay. *Este es un antibiótico. Usted debe tomar una pastilla tres veces al día. Debe tomarlas con las comidas, no entre comidas sino con las comidas.*"

"Entiendo," Mrs. Sánchez said.

"Tell her she should take the pills every day until they run out, and that she shouldn't miss a day of taking them."

Maya translated this instruction, making it clear.

"And tell her she should eat yogurt while taking the pills."

"Yogurt? Why yogurt?"

"Because antibiotics kill the beneficial bacteria in your intestines, and if you don't replace them you can get yeast infections."

"So the yogurt would replace them?"

"It would help. I could give her a probiotic, but she's already taking enough pills."

While Maya translated the instruction about the yogurt, a man who worked at the Chevron station came in and went directly to the shelf of analgesics. As if in reaction to the sound of Spanish, he turned his head and glared at Maya before resuming his search for the product he wanted. She was still talking with Mrs. Sánchez when he approached the counter.

Sensing that he was in a hurry, and not wanting to rush Mrs. Sánchez, Maya said: "*Con su permiso, voy a asistir a este otro cliente.*"

"*No hay problema,*" Mrs. Sánchez said graciously.

The man was buying a large bottle of ibuprofen, which triggered Maya's memory: he bought this product regularly, though he never said a word to her. He always handed her the bottle with a twenty dollar bill and stood there in stony silence while she rang it up.

"Hey, Eddie," Mr. Otis said pleasantly. "How're you?"

"I'm fine," Eddie muttered. He stared at Maya with cold blue eyes that clearly said: "You don't belong here."

Completing the transaction, Maya did what Judson had advised her to do in such situations—she sucked it up. Besides, there was a counter between her and Eddie, so she wasn't in a position to deliver a *mae geri* to his groin. But as she watched him leave the store she was roiled by a feeling of unrequited injustice.

"He wasn't well raised," Mr. Otis said as if he had noticed the way Eddie stared at her.

"He's like those men at the meeting last night."

"He would have benefited from serving in the military."

She resumed talking with Mrs. Sánchez. She knew that Mr.

Otis appreciated her ability to relate with customers, and he evidently understood that in her culture you didn't just take a customer's money and leave it at that. Since she also lived in Mr. Otis's culture she knew it wasn't different from hers in that respect, though there were exceptions to the norm of civility like the man who had just bought a bottle of ibuprofen.

"When do you start at the university?" Mrs. Sánchez asked.

"The first week of August."

"Isn't that early?"

"We have soccer practice. We have a match in the middle of August."

"*Bueno, eres una buena chica. Estoy seguro de que el señor Otis te echará de menos.*"

"I think I understood that," Mr. Otis said. "If you said I'll miss Maya, you're right. She's the absolute best."

Conscious of how little it took to lift her up and put her down, she wondered if she would always be this way.

A few minutes before eight Shelby came into the store. She was glad to see him, and she looked forward to hanging out with him. She was also hungry.

"Hey, Mr. Otis," Shelby said. "How're you?"

"I'm fine, Shelby. How're you? And how's your family?"

"I'm fine, and they're fine. If you can believe it, my daddy and I played golf this afternoon."

"In this heat? You must love the game."

"I do love it, but if I'd had a choice I wouldn't have been out on that course today."

"Well, you kids can run along. I'll lock up the store."

"Are you sure I can't help you?" Maya asked.

"I'm sure. Thank you."

As they walked out of the store into the summer evening Shelby asked: "You want to go to Sonic?"

"Yeah. I feel like a burger and fries."

They strolled to his car, which was parked only a short distance down the block. At this hour there was no shortage of parking spots.

His car was a brand new Corvette convertible, which he had received as a graduation present. The body was silver metallic, and the top was gray. He had left the top up, presumably to retain the cool air provided by the air conditioner.

When they got into the car he asked: "Should I put the top down?"

"Yeah, if you want to. It's not so hot now."

He pressed a button, and the top retracted. You could make this car do anything by pressing a button. There were even some things it would do without your pressing a button.

As they headed up Main Street she felt the breeze lifting her hair. She wore her hair short for soccer and karate, but she had enough hair to feel it lift, and she closed her eyes, pretending for a moment she was one of those blonds who rode around in convertibles.

"You like this car?" Shelby asked.

"I love it," she said. "I mean, as much as I could love a car."

"I don't know if I should take it to college."

"Really? Why wouldn't you?"

"There are some rough areas in Tuscaloosa, and I wouldn't want it to get stolen."

"You have insurance, don't you?"

"Yeah. But they wouldn't pay me the full value. They'd pay me the depreciated value."

"Even for a new car?"

"Well, technically it's not new. It's used, though I've driven it only—" He leaned forward to check the dashboard "—two hundred and one miles."

"What percentage of the full value would they pay?"

"If the car was stolen now, they'd probably pay only eighty percent of its full value."

"That's not right. If you've driven only two hundred and one miles, then they should pay you almost its full value."

"It doesn't work that way."

"It should."

"A lot of things don't work like they should."

Since she didn't want to go into it yet, she didn't take the opening. Instead, she leaned her head back and closed her eyes and pretended she was one of those blonds.

Sonic was just beyond the sign that invited you to come again to Harperville, where Main Street became a highway and the speed limit went up to fifty. It looked like a feed lot for cars, and you pulled into a stall, looked at the pictures of food, pressed a red button, and within a few minutes a carhop delivered the food to the driver's window.

Maya wanted a Sonic burger, well done, and a side of fries. Shelby liked his burger medium, but otherwise he ordered the same thing. She had him ask for extra napkins to protect the seats from spilled catsup, mayonnaise, or mustard, though they looked impervious to food stains.

As they waited for their orders Shelby said: "Now, tell me about the immigration law."

"All right." She took a long deep breath. She had told Shelby about her family's status early in their relationship because she trusted him and wanted to share her concerns with him. She was confident that he would never tell anyone about it, just as he could be confident that she would never tell anyone about the things he had shared with her. "For one thing, the law will make it a crime for my parents to work."

"Don't worry. Their employers won't report them."

"But what if they're caught? They'll be arrested."

"Their employers won't let them be arrested. Judson and your mother's clients are important members of the community."

Maya was heartened. "So their employers could protect my parents from the law?"

"Yeah. They could stop it from being applied to them."

Since she was getting another perspective on the situation, Maya kept going. "The law will also prohibit me from attending the university."

"You've already been admitted. And if there ever was a problem, the athletics department would fix it. They want you for the soccer team."

"Well, maybe the law won't affect us right away, but it will eventually. And it makes me feel like we don't belong here."

"You belong here," Shelby assured her.

"There are people who think we don't belong here. A man at the meeting actually said we don't belong here."

"I'm sure he was a redneck."

"He did have a red neck."

"That's why they're called rednecks. They have red necks."

"Why do they have red necks?"

"From working in the fields and being in the sun."

"But they don't work in the fields."

"They used to."

"We work in the fields," Maya said after thinking about it. "So if we were white, would we be rednecks?"

"No. That wouldn't be enough to make you rednecks. You'd also have to be bigoted."

"Then the guy who comes into the pharmacy and buys big bottles of ibuprofen is a redneck."

"What guy are you talking about?"

"A guy who works at the Chevron station. He heard me speaking Spanish to a customer, and he stared at me in a way that told me I don't belong here."

"I know who you mean. Yeah, he's a redneck."

"It's a good thing there was a counter between him and me," Maya said, letting it out. "I felt like kicking him in the *cojones*."

"He would have deserved it," Shelby said.

That lifted her, and later when they were parked in their usual place by the river she let him know through kissing how grateful she was for his support.

At one point Shelby tried to go beyond kissing. Maya loved him, she loved being with him, and she loved kissing him, but she wasn't ready to make love with him or with anyone. She had made this clear the first time he had touched her breasts, so she didn't often have to stop him from trying to go beyond kissing.

"No," she said, removing his hands. "I'm not ready."

"When will you be ready?"

"I don't know. I just know I won't be ready for a while, so don't get your hopes up."

"I don't understand why you're not ready. You're eighteen, and we love each other. So why shouldn't we express our love?"

"We have other ways of expressing our love."

"It's not because you're a Catholic, is it?"

"That has nothing to do with it," Maya said truthfully. If she had been ready, her religion wouldn't have stopped her. If there was a reason why she wasn't ready, it was that whenever she considered making love with Shelby she faced the question: then what? She tried to explain this obstacle by saying: "I can't see what would lie beyond our making love."

"I can," he said. "A lifetime of making love."

"There's more to it than that."

"I know there is. We'd get married and have children—"

"But we have to complete our education first. And right now I don't even know if they'll let me attend the university."

"If we got married," Shelby said after a silence, "you wouldn't have to worry about that law."

"We'd get married to solve the problem?"

"No. We'd get married because we love each other and want to spend our lives together. But it would also solve the problem."

"We're too young to get married."

"No, we're not. People our age get married all the time."

"They do, and they get divorced all the time. And the children are left with single mothers." She had seen it happen in her own community, and she knew it happened in other communities, including the one that Shelby belonged to.

"I'm not saying we should get married now. I'm only saying it could be a fallback."

"You mean if nothing else solved the problem?"

"Yeah. So don't worry," Shelby assured her.

"What about my parents?"

"If you were legal, then your whole family would be legal."

"Is that how it works?"

"I think so. The guy in your neighborhood who became legal

by serving in the army brought his mother here from Mexico, didn't he?"

"Yeah. His mother was the customer I was speaking Spanish to when that redneck came into the store."

"Well, there you go. So you have a fallback."

She wasn't completely reassured by this fallback. Though it sounded reasonable, she had doubts about whether it would solve the problem her parents would have if the law was signed and implemented. And even if it did solve the problem Maya knew that as much as she loved Shelby, she wasn't ready to get married.

THREE

AT MASS THE next day Father Philip used his homily to explain the church's position on the immigration law, which he said violated the second commandment—to love your neighbor as yourself. He assured the congregation that their church was working with other churches and synagogues to stop the law from being signed, and if it was signed, to stop it from being implemented. He encouraged them all to let the governor know how they felt about the law by calling him and emailing him.

The next morning Maya and her father met with Trevor, whose office was on the second floor of a building on Main Street, above the branch of a bank from Montgomery. Trevor owned the building, which he had inherited from his father, and Shelby's father was still annoyed at him for renting the storefront space of his building to a competitor.

Trevor had gone to Harvard Law School and worked with the Justice Department in Washington before joining the district attorney's office in Birmingham. About twenty years ago he moved back to Harperville and took over his father's law practice, happily becoming a small town lawyer. He had two grown-up sons: one lived in Atlanta and the other in San Francisco. It was rumored that the latter was gay, which may have explained Trevor's advocacy of gay rights, though it may have simply reflected his position on rights for all people, including illegal immigrants. Trevor once confided to Maya that his only regret was being born too late for the civil rights action of the 1960s.

The receptionist in Trevor's office was a Latina in her late twenties who was perfectly bilingual. In addition to taking phone calls and making appointments, she managed the office and acted as an intermediary with the Latino clients. There was one other lawyer, a woman in her thirties, who handled wills and trusts and divorces and other family matters. Trevor focused on his business clients and on his pro bono activities.

They met in a paneled conference room that had bookshelves built into the walls. The books were volumes of legal records going back many years. Like the paneling and the shelves, the table and the chairs were oak, creating an impression of solidity and longevity.

Trevor was a few years younger than Judson, but the deep lines in his face made him look older. His long dark hair was streaked with gray, and it would tumble over his forehead, so from time to time he would sweep it back with a motion that carried his hand over the top of his head as if he was clearing his brain.

"Hey, y'all," Trevor greeted them. "Have a seat and make yourselves comfortable. Would you like a coffee? Or a coke?"

"No, thanks," her father said, sitting down.

Maya sat next to her father while Trevor sat across from them. Moving the folder on the table in front of him to one side, Trevor said: "This law is trying to reverse the process that made our country great. It's trying to turn America into a gated community."

"Could the federal courts stop it from being implemented?" her father asked.

"They could. In my opinion, parts of this law are open to challenge. But the law states that if any part is declared invalid, the other parts will remain in effect. So the courts might stop only some parts from being implemented."

"What parts are open to challenge?"

"The parts that conflict with federal law. For example, the Alabama law makes it a crime for illegal immigrants to work as well as for employers to hire illegal immigrants. Under federal law it's a crime for employers to hire illegal immigrants but it's not a crime for them to work. So there's a conflict between the state law and the federal law. The Arizona immigration law had a similar provision, and it was stopped because of that conflict. The basic principle," Trevor explained, "is that state laws should not interfere with the federal law on immigration."

"I understand. But if it's already a crime under federal law for employers to hire us, what's the purpose of Alabama making it a crime for us to work?"

"If you commit a crime by working, then they have grounds for deporting you. It puts you on the list of immigrants who have committed crimes."

"So it helps them deport us."

"That's the purpose of this law."

Her father pondered and then asked: "If they caught Judson employing me, what could they do to him?"

"They could fine him."

"Could they arrest him?"

"They could," Trevor said, "but they probably wouldn't. He's an important member of the community."

Her father nodded as if he understood. "What other parts are open to challenge?"

"The part that makes it a crime to harbor or transport illegal immigrants. I know the churches will challenge that since it interferes with their mission to help people."

"What other parts?"

"Well, in my opinion the part that requires law enforcement officers to determine the status of people they stop, detain, or arrest is open to challenge. I think it gets the state into an area where the federal government has jurisdiction. But a federal judge might not see it that way."

"What about the part that makes it a crime to rent to illegal immigrants?"

"In the preamble," Trevor said after sweeping hair off his forehead, "the law talks about prohibiting a landlord from knowingly entering into a rental agreement to harbor an illegal immigrant, but the only specific reference to that in the body of the law is the part that makes a contract with an illegal immigrant invalid if the other party knew the immigrant was unlawfully present at the time the contract was entered into. In your situation, the landlord had no idea of your immigration status. He didn't ask, and he didn't want to know."

"So that part might not affect us?"

"It wouldn't be my most immediate concern."

"Regarding that contract," her father said, shifting in his chair, "my wife wanted me to ask you how we could get the money we've invested in the house."

"You could buy the house and sell it," Trevor said as if it were that simple.

"We don't have money to buy the house."

"You don't need money. You could buy the house from the landlord and immediately sell it back to him. It would just be paperwork. And if you want to do that, it would be a good idea to do it before this law is implemented."

"I understand. Now, what about the part that prohibits illegal immigrants from attending public universities?"

"That would be my most immediate concern," Trevor said, frowning. "I think it's the least open to challenge, and it becomes effective on September 1."

"Why do you think it's the least open to challenge?"

"Well, I don't know of any federal law that gives illegal immigrants an equal opportunity for higher education. So I don't see a conflict between this part of the law and the federal law."

"But Maya has already been admitted to the university. How can they apply a law to something that happened before it was passed?"

"They can make laws retroactive. But if they apply this law to Maya we'll have grounds for a challenge. You know," Trevor added, "the law doesn't require public universities to report the immigration status of existing students, as it does with public schools. So if no one brings Maya's status to their attention, she might not have a problem."

"What about her scholarship?"

"According to the law, she's not eligible for a scholarship. But she already has a scholarship, which she was awarded before this law was passed. So if they take away her scholarship, we'll have a legal argument."

"Would we win that argument?"

"You never know. It depends on the judge."

Her father reflected. "What would you advise us to do?"

"I'd advise you to get your money out of that house," Trevor said after sweeping hair off his forehead again. "But other than that, I'd advise you to carry on with your life until we see how things play out."

"Do you think the governor will sign this law?"

"I think he will. When he ran for office he promised to pass an immigration law. Of course politicians rarely keep their promises, but every now and then they do."

"What will happen after he signs it?"

"The next day we'll begin the process of challenging it and trying to stop it from being implemented."

"Do you think you have a good chance of stopping it?"

"I think we have a very good chance where the law gets into the federal government's area of jurisdiction. By passing this law," Trevor told them, "the state of Alabama is claiming the right to control immigration. It's asserting the rights of states over the rights of the federal government, as it did with civil rights. In fact, the part that prohibits illegal immigrants from attending public universities reminds me of George Wallace standing in the schoolhouse door."

"The schoolhouse door?" Maya asked.

"Wallace was governor, and a federal judge ordered him to let two black students attend the university. Wallace refused, and he stood in the door of the auditorium where students were being processed for admission. When Nicholas Katzenbach, the deputy attorney general, ordered him to step aside, Wallace replied that he was upholding the constitutional right of states to operate public schools, colleges, and universities. Katzenbach called President Kennedy, who federalized the Alabama National Guard to deal with the crisis, and Wallace finally stepped aside. Of course he did the whole thing for show, but he meant every word when he declared: 'Segregation today, segregation tomorrow, segregation forever.' And he used the doctrine of states' rights to support his position."

"We didn't cover that in our history course."

"I'm not surprised," Trevor said wryly. "And you know what happens when you don't know history? You repeat it, as they're doing now."

"From what you say," her father said, "our best hope is that the federal government will stop this law from being implemented."

"That *is* our best hope. But immigration is trickier than segregation. We had a federal policy against segregation, and we had some court rulings against it. But on this issue we don't even have a federal policy. The federal government has put immigration on the back burner."

"I thought it was one of Obama's priorities."

"It was. But healthcare became a higher priority, and he used his political capital to push healthcare reform through Congress. There's also the recession and the unemployment. You heard what Fraser said at the meeting about protecting the jobs of Americans. They're using the problem of unemployment to gain support for this racist law."

"Is it working?"

"I'm afraid it is. If there's one problem that brings racism to the surface, it's unemployment. And the sad thing is, people can feel righteous when they say that illegal immigrants are taking their jobs. But it's not about jobs."

Without his saying it, Maya knew what it was about, and it made her angry. It made her wish she had kicked that redneck at the pharmacy.

"Oh, there's one more thing," her father said as if he hadn't wanted to mention it. "If we decide to go back to Mexico, we'll need our passports."

"You and your wife and Maya have Mexican passports, which have to be renewed. The kids can get American passports."

Her father shrugged as if it wasn't a major concern. "Whatever we need to cross the border."

"Okay. I'll handle it," Trevor said. "It could take a while, but we have time."

Maya practiced breaking boards on the picnic table in her backyard between then and the *shiai*, which was scheduled for Wednesday evening. By that afternoon she was confident of her ability to break the boards, but she worried about a lapse in focus, so she tried to put out of her mind everything that might distract her.

The event was being held in the middle school gym at six thirty. Students were supposed to be there fifteen minutes early, so around six Maya put on her white *gi* and tied her purple belt around her waist. She reflected on the fact that as you moved toward higher levels of karate, the belts got darker, with white at the lowest level, brown at the next to highest level, and black at the highest level, whereas in society it was the opposite.

She had been doing karate since she was twelve when her parents decided that she needed an activity that would help her control her violent feelings. She wore her hair longer then, and the only thing that kept it in place was an elastic headband. Now, with shorter hair, she folded a blue and white bandana into a strip and tied it carefully around her head. She removed the lanyard with the wooden cross she wore around her neck as well as her watch and her earrings. Jewelry of any kind was prohibited in karate.

Maya walked to the school with her family, and when they arrived she joined her fellow students on the gym floor while her parents and siblings found seats in the stands. There were more than twenty students, with three *sensei* (teachers) including Judson, the *shihan* (master teacher). Maya bowed to the *shihan* and the *sensei*, who returned her bow, and then she began to warm up. As she was stretching her hamstrings she noticed two of her girlfriends from school in the stands with Shelby. The two girls were on the soccer team, where her friends were mostly concentrated. It made her feel good to see them there.

By the time the students began the formal warm-up exercises there were more than a hundred people in the stands, mostly family and friends. The exercises were led by Sensei Rick, a man in his early twenties who worked as a paramedic for the fire department. Rick was cute, and he always made the classes fun, though he worked you hard and made you follow the strict discipline of karate. She hoped she would get him for sparring.

"*Yoi!*" Rick said, calling them to attention. He started with the usual arm exercises, and then he commanded them to take a *kiba dachi* (horse stance). As they assumed the stance they did a *kiai*, which the gym seemed to amplify.

"*Ichi, ni, san, shi*," Rick counted in a loud voice as Maya stretched her hands to her left foot. She had no trouble with the stretches since she was in good shape from soccer, but if they did American pushups she knew she would have to struggle to do thirty. This was the only exercise that boys could do more easily than girls, presumably because they had stronger arms and less weight in their butts.

There were five girls in the class, all of them younger than Maya. The youngest girl was Jenny, who was only ten. She was extremely shy and hesitant to punch or kick another person. Her parents must have hoped karate would help to make her more aggressive.

Maya was relieved when Rick only made them do Japanese pushups, which were easier than American pushups. She had no trouble doing thirty of them, but was still glad when he didn't make them do more.

After the warm-ups the students were paired off for *ippon kumite* (basic block and counter exercise). They often paired a white belt with a higher-level belt so that the former could learn from the latter, and Maya wasn't surprised when they paired her with Jenny. They were on the floor with another pair, and Maya spotted the younger girl's parents in the stands, maybe wondering why they had gotten their kid into this situation.

For the exercise the lower-level belt assumed a stance that resulted from doing a *gedan barai* (downward block), while the higher-level belt assumed a defensive stance. When the *sensei* told them to begin, the lower-level belt was supposed to throw a punch at the other person's *jodan* (head), which the higher-level belt was supposed to block with an *age uke* (upward block) and then counter with at least two punches or a combination of punches and kicks.

Before beginning, the person who would throw the first punch measured the distance to the other person's head, with the fingers extended to provide a few inches to spare when the fingers were retracted into a fist. You wanted to come as close as possible without actually hitting the other person.

"*Hajime*," Rick said, which meant to begin.

Jenny tentatively threw a punch that landed far short of Maya. In fact, it was so short that Maya had to lean forward to block it. Then gently she threw a counter punch at the girl's stomach and another at her ribs. When she got close to the girl she whispered: "Throw your punch all the way out, and don't worry about hitting me."

Jenny's next punch went farther, and after countering with a punch that sailed by the girl's ear and an elbow that comfortably missed her chin, Maya whispered: "That was much better."

The girl glowed, and Maya could remember being her age and realizing that she could do this. By the end of the exercise she really had to block the girl's punches.

They paired her later with Sensei Don, a tough young man who worked at the hardware store. Unlike Rick, he never smiled during karate, but he was an equally good teacher in his own way. As the lower-level belt in this situation, Maya threw the first punch, which Don blocked and then countered with a *mawashi geri* (roundhouse kick) at her rib cage and a hold that could have broken her arm in a real-life situation. When it was her turn to block and counter she aimed a *mae geri* (front kick) at his groin and then a flurry of punches at his undefended head. She could tell that her attack almost made him smile.

In the next section of the event students demonstrated their ability to perform a series of solo exercises or *kata*. To advance to a higher-level belt you had to master more *kata*, so they lined up all the students on the floor, with lower-level belts in back, and ran them through the *kata*, starting with *empi kata*. After performing the last *kata* they had learned, the students retired from the floor until only Maya was left. She demonstrated her mastery of the *kata* she needed for a brown belt, and when she had finished the crowd applauded.

Then she had to break the boards. She watched as Judson, in a black *gi*, brought out the materials and set them up. Before leaving her alone on the floor, he patted her on the shoulder and whispered: "You can do it. And make them hear your *kiai* in Montgomery."

She approached the boards and studied them. She cleared her head of all other thoughts and summoned her violent feelings as she raised her hand and lowered it twice, preparing to strike. And then with a *kiai* she wanted them to hear not only in Montgomery but also in Washington, she broke the boards.

The crowd cheered, and feeling like she did when she scored a goal in soccer, she looked at her father, who raised his fists in triumph, and at Judson, who bowed to her in respect, and finally at Shelby, who along with her friends was giving her a standing ovation. She bowed to the crowd, and then helped the *sensei* pick up the pieces of wood.

In the final section she got her wish to spar with Rick, and they entertained the crowd with a joyous round of punches and kicks and holds and maneuvers. Her best round was a *mawashi geri* (roundhouse kick) at his butt that threw him off balance and enabled her to pummel him in the *chudan* (stomach). From the beginning he had always invited her not to hold back with punches to the *chudan*, so she really hit him, encountering the hard wall of his abs. And he countered with a *nidan mae tobi geri* (double flying front kick) that sent her reeling.

At the end of the sparring they bowed to each other and said: "*Arigato gozaimasu*," which meant "Thank you for teaching me."

And though it was a formality, she felt that Rick meant it, which made her feel great.

The students then all sat down on the floor in rank order, with Maya at the head, while Shihan Judson had them come up one by one for praise and awards. The first was Jenny, who got a yellow stripe on her white belt. Next were three kids who went from white belt to yellow belt, and two kids who went from yellow to green, and one who went from green to purple. Maya was last, and Judson presented her to the crowd before giving a speech about her.

"Maya started with us," he said, "when she was twelve. She wasn't sure she could do karate, being a girl, but she kept at it. And now she's eighteen, about to go off to the university in Tuscaloosa. Most of you know what she contributed to the high school soccer team, but only Maya and her teachers know what she put into karate. By earning her brown belt, she's made it to the second highest level. If we had her for another year, I know she'd earn her black belt. Maybe she can work on that in her spare time at the university, but in the meantime she's a model for you other girls. With discipline and hard work you can all make it to a higher level."

The crowd applauded with enthusiasm.

"Here it is," Judson said, handing the brown belt to her. It was folded and packaged in cellophane.

"*Arigato*," Maya said, taking it.

Judson gave her a big hug, and he stood there with his arm around her shoulder while the ditzy woman from the town newspaper took pictures.

Maya felt nothing but good will from the crowd.

After the *shiai* Judson took her family and Shelby to dinner at Erna's Café, which a lot of people considered the best restaurant in town. Except for the fast food and takeout she had with her boyfriend, Maya never ate out, nor did her family since they couldn't afford to go to restaurants, so going to Erna's was a special treat. It was also a new experience for her family, who lived on the home cooking they had brought from Mexico, and when they looked at the menu they had a lot of questions.

"This is real Southern cooking," Judson explained. "It's what people used to eat before the national chains came into the area."

"We still eat it," Shelby said, "whenever we can."

"We do," Judson said amiably. He was sitting at the head of the table with Maya on his right and Shelby on his left. Maya's parents were in the middle, sitting across from each other, and the kids were at the other end.

"What do you recommend?" her mother asked.

"They're noted for the pan-fried chicken. It's served with mashed potatoes, vegetables, and cornbread."

"What kind of vegetables?" Selina asked suspiciously.

"You usually have a choice of collard greens or butter beans."

"Collard greens are like spinach," her mother said.

Selina made a face that ruled out collard greens.

"The catfish is also good," Shelby said. He went out a lot with his family.

"What's a chicken-fried steak?" Victor asked.

"It's steak fried like chicken," Judson said.

"Are the pork chops good?"

"They're very good."

Maya and her parents and Selina had pan-fried chicken, mashed potatoes, and butter beans, while Shelby had the catfish and Victor had the chicken-fried steak. They all had iced tea to drink, except for the kids who had cokes.

"It's so nice of you to take us out," her mother told Judson.

"It's my pleasure," Judson said. His short gray hair was already dry from the shower he had taken at the school before changing. Maya's hair was still wet from the shower, but she didn't mind. Her boyfriend had seen her sweaty and dirty and bruised after a soccer match. At least she felt fresh and clean now.

"I like the way you sparred with Rick," Shelby said.

"You gave as good as you got," Judson said.

"I always have fun sparring with Sensei Rick," Maya said.

"That's what it's about," Judson said. "To work and have fun at the same time."

"It looked like they had fun fighting," Shelby said.

"They did," Judson said. "But it's not about fighting. It's about engaging with other human beings in disciplined activity, which you have to work at."

"That applies to soccer, doesn't it?" Maya said.

"It does. Unless you work at it, you can't have fun."

"I think you should coach soccer," Shelby said. He hadn't been happy with the coach of the high school boys' team, so he had quit and switched to golf.

"I never played soccer," Judson told him, "so I don't know enough about it."

"What did you play?"

"Baseball."

"What position?"

"Short-stop."

"Did you play in college?"

"I didn't go to college after high school."

"What did you do?"

"I enlisted in the army."

"Judson served in Vietnam," Maya told Shelby.

"You did? What was it like?"

Judson glanced at her parents, who were having a discussion in Spanish, before he said: "It was like looking at a baboon's asshole."

Shelby flinched, but then he said: "Are you against war?"

"You know what that Yankee general said after wrecking the South on his march to Georgia? 'It is only those who have neither fired a shot nor heard the shrieks and groans of the wounded who cry aloud for blood, for vengeance, for desolation. War is hell.'"

"So you're against the wars in Afghanistan and Iraq?"

"There's no good reason for either of those wars. A lot of

innocent people, including a lot of civilians, have been killed for nothing."

"Was there a good reason for the Vietnam War?"

"When I was your age," Judson said, "I thought there was, but I was wrong. As the Yankee general said, I had neither fired a shot nor heard the shrieks and groans of the wounded. In that sense I was like the man who got us into Afghanistan and Iraq."

"Well, we were attacked."

"We were, but his response was out of all proportion to the attack. He was out of control."

"Like I was," Maya said, "before karate."

"Yeah," Judson said, clapping her on the shoulder. "That wannabe warrior could have learned a lot from karate."

After dinner Shelby asked her to go for a drive with him, but she was tired from the *shiai* so she gently declined and went home with her family.

Lying in bed, she thought about the conversation at the restaurant, and she remembered the last time she had gone out of control. She had just turned twelve, and she was at the middle school, in seventh grade. They were having recess, and several kids were on the field kicking a soccer ball around. She had the ball, and three boys ganged up on her and tried to take it away from her. With her skillful footwork she managed to keep it, and one of the frustrated boys said: "Give us the ball, you greasy spic."

She abandoned the ball and went straight to him and punched him in the mouth, breaking his lip and drawing blood.

When he started crying she refrained from calling him a baby, but she had the thought that if you can't take it, don't dish it out, and she stood there defying the other two boys to retaliate. Instead, they went with the wounded boy to the principal and accused her of attacking them for no good reason.

She was called into the principal's office, where she had to confront her accusers.

"They say you attacked Brandon," the principal said. He was a mild man who obviously didn't like having to deal with violence.

"I had a reason," Maya said.

"What was the reason?"

"He called me a name."

"Well, you know what they say," the principal said. "Sticks and stones may break my bones, but names can never hurt me."

"That's not true."

"What's not true?"

"That names can never hurt you."

"What did he call you?"

Maya hesitated, and then she blurted out: "A greasy spic."

The principal turned to Brandon and asked: "Did you call her that?"

"No. I didn't. I didn't call her anything."

The two other boys supported him, swearing that he hadn't called her anything and claiming that she had attacked Brandon without provocation.

"We seem to have two different stories here," the principal said, clasping his hands.

"We're telling the truth, and she's lying," one of the boys said.

"I'm not lying. You're lying," Maya said, feeling the rage that had made her hit Brandon. "He couldn't get the ball away from me, so he called me a name."

"You're not going to believe her, are you?" Brandon said to the principal.

"Why shouldn't I believe her?"

"You know why."

"No, I don't know why," the principal said, beginning to show some backbone. "Why shouldn't I believe Maya?"

The boys were silent.

"If you mean what I think you mean, I'm inclined to believe her. You might as well have called her a name just now."

"We didn't call her anything," one of the boys said.

"Get out," the principal told them in disgust. "The next time you call someone a name like that, I'll have you suspended. You hear?"

The boys were again silent.

"And you better have a doctor look at your mouth. You may need stitches."

When the boys had left, the principal said: "Their behavior was unacceptable, but so was yours. If someone calls you a name, you can't just punch him in the mouth."

"Well, he hurt me, so I hurt him."

"Is that what your pastor would tell you to do?"

"No. But no one's ever going to call him a greasy spic."

"I have to admit," the principal said, "I don't know what it's like to be called a name like that. I can only imagine. But hitting people won't solve the problem."

"What will solve it?"

"Ignoring them and acting with dignity. I hope no one ever calls you a name like that again, but if someone does, just ignore it. Rise above it."

"How can I rise above something that drags me down?"

"That's a good question," the principal said, "but I think your pastor has the answer."

"I know what he'll say. He'll say to turn the other cheek."

"Then you already know what you should do."

"I know what I should do," Maya said, "but I still want to hit people when they deserve it."

The principal looked interested. "How often do you want to hit people?"

"I don't know. I guess about once a week."

"Do people call you names that often?"

"No. But they say things and they do things that make me feel—" Maya wondered if she could trust the principal.

"Make you feel what?"

"That I don't belong here."

"So you want to hit them when they say things or do things that make you feel you don't belong here?"

"Yeah. I do. I usually stop myself, but not always."

"If you don't mind," the principal said, "I'd like to talk with your parents about this. I'd like to find a way to channel your violent feelings into some activity."

"I don't mind," Maya said. "I'd rather not hit people. For one thing, it hurts my hands."

The principal smiled. "I'm sure it does. It also hurts you in other ways."

The governor was expected to take action on the immigration law by the end of the week, and though Maya hoped that people like Judson and Trevor and Father Philip would convince him not to sign it, she remembered what the big man with the red neck had said at the meeting and how the guy from the Chevron station had stared at her when he paid for the bottle of ibuprofen and what the boy at middle school had called her, so she wasn't surprised when the governor signed the law on Thursday.

With her family that evening Maya felt like she was at a wake for her father's dream of living in America. Always optimistic, her father reminded her that the law would be challenged and would probably never be implemented, but she was despondent. The day after earning her brown belt she had fallen again from the euphoria of achieving something, and she wondered if there was any use trying.

FOUR

THE NEXT DAY her father contacted the landlord and began the process of trying to get his investment out of the house. The landlord was willing to pursue a deal, subject to their getting an appraisal of the house's current market value. That took a week, and meanwhile the landlord's accountant reviewed the material her father presented to support the value of the improvements he had made. The total was ninety-one thousand two hundred thirty dollars, and the landlord agreed to a rounded value of ninety thousand. It took another week to work out all the details with the landlord, who brought his lawyer to Trevor's office for several meetings. Maya attended all the meetings since her father wanted her to know what was happening.

They closed the deal on July 1 with her father buying the house at the option price and immediately selling it back to the landlord at the market price, collecting the difference of ninety thousand dollars, which the landlord financed with a loan that Trevor arranged with the bank on the main floor of the building. They transferred the money to a dollar account that Trevor helped her parents open with Banco Nacional, an affiliate of Citibank, with which he had a relationship. Trevor said it would be prudent for them to have the money there.

With the money in hand, her mother began urging her father to return to Puebla before the immigration law was implemented. The timing would be right for Selina and Victor, who were on summer vacation now, and they could get settled before school started in Mexico. Maya could start at the university, and if all went well she could live there in a dormitory as planned, but if anything happened she would have a home in Puebla.

Her father pointed out that if they left Maya and if all went well they wouldn't see her for at least four years since she couldn't go to Mexico and then come back. Her mother suggested that Maya get a visa and become an international student. Her father asked Trevor about that, and Trevor said it was possible but would require Maya to redo the process of being admitted to the university. Though it might set her back a year, Maya was willing to do this for the sake of her family, but her father refused to give up his dream, and he decided that they should stay in America and hope that the federal government would stop the law from being implemented. So despite her mother's strong misgivings he entered into a one-year lease with the landlord, who still didn't know they were illegal immigrants.

Meanwhile the Southern Poverty Law Center in alliance with the American Civil Liberties Union, the National Immigration Law Center, the Asian Law Caucus, and the Hispanic Interest Coalition of Alabama filed a lawsuit in the U.S. District Court for Northern Alabama asking it to declare the law unconstitutional. Churches mobilized against the law, and the Birmingham City Council unanimously passed a resolution calling for repeal of the law. So it looked like many people, if not most people, were against the law.

For the next few weeks Maya followed the Women's World Cup in soccer, watching as many of the American team's matches as she could. She was elated by their victories against North Korea and Colombia, she lamented their defeat by Sweden, and she shouted with joy when they won the shootout against Brazil. She was relieved when they defeated France, but she was shocked when Japan tied the championship match with only a few minutes to play, and she moaned when they lost the shootout. Still, she felt they had played well, and she was especially proud of the fact that there was a Latina on the team. And she didn't begrudge the victory to Japan after all they had suffered from the earthquake and the tsunami.

She would have liked to watch some matches of the Copa América, which were being played during July, but she wasn't able to find them on television, so she had to read about them in the paper. She was disappointed that Mexico lost all three matches in the first round, and she didn't have a preference in the final match between Paraguay and Uruguay since they were both small countries and after Mexico was eliminated she wanted a small country to win.

Her last day of work at the pharmacy was Friday, July 22 so that she would have a full week to get ready for college. She had helped Mr. Otis find a replacement, a girl who played on the soccer team and would be a junior in the fall. At the request of Mr. Otis she went to the store at four on Saturday, and he had a little party for her, wishing her well and giving her an envelope with two hundred dollars in cash.

The following Monday her mother took her shopping for things she would need for college, including a suitcase. She already had a bag she had used when the soccer team played away matches. On those occasions she had traveled short distances from home, but except for a few nights in a hotel at the state tournament she had never slept away from home, so she was anxious as well as excited about living in a dormitory.

That Saturday, the day before she was due at college, her mother had to clean the house of a longtime client who was having a party. Since her mother had promised to take the kids to the swimming pool, she asked Maya to take them. Maya was already packed, so she had nothing else to do, and after a lunch of hot dogs and potato salad they headed for the pool. They wore their swimsuits, with Maya and her sister in covers and her brother in a tee-shirt. Maya carried their towels in a bag her mother used for that purpose.

The pool was a twenty-minute walk from their house in an area where white people still lived. About forty years ago when black people started using the pool, white people stopped using it. The town then built a new pool far enough away so that black people had trouble reaching it. So you didn't see many white people swimming in the old pool. What you saw were blacks and Latinos in about equal numbers. They mixed in the water, but when they got out they joined their own groups and stuck together, as they did at school.

As soon as they got to the pool Victor tore off his tee-shirt and dove in, while Selina carefully removed her cover and dipped a toe into the water. Selina always took forever to get into the pool and always kept her hair dry. Maya plunged in from a sitting position at the edge of the pool and swam a few laps, keeping an eye on her brother and sister. At one point a black boy who looked younger than she was started racing against her, and immediately rising to the challenge, she accelerated her pace and beat him.

"You good," he told her.

"You are too," she told him.

"You on the swimming team?"

"No. The soccer team."

He nodded, impressed, and then swam away.

They stayed for a few hours, mostly in the water. There was no reason to sunbathe since they were already brown.

They were walking home, still in the white neighborhood, when they passed three white guys who were sitting on a wall. They looked about Maya's age.

"I smell something," one of the guys said.

"I do too," another guy said. "I think it's grease."

"They look like they've been swimming," the other guy said.

"Yeah. Swimming with niggers."

Selina moved closer to Maya, leaning against her, while Victor stared straight ahead.

"Who the hell gave you permission to walk through our neighborhood?" the first guy asked, rising from the wall and blocking their way.

"We don't need permission," Maya said, facing him. "This sidewalk is public property."

"It's public property for Americans, but not for you."

"We're Americans as much as you are."

"You don't look like Americans. You look like greasy spics."

"You look like dumb rednecks," Maya told him, unable to stop herself.

"What did you call us?" the guy said with murder in his eyes. He came closer, defying her to repeat what she had said.

"You know what I called you, and if you don't get out of our way, you'll be sorry. I have a brown belt in karate."

"A brown belt? What does that mean?"

"It means I could hurt you."

"If she has a brown belt in karate," the second guy said, "she *could* hurt you."

"Are you saying I should be afraid of this pissant girl?"

"I'm only saying you should respect her."

While they were talking Maya imagined shedding her flip-flops and doing a *yoko geri* (side kick) on her aggressor, breaking his ribs with the knife-edge of her foot. But she hoped he wouldn't provoke her into kicking him since it would get her family into trouble.

After some consideration the guy said: "I'll tell you what. If you take back what you called us, I'll let you walk by."

"I'll take back what I called you if you take back what you called us."

"I'm not going to take back what I called you."

"Then at least get out of our way."

"Why should I?"

"Because if you don't," Maya said, planning the punches that would follow her kick, "I'll leave you on the sidewalk with broken bones."

The guy laughed nervously. "You think you can bluff me?"

"I'm not bluffing you. I'm warning you."

"I think you better let them walk by," the second guy said. "It's no big deal."

There was a long silence during which Maya and the first guy stared into each other's eyes. She knew from the weakness she saw in him that he would be no match for her, and for a moment she hoped he wouldn't get out of their way so that she could satisfy her urge to make him pay for what he had called them. But then she thought of the consequences, and with one arm around her sister and the other around her brother, she guided them around the guy.

"You greasy spic," he called her from the safety of distance.

Maya ignored him and silently prayed: "Lord, make me an instrument of your peace."

On Sunday, July 31, Judson drove Maya and her parents to Tuscaloosa, which was about an hour and a half from Harperville. Maya had selected her dormitory room online and had printed a campus map, so with her navigating in the passenger seat they had no trouble finding Tutwiler Hall, a female dormitory on the southwest side of the campus.

Maya had been in contact with her roommate, who was planning to arrive today in the late afternoon. Her roommate, Erin, also played on the soccer team, and like Maya she had to be there for training camp, which began on Wednesday, August 3. From their exchange of messages Maya knew that Erin was from Pelham, New York, a suburb of New York City, and that her father was a doctor. Her mother had been a nurse but now worked at home raising her children. Erin had two younger sisters, one of whom sounded like Selina.

The dormitory was taller than any building Maya had seen before, and gaping up at its higher floors she was momentarily overwhelmed. Then with Judson and her father each carrying a bag, she wheeled her suitcase into the building, checked with the receptionist, and headed for the elevator as if she were used to such buildings.

Her room was on the fifth floor, and it was furnished with two twin beds, a desk, and two chairs. There were two built-in wardrobes as well as a built-in dresser and a built-in desk. She and her roommate would have to share the dresser, and they would have to decide how to allocate the desks. There was no sign that Erin had arrived, so Maya refrained from taking a wardrobe or a bed since it would be better to work that out together.

"It's a nice room," Judson said.

"It should be big enough for both of you," her mother said.

It was bigger than the room Maya shared with her sister, so it would be fine.

As they stood there making conversation to mask the anxiety of parting, the door opened revealing a girl with blond hair and rosy skin and bright blue eyes whom Maya recognized from an exchange of photos.

"Erin?"

"Maya?"

They both laughed at how dumb they must have sounded. Then Erin advanced into the room, followed by two people who looked like parents.

There were introductions, and for a while the conversation was dominated by the parents, with the men talking about how they had gotten to Tuscaloosa and the women talking about how the room could be decorated.

Then Judson said: "I think it's time we headed home."

As if they had clearly received this signal that it was time to leave the girls alone so they could begin working things out, both sets of parents hugged their daughters and said goodbye and left the room.

"It suddenly got quiet," Erin said. She spoke fast, sounding like the people in detective programs set in New York.

"It did, didn't it," Maya agreed, wondering what she sounded like to Erin. According to Shelby, she didn't have a Southern accent, she had a Latino accent.

"Which bed do you want?" Erin asked.

"I don't care," Maya said. "Which bed do *you* want?"

"I don't care either," Erin said.

They each ended up taking the bed that was nearest to where she was standing.

"If you want," Maya said after lifting her bags up onto her bed, "you can have the top drawers in the dresser. I don't have a lot of clothes."

"I don't either," Erin said. "I'll take the bottom drawers."

In this spirit it didn't take long for them to allocate the room's resources, and it didn't take long for them to unpack and put their clothes in the wardrobes and the dresser. Neither of them had a lot of clothes, so there was plenty of room for them. In fact, Maya had never had so much room for her things.

By now it was after five and they were both hungry. There was a snack bar in the building, but they wanted something more substantial and they also wanted to explore the campus, so they went out and headed toward University Boulevard, where they hoped to find a restaurant.

They asked a guy who looked like a student where they could get a good hamburger, and he directed them to a place called Buffalo Phil's, a few blocks west on University Bloulevard.

The place wasn't crowded, maybe because it was early or maybe because most of the students were still on vacation. In any case, they easily got a table, and they considered ordering the buffalo wings for which the place was famous, but they finally ordered burgers.

As they waited for their food Maya felt the vibration of her phone in the pocket of her jeans. It had vibrated while she was in the dormitory room, but she had ignored it, assuming it was Shelby and believing it was rude to pay attention to the phone while she was with people. Again, she ignored it, but Erin apparently could tell by the expression on her face that her phone was alerting her.

"If that's a message, you can check it," Erin told her.

"I don't need to. I know who it is. It's my boyfriend," Maya added, deciding not to leave her roommate in suspense.

"Where is he?"

"He's here in Tuscaloosa."

"He's going to the university?"

"Yeah. He's here now to try out for the golf team."

"Well, I'm glad my boyfriend isn't here. I need a break from him. Things were getting too serious."

"Is he going to college?"

"He's going to Holy Cross," Erin said, "so I won't see him until Thanksgiving."

Maya didn't know where Holy Cross was, but she thought it was somewhere in New England. "Won't you miss him?"

"I will, but I can live without seeing him for a few months."

When their food arrived they stopped talking for a while, and then Maya asked: "When you were at home how often did you see your boyfriend?"

"Every day."

"I saw my boyfriend every day except Sunday. We went to different churches."

"We went to the same church."

"Well, I don't think I can see my boyfriend as often here. I'm on a scholarship, so I have to do well in my courses."

"How often does he expect to see you?"

"I don't know. I guess every day."

"Then he has to understand your situation."

"Can I ask you a question?"

"Yeah. Sure."

"Do you feel bad about needing a break from your boyfriend?"

"No. You see, I realize that unless you have your own space," Erin said, talking fast, "you can't develop your own identity. And until you have your own identity you can't really love anyone, not even yourself."

"That's what I think," Maya said, impressed, "but I never could have put it that way."

"So don't feel bad about not seeing your boyfriend as often as you did at home. What's good for you is good for him."

They returned to their room and made their beds, using the sheets that had been left for them on top of the dresser. While they were doing this she felt her phone vibrate, but she ignored it until they were finished. Then she sat down on her bed and checked her messages. "I'm here. Are you?" "How's your room?" "I heard about a great place to eat. Can I pick you up?" In all there were seven messages from Shelby, with the last one asking: "What are you doing?"

She texted him back: "I just finished making my bed. I'm really tired so I'm going to sleep. I'll see you tomorrow. I love you."

Within a minute he replied: "Okay. I love you too."

The bathroom was communal, which Maya didn't mind after living in a house with only one bathroom. She and Erin headed there together, and on their way back they met two girls who also played soccer. They were sophomores, and their names were Dana and Jackie.

Before slipping under her sheets she turned off her phone in case Shelby decided to text her during the night. She didn't want to be disturbed in any way.

They were both in bed with the lights out when Erin asked: "What time do you usually get up in the morning?"

"For school I had to get up at six, but I don't like to get up that early."

"I don't either. I'd like to sleep late tomorrow, but I have a meeting with my adviser."

"What time is your meeting?"

"It's at ten," Erin said regretfully.

"Then we can sleep until eight tomorrow."

"You have a meeting too?"

"No, but I'll get up with you."

"You don't have to."

"I want to. And if I sleep too late, I'll never wake up."

"So I'll set my alarm for eight. Okay?"

"Okay," Maya said. She closed her eyes while Erin turned on a light and set her alarm.

After turning off the light Erin asked: "Do you have classes early in the morning?"

"I don't have any before ten."

"I don't either. So we won't have to get up early during the week, and we can sleep late on the weekends—unless you have a Saturday class."

"I don't. Thank God."

They said goodnight, and being so tired, Maya expected to fall asleep right away, but she was kept awake for a while by the fear that her happy situation could be abruptly ended by the part of the law that prohibited illegal immigrants from attending public universities.

She awoke before Erin's alarm went off, and together they staggered to the bathroom, where they ran into Dana and Jackie.

They learned that the best place to eat was Burke Dining Hall, where you could get anything including healthy food, and the most convenient place was Julia's Market, which was right in Tutwiler Hall. But they weren't serving breakfast yet at Burke, and Julia's was takeout, so they suggested going to Starbuck's, where they could get muffins or bagels with a good cup of coffee. Maya didn't drink coffee, but she liked muffins, and when they were ready the four of them headed for Starbuck's, which Dana said was a twenty-minute walk.

From their exchange of information Maya learned that Dana was from Mississippi and Jackie was from Georgia, and that they were both midfielders. Since she and Erin were both forwards, in theory they could all play together.

As they walked at a leisurely pace to Starbuck's they talked about the team orientation meeting, which was the next day, and about the coach.

"What's he like?" Maya asked.

"He's tough but fair," Dana said.

"He understands females," Jackie said.

"That's good," Erin said. "I had a coach who didn't know the difference."

Starbuck's was in Ferguson Student Center, which offered a wide range of services including a food court and a supply store. Erin got a plain bagel which she smeared with cream cheese, and Maya got a blueberry muffin.

They hung out there for a while, but then Erin had to leave in order to make her ten o'clock meeting. Maya lingered after the two other girls had left, exploring the center. Among other things she noted that there was a place where you could watch television. She didn't watch television much, but she liked watching sports, unlike her sister who liked watching things like "Project Runway" and "America's Next Top Model."

She was strolling back to the dormitory when her phone

vibrated. She stopped and saw that it was Shelby, who asked: "Can I give you a tour of the campus?"

Maya had no appointments since she had done everything online, including her registration and her financial aid, so she texted back: "Sure."

"Where are you?"

"I'm on University Boulevard."

"Where on UB?"

"Between the student center and my dorm."

"Wait on the north side of UB and I'll look for you."

She stopped where he could easily spot her, and she waited for him. In less than five minutes she saw his car, which pulled over in front of her.

She got in and buckled her seatbelt.

"Are you settled in your dorm now?" Shelby asked as they drove away.

"More or less."

"Is your roommate here?"

"Yeah. And she's really great. She's from New York. She has an accent and she talks very fast."

"So she's a Yankee."

"I guess, but I like her."

"What have you seen of the campus?"

"Not much. Only my dorm and the student center."

"Then I'll take you to the soccer complex," Shelby told her. "That's where you practice and play your matches."

"Is it far from here?"

"It's too far to walk from your dorm. You should have picked a dorm that's closer."

"There are at least three other girls in my dorm who play soccer, so I'm not the only one. They must have had a reason for advising me to live there."

"You asked for a female dorm. You could have been in a co-ed dorm."

"I didn't want to be in a co-ed dorm."

"Well, I'm sure there's a bus that'll take you to the soccer complex."

As he drove around the block she put on the radio and looked for a station that played the kind of music they liked. For a while she got only country music, but she finally found a good station, which was playing "Just the Way You Are" by Bruno Mars. The song had a special meaning for her since it was playing when Shelby first told her he loved her, and it reinforced her hope that he loved her just the way she was, a brown girl regarded by the white girly-girls as a tomboy and by rednecks as a greasy spic. It had also pleased her to learn that Bruno Mars had a Puerto Rican father and a Filipino mother.

Shelby gave her a grand tour not only of the campus but also of Tuscaloosa, except for the area where people might want to steal his car. After more than an hour of riding around he invited her to lunch at Buffalo Phil's, which they had just passed.

"I ate there last night with my roommate," she said, "but it was good, so I don't mind eating there again."

"We could try another place," he said amenably.

"Do they have a Sonic in Tuscaloosa?"

"They must. Here, look for one." He handed her his phone, which could do anything a computer could do.

She found more than one Sonic in Tuscaloosa, and they headed for the one on University Boulevard East, with Shelby using his GPS to navigate there.

Eating at Sonic gave her a feeling of comfort, but it didn't take away the fact that they were in a different situation now without their families setting limits. And she could anticipate a conflict between Shelby's need to see her often and her need to have time for herself.

This conflict emerged when he stopped to let her off at Tutwiler around three and said: "Let's do something tonight. Okay?"

"I told my roommate I'd do something with her," Maya said, though it was an intention rather than an arrangement.

"What are you going to do with her?"

"I'm going to have dinner with her."

For a moment Shelby looked as if he might ask if he could join them, but then he said: "Well, how about tomorrow night?"

"I can see you then, but I can't stay out late. We have our first training session the next day."

"Don't worry. We won't stay out late."

She leaned over and kissed him tenderly.

"I love you," he said.

"I love you too."

She was glad to find Erin in their room, and they hung out there for the rest of the afternoon.

Not knowing if Maya would be with her boyfriend, Erin had told Dana and Jackie she would join them for dinner, so around six the four of them walked to Baker Dining Hall, where they hung out for the next few hours. Being with them, Maya didn't miss being with Shelby. She would see him tomorrow, and somehow she would find a way of balancing things.

They had just returned to their room when her phone vibrated. She assumed it was Shelby, but when she checked the screen she saw it was her father.

She answered, saying: *"Hola, papá."*

"Hola," he said. *"Cómo están las cosas en la universidad?"*

"Bien. Qué noticias hay?"

"Well, I thought you'd want to know that today the federal government filed a lawsuit against the state of Alabama."

"They did?" She was standing in the middle of the room, conscious of Erin, who had flopped down on her bed. She hadn't told Erin about her situation, even though she already felt she could trust her roommate with her life.

"The lawsuit says that the state of Alabama can't have its own immigration policy."

"So it can't implement that law?"

"The federal government says it can't," her father said, "and the state says it can. The courts will have to decide who's right."

"How long will that take?"

"I asked Trevor, and he said it might not take them long. He said it didn't take them long to rule on the Arizona law."

"I hope it doesn't take them long."

"Also today the churches filed a lawsuit against the state. They say that the law makes it a crime to follow God's commandments."

"Was Father Philip involved?"

"Oh, yes. And he sends you his blessings."

"Does mom feel better?"

"No, not really. She still doesn't trust the government. You know your mother."

Maya as usual was caught between them, feeling better but at the same time not trusting the government.

"Have you gotten settled?' her father asked after a pause.

"Yeah, I have. And I have a great roommate." She smiled at Erin, who was looking through the packet of material that the athletics department had sent them.

Erin smiled back as if she felt likewise.

"I'll let you know when there are more developments," her father said.

"Okay. I love you. Say hi to mom."

"Te amo, hijita. Y nunca pierdas tu fe en Dios."

After ending the call she sat down on her bed, wondering if she should tell Erin about her situation. She didn't want to burden her roommate with information that could make her worry or get her into trouble, but as far as she knew, the law didn't make it a crime to room with an illegal immigrant, and it didn't feel right to withhold such information from Erin, so she began by saying: "That was my father."

"Is everything all right?"

"Yeah. There's something I should tell you. I'm an illegal immigrant," she said, talking faster than usual, "and the state of Alabama passed a law that prohibits illegal immigrants from attending public universities."

"I heard about that law," Erin said. "Will it affect you?"

"I don't know. They admitted me before the law was passed, and they didn't ask for proof of citizenship. They asked for transcripts and SATs and recommendations."

"They must have assumed you were a citizen."

"They must have. And our lawyer says that the law doesn't require them to report my status, as it does for students in public schools."

"Then you should be okay."

"I should be," Maya said. "But I still worry about it."

"My father says the federal government will never let them implement that law."

"Yeah, my father says that too, and he believes it. But he's an optimist."

"You're not an optimist?"

"Sometimes I am," Maya said, "and sometimes I'm not."

"I understand. It depends on whether you have a reason to be optimistic."

"My father called to tell me that the federal government has filed a lawsuit against the state of Alabama, and so has a group of churches."

"Then you have a reason to be optimistic."

"I guess I do," Maya admitted, drawn toward her father's position. "The last thing my father told me was never to lose my faith in God."

"Are you a Catholic?"

"Yeah. Are you?"

"I'm Irish, in case you didn't guess."

"I'm Mexican, in case you didn't guess."

They laughed compatibly.

"I like the name Maya," Erin said.

"My actual name is Mayahuel."

"What does it mean?"

"It's an Aztec goddess of fertility," Maya explained, drawing on what she had learned from her mother. "She has many breasts to feed her many children. She's associated with the maguey plant, which they use to make *pulque*, an alcoholic drink like beer."

"Breasts and beer. The guys would love her."

They laughed again.

"What does Erin mean?"

"It means Ireland. The funny thing is, people in Ireland don't have that name. Only people in America have it."

"I guess our parents wanted people to know our origins."

"I guess they did. Well, I'm proud of my origin, but I'm an American."

"That's how I feel. But there are people who make me feel I don't belong here."

"My father says they made the Irish feel they didn't belong here. But we survived, and you will too."

"If you don't want to room with an illegal immigrant," Maya said after a silence, "you can ask for a change. You can tell them I'm a slob."

"You're not a slob," Erin said firmly. "And I don't want to room with anyone else."

The team orientation was the next day at three. The packet of material told them how to get to the soccer complex from the different dormitories. The easiest way for Maya and Erin was to take a bus that stopped at Tutwiler. There was more than one line in the network called the Crimson Ride, and they were instructed to take the Blue Line. So around two thirty they got together with Dana and Jackie and went to the bus stop, where they met several other girls from Tutwiler who were going to the soccer complex.

They got there about ten minutes early and found the room where the meeting was. As they entered the room, which was filled with girls, they were stopped by a man who was holding a clipboard. He had a reddish blond hair and cheery blue eyes, and he looked very glad to see them though he couldn't have possibly known who they were.

"Welcome, ladies," he said with an accent. "I'm Tom Hogan. Who are you?"

"I'm Erin Healy."

"I'm Maya Méndez."

He checked their names on his clipboard, saying: "I see you're freshmen."

"Right, sir," Maya said.

He smiled at her. "I like it that you show respect, but you don't have to call me sir. You can call me coach. I also see you're forwards."

"Right," Maya said.

"Are you roommates?"

"Yes," Erin said.

"Good. If you can live together, you can play together."

They moved on and took seats in the back row.

Whispering, Maya asked Erin: "What kind of accent does the coach have?"

"Irish. He's from Ireland."

They waited until about thirty girls were in the room, and then the coach welcomed them and introduced his staff, which included a male assistant coach and a female assistant coach. He reviewed the team's record last year, which was 8-8-2 overall and 3-6-2 in the conference. He praised the returning players but said he expected the team to do better this year. In fact, he set a goal of a winning record both overall and in the conference.

He then handed out a schedule of the training sessions between then and their exhibition match against Clemson on Sunday, August 14. The first session was the next day, early in the morning. After that they would have sixteen training sessions, including six double-day sessions leading up to the match.

The meeting was followed by a tour of the facilities conducted by the assistant coaches at the end of which the players were assigned lockers.

As they rode the bus back to Tutwiler they talked about the coach.

"I like him," Erin said.

"I do too," Maya said.

"Then you'll play for him," Dana said.

"We have to like our coach to play for him?" Jackie asked.

"No, but it helps."

"When I play for the coach," Erin said, "it brings out the best in me."

"You need a coach to bring out the best in you?"

"I guess I do."

"What about you, Maya?"

"I need a coach to bring out the best in me," Maya admitted. "But I also play for my father and my *sensei*."

"Your *sensei*?"

"My karate teacher."

"You do karate?"

"Since I was twelve. I needed to channel my violent feelings into a disciplined activity."

"You have violent feelings?"

"Sometimes I do."

"Well, if you have violent feelings while you're playing soccer," Dana said, "I hope you don't commit fouls."

"I don't. I never got a red card, or even a yellow."

"That shows you play for the team."

Maya understood. If you played for the team you resisted the urges to push or trip opponents with the ball since those actions could draw a penalty kick or leave your team a player short.

"Have you ever had to use karate?" Jackie asked.

"I almost have. But you're only supposed to use it for self-defense."

"You may need to use it on some of the guys here."

"Yeah, there are some real animals here," Dana said, "especially in the frat houses."

"There are also some on the football team," Jackie added.

"Maybe you can teach us karate."

"I can show you how to do some punches and kicks," Maya said, doubting they would take her up on the offer.

"That sounds good. You can do that after the soccer season."

At six thirty Shelby picked her up in front of her dormitory, and out of habit they went to Sonic. She still liked the food, but as she was eating the familiar hamburger she wished they had gone somewhere else. She wasn't excited by the prospect of eating at Sonic two or three times a week over the next four years.

After they left the restaurant Shelby drove around for a while looking for a place to park, and not finding one, he said: "Let's go to my room."

"Oh, I don't know," Maya said, having reservations. She didn't want to be in a situation where it would be harder to stop at kissing.

"I want you to see it. And I don't know where else we can have some privacy."

"If I go to your room, I won't make out with you there."

"You won't let me kiss you?"

"I will, but things haven't changed just because we're away from home." Of course things had changed, and that was the problem.

He parked in an area reserved for his dormitory, and he led her into the building. Immediately she could feel the difference between a male dorm and a female dorm, and it made her feel she didn't belong here.

His room was on the third floor. It was a suite with two bedrooms and a small common area. In his bedroom there was a bed, a desk, and a chair. He shared a bathroom with his suitemate, which wasn't exactly the same as a roommate since they could both lock the doors of their bedrooms for whatever reason.

As she surveyed the room she realized that the only place you could make out here was on the bed, and she could imagine what might happen.

"This is luxurious," she told him.

"It's not bad," Shelby allowed. "My suitemate won't be here until the semester begins, so I have this place all to myself."

"He's not an athlete?"

"He's an engineer."

"Well, I don't see how we can hang out here," she said after a silence. "There's no place to sit except the bed."

"We could lie on the bed and watch television."

"Sure. And anyway I don't like watching television."

He came to her and put a hand on her shoulder, turning her toward him and saying: "I just want to kiss you."

She let him kiss her, and she kissed him back. She still liked kissing him, but she was uneasy about doing it in his bedroom. Yet it would be ridiculous to leave the room and go down to his car and kiss there.

When he touched a breast she removed his hand. "I'm still not ready to make love with you. And I'm sorry if I gave you the wrong idea by coming here."

"You didn't give me the wrong idea. It came from me."

Suddenly feeling bad for him, she reached out and touched his cheek. "When we adjust to this new situation, everything will be all right."

He looked as if he believed her.

"Now, I don't know about you," she said, "but I have a training session tomorrow, early in the morning. So I need to get some sleep."

"Okay. I'll drive you back to your dorm."

"I can walk. I need the exercise." She kissed him tenderly, running a hand through his soft hair and feeling maternal.

"We'll see each other tomorrow?"

"Yeah." At some point she would have to help him understand why it wouldn't be good for either of them to see each other every day, but now wasn't a good time for that discussion.

FIVE

THEIR FIRST TRAINING session began with exercises whose purpose was not only to determine their level of fitness but also to start getting them into shape. Thanks to karate, Maya breezed through the exercises, actually enjoying them since physical exertion took her mind off the things that were worrying her.

When they did wind sprints the coach had the six new players race against each other. Maya and Erin finished way ahead of the others, and to test them against team standards the coach had them race against the two fastest members of the team. They won, finishing in a dead heat, which prompted the coach to say: "Welcome, ladies. We can use your speed."

They then did ball touches, with a ball for each player. The coach said he wanted them to do a thousand ball touches per day, which didn't seem possible to Maya when she did the math, but it gave her an idea of what the coach expected.

They worked on dribbling and then on passing, with two girls sharing a ball. The coach paired Maya and Erin, and he watched them intently. Maya was happy to see how well they worked together. It was as if they had played together in high school.

"Good pass," the coach told Maya. "You led her well."

They finally broke up into squads for small-sided games. The coach put the freshmen together against a squad of veteran players.

At one point Maya got control of the ball and passed it over to Erin, who passed it back to Maya as they advanced on the goal. Maya had a chance for a shot, but she thought Erin had a better chance, so she passed it back to Erin, whose shot was blocked by a defender.

When the play stopped, the coach took Maya and Erin aside

and told them: "There's a time to pass and a time to shoot. You made a good pass, Maya, but that was a time to shoot. In a match you won't get many shots on goal, so you have to take advantage of them."

"I understand," Maya said, nodding.

"I should have gotten my shot off sooner," Erin said.

The coach patted them both on the shoulders, saying: "If you learn from your mistakes, you'll get better. That's the purpose of making mistakes."

They spent the rest of the week on fitness and fundamentals, and in the next week they did more scrimmages, preparing for the exhibition match. In the scrimmages Maya and Erin played together with Dana and Jackie along with two other midfielders and four defenders who were veteran players. As the two forwards, Maya and Erin led the attack, and they were learning when to pass and when to shoot.

On Sunday Erin wanted to watch the game between the Yankees and the Red Sox that was on Sunday Night Baseball. Maya didn't know much about baseball and wasn't a fan of any team, though Shelby was a fan of the Braves. She remembered seeing a room with television at the student center, which they now called "the Ferg," so they headed there at six thirty since the game started at eight Eastern Time. On the way she learned from Erin why watching this game was so important.

"My father's from the Bronx," Erin explained, "and when you're from the Bronx the Yankees are your pride. In fact, there were times when people from the Bronx had nothing else to be proud of."

"Was your father poor?"

"He wasn't rich. He came from a family with seven children."

"You must have a lot of cousins."

"I have eighteen cousins."

"Do they live in the Bronx?"

"They mostly live in Westchester now."

"My cousins live in Puebla. I wouldn't know any of them. I

haven't seen them since I was three, and I don't remember anything from that age."

"I don't remember being three. But I remember going to Yankees games with my father when I was five. My mother didn't want to go, so he and I went."

"Did you play baseball?"

"I played softball. I was a shortstop, and the best thing I did was steal bases."

"You stole bases?" Maya said, not understanding.

Erin laughed gently. "It means that when you're on base you sneak to the next base when the pitcher isn't looking."

"I guess I should learn more about baseball."

"You'll see the best two teams tonight. The Phillies are good, and the Giants are good, but they play in the National League, which isn't as tough as the American League."

"I heard a lot of Latinos play baseball."

"Oh, yeah. There are hundreds of Latinos playing baseball. For the Yankees we have Alex Rodriguez and Robinson Canó and Bartolo Colón and Ivan Nova and Hector Noesí and Rafael Soriano and Eduardo Nuñez," Erin said, reeling off the names in passable Spanish, "who are all Dominicans, and Mariano Rivera, a Panamanian, and Jorge Posada, a Puerto Rican, and Freddy García and Francisco Cervelli, who are Venezuelans, and Luis Ayala, a Mexican."

"It sounds like Latinos are the whole team."

"They practically are."

"Is Ayala the only Mexican?"

"Well, Eric Chávez is of Mexican descent," Erin said, "so you can count him."

It made her proud of being a Latina. It also made her realize that if you had talent at sports you wouldn't have a problem with the immigration laws.

As they watched the game she was impressed by Erin's knowledge of baseball, which included statistics like batting averages and earned run averages. She could see how Erin would do well in the biology and chemistry courses she had to take in order to pursue a career in medicine.

It was a close game, and Maya got emotionally into it, rooting for the Yankees and in particular rooting for their Latino players. So she shared Erin's disappointment when Rivera blew the save in the ninth inning and Hughes lost the game in the tenth.

"We shoulda won it," Erin said in the accent that Maya now realized came from the Bronx. "We had them by the—how do you say it?"

"*Cojones*," Maya said, a converted Yankees fan.

Though her main activity now was soccer, Maya didn't want to lose what she had achieved in karate, so she found a place where she could practice two or three times a week. It was a patch of lawn behind Tutweiler that bordered on the narrow end of the parking lot. Since the grass was matted down from people walking over it to get to their cars or to 10th Avenue, it was all right for doing the footwork, and since there was no one around at seven in the morning, she had the place all to herself. Occasionally, a Latino maintenance man would come by and stop and watch her, and one of them commented in admiration for her having earned her brown belt, saying: *"Debes ser muy buena tener el cinturón marrón."*

She eased Shelby into a pattern of seeing her two or three times a week, and he stopped pressing to see her more often. They still went to Sonic, but more often they ate at Bryant Sports Grill, where she could use her meal plan, and on those occasions he didn't suggest that they go to his room. By then they had found a place by the river where they could park.

She spent a lot of her free time with Erin, not only in their room but also at other places on campus. Their first Sunday, mindful of admonitions from their parents, they went to the eleven o'clock mass at St. Francis, which they could walk to. From talking about it they discovered that religion played a similar role in their lives—it wasn't something they thought about much but it was something they couldn't live without. So they planned to go to mass on Sunday unless they were on the road for a match. Since the home matches on Sunday would usually begin at one and there wasn't a mass at ten, they would have to go to the nine o'clock during the season, which meant they would have to get up at eight.

The exhibition match against Clemson was on Sunday, August 14 at six in the evening. Judson drove her father to Tuscaloosa, and they were in the soccer stadium with a small partisan crowd to watch the team in its first encounter of the season.

As untried freshmen, Maya and Erin weren't in the starting lineup, but they expected to play in the second period. So they were surprised when the coach put them into the match with about ten minutes remaining in the first period and the score tied at 0-0. Maya was nervous, and she faltered in her first attempts to move the ball into scoring position, but she got ahold of herself and a few minutes before the end of the first period she passed to Erin, who was streaking down the middle. Maya danced around a defender to become open on the right, and she took a pass from Erin, who then got into a better position. After briefly debating whether to shoot or pass the ball back to Erin, she remembered what the coach had said about there being a time to pass and a time to shoot, so she faked a pass to Erin, drawing the goalkeeper back toward the middle, and she kicked the ball into the right upper net.

She and Erin slammed together in a wild hug while the other players churned around them and the crowd cheered. From the center of a mass of excited girls she saw her father and Judson and Shelby in the stands, gesturing happily. She had told her father it really wasn't necessary to drive all that way for an exhibition game, but now she was glad he had come.

As the team left the field for the half-time break the coach put his arms around her and Erin and told them: "Great play, ladies."

In the second period they had a few more chances to score, and Erin made a perfect kick that hit the post, with the goalkeeper vainly trying to stop it. Their team scored another goal late in the match, and they were happy with a 2-0 victory.

After the match the coach told the team what they had done well and what they still needed to work on, and he reminded them of the training session the next day.

When they had showered and changed, Maya and Erin met her father and Judson and Shelby outside. To celebrate their victory Judson took them to the Cypress Inn, a restaurant they never would have gone to on their own since it was out of their price range. Maya and her father and Erin went in Judson's car, and Shelby followed them in his car.

It was after ten when they left the restaurant, and Maya and Erin were dead tired. Judson drove them back to Tutwiler, and Shelby drove by himself to his dormitory. Before parting, Maya had given him a tender kiss.

On Friday evening they played Kennesaw State at home, and they won 7-1. The coach started Maya and Erin, and within the first minute they produced a goal. Receiving a pass from her roommate, Maya was in a good position on the right, but she saw that Erin was in front of the goal, and remembering what the coach had said, she decided it was a time to pass, so she passed to Erin after faking a shot, and Erin coolly kicked the ball into the left side of the net. In a later play Maya scored on a perfect pass from Erin, and they each had assists on the goals scored by four other players. As the coach said after the match, it was a lovely way to open the season.

On Sunday evening they played Samford in Birmingham. After fourteen minutes of the first period Erin scored a goal on a pass from Maya. Five minutes later Maya scored on a pass from Erin, and they took a 2-0 lead. But they didn't play so well in the second period. Samford outshot them and scored a goal. So the final score was 2-1.

After the match the coach told them he liked the way they played in the first period but he wasn't happy with the second period.

"It looked like you were coasting in the second period," he

told them, "and you gave them a chance to make a comeback. From now on I want to see you play two good periods, instead of just one. Is everyone on board?"

They murmured in assent. Maya didn't know how her teammates felt, but she felt she had let them down, and she vowed not to do it again.

Classes began on Wednesday, and the campus suddenly filled with people. There was more going on, and they were now on tighter schedules. It wasn't all about sports now, it was also about academics.

During that week Shelby told her he hadn't made the golf team. They were in his car, parked in the secluded spot they had found near the river, and feeling bad for him, she tried to comfort him. Then he admitted that he really hadn't wanted to play on the golf team, he was only doing what his father wanted. In fact, he didn't really like golf. So she encouraged him to do something that *he* wanted, believing that if he did well at it his father would be proud of him.

On Friday evening they played Memphis at home. The coach had prepared them for a tough match, and as soon as it started they could tell they were up against the best team they had played so far. The first period was scoreless, though Alabama had some opportunities. Erin had a shot that the goalkeeper blocked, and Maya had one that was just a little high. It looked like the match would be a draw, but twenty minutes into the second period Memphis scored the only goal, so the final score was 0-1.

"I'm proud of you," the coach told them after the match. "That team is highly ranked, and you played as well as they did tonight. The match could have gone either way. So let's make the next match go our way."

The next day at practice they worked on some things they could have done better in the match with Memphis, including defense. Memphis had outshot them, and that had been a determining factor in their loss, so they focused on reducing the other team's opportunities to score, which involved everyone from the forwards to the defenders.

On Sunday at noon they played New Mexico at home. They were outshot in the first period, but their defense held, and they did better in the second period. But they didn't score, and after two overtime periods neither team had broken the draw. So the final score was 0-0.

Sitting in the locker room after the match, they were dispirited. Maya felt she should have scored on a shot she had taken in the first overtime, and she blamed herself for not getting the ball past the goalkeeper. If she had only placed it a little further to the left, it would have been out of the goalkeeper's reach, and they would have won.

"Our defense was better," the coach told them. "It looks like that extra work paid off. Our offense was a little sluggish in the first period, but it picked up in the second period. We created a lot of good opportunities. We just couldn't score."

"I should have scored on the shot I had in the first overtime," Maya said.

"I blew my chance in the second overtime," Erin said.

"Well, think about how you could have scored on those shots," the coach told them, "and do it next time."

Judson hadn't been able to drive to Tuscaloosa for the match, but Shelby was waiting in front of the building when she and Erin came out.

"You played well," he told them.

"We could have played better," Maya said.

"Do you want to go to the Cypress Inn?"

"You can't take more than one passenger in your car."

"Erin could sit in your lap."

"No, thanks," Erin said. "I'm going back to the dorm now. I'm exhausted."

"I am too. We played a hundred and ten minutes."

"Then I'll take you back to your dorm," Shelby offered.

"You want to sit on my lap?" Maya asked Erin.

"Okay. I'll do it once," Erin said, "just so I can say I've ridden in a Corvette."

It was cramped, but it was fun, at least for the ten minutes it took them to get to Tutwiler, and when they got out they were no longer feeling so down.

"Thanks for the ride," Erin said to Shelby.

"Do you want to do something tomorrow?" he asked Maya.

"Sure," she said. "I'll see you tomorrow."

The next evening Shelby took her to Buffalo Phil's, where he gave her an update on his efforts to organize an intramural soccer team at his dormitory. Then he told her he was going to join a fraternity.

Since her impression of fraternities had come from movies, Maya asked: "Why? You want to spend your time at college drinking?"

"That's not what fraternities are about. They do good things. In fact, one of the fraternities I'm considering won an award for helping people in Tuscaloosa after the tornado last spring."

"Then maybe I'm wrong about them."

"You are. And there are advantages in joining a fraternity. You make contacts, and my father says it's important for me to make contacts while I'm at college."

"Would you live at the fraternity?"

"No. I'd stay in my dorm. But I'd socialize at the fraternity."

"You mean go to parties?"

"Socializing isn't only parties. It's also hanging out with people and getting to know them."

"Well, I hope you don't expect me to join a sorority."

"You don't need to. You have the soccer team."

She understood, and she ended up supporting the idea of his joining a fraternity. She just hoped he joined a good one.

On Monday, August 29 a federal judge temporarily stopped implementation of the state's immigration law, saying she needed more time to decide whether it was constitutional. She said she would issue a ruling by September 28.

As soon as she heard about the judge's action Maya called her parents. She talked first with her father, who answered the phone when he and her mother were both at home because his English was better. He said the judge's action confirmed his belief that most people in America were good, and that everything would be all right. She got a different perspective from her mother, who focused on the fact that the judge hadn't struck down the law, and that it could still be implemented. After listening to her, Maya felt that her mother would have been happier if the judge had ruled in favor of the law since it would have confirmed her belief that their family didn't have a future in America. Now her mother would have to endure another month of uncertainty about their status.

That night, as they were talking in the dark after going to bed, she told Erin about the judge's action. "So at least for a month I don't have to worry about my family being deported."

"Do you worry a lot?" Erin asked.

"Yeah. And I hear voices."

"You mean like Joan of Arc?"

"No. She heard voices of angels and saints. I hear rednecks."

"What do they tell you?"

"They tell me I don't belong here."

"They're wrong. You belong here as much as anyone. When did you start hearing them?"

"As far back as I can remember. But I started hearing them more often after they passed the immigration law."

"But that judge stopped them from implementing it."

"She only stopped them temporarily. She could still let them implement parts of it."

"She could. And I know which part you worry about most."

"I worry about the other parts, but according to our lawyer that part is the least open to challenge."

After a silence Erin said: "When you first told me about your situation you said that the law doesn't require the university to report your status."

"It doesn't," Maya said. "But they might check my status for some other reason."

"What other reason?"

"They might need more information for my scholarship."

"They have all the information they need. If they didn't, they wouldn't have given you the scholarship. So don't worry."

"But what if they found out that I'm illegal?"

"The coach wouldn't let them kick you out. You're a key member of our team."

"You think he has that kind of power?"

"Of course he does," Erin said definitely. "Coaches of sports teams are the most powerful people in Alabama. The stadium, a major street, and your boyfriend's dorm are named for a coach—Bear Bryant."

"He was a men's football coach."

"Well, under the law that makes women's sports equal to men's sports, our coach should have equal power."

Maya was impressed by this argument. "So if they found out that I'm illegal, you think our coach would protect me?"

"I know he would. The coach is Irish. He understands what it's like to be an underdog."

For some reason this conversation with Erin reassured her more than conversations with her father or Judson or Trevor or Shelby, maybe because her roommate brought a new perspective to the situation.

On Thursday the team traveled to San Diego for two matches over Labor Day Weekend. On Friday evening they played San Diego, which scored within the first minute and never let them catch up. With another goal in the second period, San Diego clinched the match, and the final score was 0-2.

The lesson, which the coach impressed on them after the match, was not to let the other team score an early goal. In other sports you might get away with letting the other team take an early lead, but in soccer it could be lethal. The coach also noted that they were outshot 13-3, which didn't speak well for their offense. Maya took this comment to heart and vowed to do better in the next match.

On Sunday afternoon they played San Diego State, and they bounced back from their loss on Friday. They did what San

Diego had done to them—they scored an early goal. On a corner kick by San Diego State their goalkeeper punched out the ball, and Maya got it and took it up the field. She eluded the defense and approached the goal, with Erin accompanying her. They were two on one, and deciding that this was a time to pass, she passed to Erin, who deftly kicked the ball into the net. Though they were outshot in the match, their goalkeeper stopped the other team from scoring, so the final score was 1-0.

"You showed a lot of character," the coach told them after the match. "You're on the road, a long way from home, and you didn't play your best on Friday. But today you showed what you can do, and you did it against a highly ranked team. This is a big win for you, and you should feel good about it."

Back in Tuscaloosa, Maya called her parents and told them about the trip. When her mother got off the line she continued talking with her father, who told her about the effects of the immigration law. He said there was a shortage of workers to harvest crops since illegal immigrants had responded to the law by moving to less hostile states or going back to Mexico. He had been able to find workers to pick Judson's peaches, but the farmers who had planted squash and tomatoes weren't able to harvest them, so their crops were rotting in the fields. For some farmers the loss of income would put them out of business.

Maya felt bad for the farmers, who were unintended victims of the law. At the same time she wondered what would happen to Judson if he couldn't find workers to pick his peaches next year. Though she had worried about her parents, she had never worried about Judson before, and it made her realize that no one in this world was secure.

She spent the week catching up on her studies, and she saw Shelby only once. She figured that if Erin could go for months without seeing her boyfriend, she could go for a few days without seeing hers.

They played UAB at home on Friday evening, September 9. It was a close match, and though Alabama outshot UAB they didn't score until late in the second period when Dana caught a rebound on a shot by Maya and drilled it into the open left side of the net. They staved off a counterattack by UAB and held them scoreless, so the match ended at 1-0.

"You did a really good job of keeping the pressure on them in the second period," the coach told them afterward. "You kept them out of it."

On Sunday she and Erin went to mass at St. Francis. It was the tenth anniversary of the terrorist attack on September 11, and though Erin had been only eight at the time she had vivid memories of how the attack had affected her community. A neighbor and the fathers of two of her classmates were lost in the World Trade Center, and in her schoolyard you could smell the grisly smoke from Manhattan.

At the mass they joined the congregation in reciting the September 11th Novena, and Maya put her heart into it, especially at the part where they prayed: "From hatred and from the demeaning of the dignity of the children of God, deliver us. From every kind of injustice in the life of society, both national and international, deliver us."

Meanwhile Shelby had narrowed his choice of fraternities to two, and he wanted her to help him make a decision. Both fraternities were having parties on Saturday before the football game with North Texas, which started at six thirty, and he asked her to go to the parties with him and give him her impressions. She told him she wasn't qualified to evaluate fraternities, but he insisted that she was. She also reminded him that she had a match the next day, but he promised not to keep her out late. So wanting to help him, Maya agreed to go to the parties.

It took her a while to decide what to wear. It wasn't that she had a lot of choices, but rather that she had no idea what to wear to a fraternity party. With Erin's help she finally decided on a simple skirt and top, which she had worn to the party after her high school graduation, and she spent more time than usual on her hair. Though she was going to the parties to make a judgment about the fraternities, she realized that the members would also make a judgment about her that would reflect on Shelby, so she wanted to look good for him.

When he picked her up he gazed at her in admiration and said: "You look beautiful."

"Thank you," she said demurely.

Always a gentleman, he opened the door of the car for her and waited until she was settled before closing it.

The first party went well. Though most of the guys had been drinking, they were under control, and when Shelby introduced her to his prospective brothers they treated her with respect. They checked out her body, but they were discreet.

The second party was another matter. It looked like there were more alumni, and the guys were less under control. The noise level was much higher, with less talking and more yelling. It didn't take Maya long to make a judgment about this fraternity, but before she could say anything to Shelby he was whisked away by prospective brothers who were evidently trying to convince him to join their fraternity.

Left alone, she was accosted by a big guy with a flushed face and a can of beer. Like so many of the guys he was overweight, and he looked old enough be an alumnus.

"Why, you're a pretty little thing," he said, leering at her with bloodshot blue eyes.

Not knowing what to say in response, she looked around for a way to escape.

"I'm J.T. Rutherford," the guy said, extending a meaty hand.

"I'm Maya," she said, not taking his hand.

"What kind of name is that?"

"It's a Mexican name."

"Are you a Mexican?"

"No. I'm an American." She refrained from adding: "Just like you."

He cocked his head, examining her. "You don't look like a Mexican. The Mexicans I've seen are short and fat."

She didn't say: "They're not as fat as you are."

"You're pretty enough to be a model."

"I don't want to be a model."

"What do you want to be?"

"I want to be a teacher."

"You're too pretty to be teacher," the guy said, closing the gap between them.

She backed away, looking desperately for Shelby and not seeing him.

The guy gripped her by the shoulder with his free hand.

"Please let me go," May said, barely controlling her anger.

"I'm not going to hurt you. I just want to kiss you."

"If you don't let me go, I'm going to hurt you."

The guy laughed. "How could a pretty little thing like you hurt me?"

"I could break your ribs or crush your windpipe."

The guy laughed again, though less heartily.

She broke his grip and turned away.

From behind he wrapped his burly arms around her and grabbed her breasts without letting go of his beer.

In a move she had practiced often she thrust her hands inside his arms and opened them, and then she pivoted and delivered a swift *teisho uchi* (palm heel strike) to his chin.

He dropped his beer and toppled backward, landing heavily on the floor amid the legs and the feet of people, who stepped away but otherwise paid no attention to him. They acted as if it wasn't unusual for guys to fall on the floor at their parties.

Satisfied that he wasn't dead but wouldn't be getting up for a while, Maya spotted Shelby and calmly walked over to him and said: "I have to go."

"Okay," Shelby agreed. "Were you talking with that guy?"

"What guy?" Maya asked dumbly.

When they were outside he asked her what she thought of that fraternity.

"I liked the other one better," she told him. "This one confirmed the bad impressions I had about fraternities."

"I liked the other one better too. But it helps to have your opinion."

She decided there was no point in telling Shelby what the guy had done to her.

By the time he dropped her off at Tutwiler she had put the incident out of her mind, and she slept peacefully.

On Sunday afternoon they played Morehead State at home. They scored within the first two minutes, and they had a lot of chances to increase their lead, but they didn't score again in the first period, and early in the second period their opponents tied the match. Alabama continued to outshoot the other team, but they didn't score again until the latter part of the second period, when Erin kicked in a rebound off the post. The final score was 2-1.

"You played well," the coach told them, "but you could have played better. It looked like after that early goal you were coasting for the rest of the period. But you came back and won after they tied it up, so you finally did what had to be done. The lesson is, when you get an early goal, build on your lead, don't coast on it."

On Monday the professor who taught her psychology course returned the papers they had handed in the previous week. The assignment was: "Choose a person who has had a major positive influence on you, and explain how that person is a role model." For Maya it had been difficult to choose among the three people who immediately came to mind—her father, her mother, and Judson—and she ended up including all of them in her paper, explaining what she had gotten from each of them: a dream from her father, a sense of reality from her mother, and a mission from Judson. She left out the fact that her family was illegal. Though she felt she could have trusted the professor with that information, she didn't want to take any chances. The paper was supposed to be three to five typewritten pages, but hers was slightly more than ten, and she hoped she wouldn't be penalized for writing too much. She could imagine what it would be like for the professor if all the students handed in papers that long.

At the end of the class the professor, a woman in her thirties, went around the room returning the papers. As students flipped to the last page and saw their grades they reacted with facial expressions or sounds. When Maya got her paper she saw her grade: A+. She also saw a note that said: "Please see me."

She waited until the other students had left the room and then nervously she approached the professor, saying: "You asked me to see you?"

The professor, standing by the podium with the papers of students who had been absent, smiled and said: "Yes. I did. Do you have a minute?"

"Sure. I don't have to be at soccer practice for a while."

"You play soccer?"

Maya nodded. She liked the professor, who had a nice smile and seemed to care about the students, but she didn't know where this was going. "I'm on the team."

"It's good to play sports. I played volleyball in college. It did a lot for me."

"I like volleyball. It's fun to watch."

"I wanted to tell you," the professor said after a pause, "how much I liked your paper. It was truly outstanding."

"Thank you," Maya said, lowering her eyes.

"I've been teaching this course for seven years, and I always assign that paper, so I've seen a lot of them. And I can tell you, most students choose their mothers, and they present a simple situation: the mother is strong, she works hard, she takes care of the family, and she motivates her children to do something with their lives. The father, if he's there at all, is behind the scenes. And there's no mention of a conflict between the mother and the father, except in cases where they're divorced, and in those cases it's only a relationship conflict."

Maya listened, feeling that the professor understood.

"But you presented a more complex situation," the professor continued, "where your mother leads you one way and your father leads you another way, and you have to decide which way to go or else find a way that reconciles the conflict."

"Writing about my situation helped me understand it."

The professor smiled. "That's what I always hope will happen when I assign this paper."

"And if I can understand my situation, then maybe I can help other people understand their situations."

"Well, I think you're on the right track toward understanding your situation. I see you want to be a teacher."

"Yes. I want to help people learn and develop."

"It's the mission you got from your karate teacher. What did you call him?"

"*Sensei*. It's Japanese for teacher."

"*Sensei*," the professor repeated. "Maybe he's the way that reconciles the conflict and retains the positions of both your father and your mother."

"Yeah," Maya said, reflecting.

At that moment several students came into the room for the next class, so they had to end the conversation, but Maya went away with the feeling she had learned something.

On Friday evening, September 23 they played Vanderbilt at home in their first conference match. In the first period Alabama outshot the other team but it took a while for them to score, which they finally did on a corner kick by a midfielder that curved around the goalkeeper and into the net. Remembering what the coach had said about not coasting, they kept the pressure on the other team through the second period, refusing to let them score. About halfway through that period Maya scored on a perfect pass from Erin, and the final score was 2-0.

"You put it all together," the coach told them after the match. "The offense was great and the defense was great. That's a good start for the conference season."

The following day the football team played Arkansas, and Shelby's parents let him and Maya have the two tickets they usually reserved for friends. An important alumnus and a major donor, Shelby's father had a box near midfield in which each seat cost six hundred dollars. According to Shelby, you couldn't get even one of those seats for a thousand dollars. You needed the kind of influence his father had.

Maya didn't want to go to the game. She didn't like American football, which in her opinion embodied the violence of the culture, and she wasn't eager to spend an afternoon with Shelby's parents. In the eighteen months that she had been going with Shelby she had seen them only a few times, starting with the time when he took her to his house specifically to meet them. She was wearing nice clothes for the occasion, and she presented herself to his parents feeling that for all her accomplishments she was at a major disadvantage.

His father, a tall handsome man with carefully tended blond hair and flashing blue eyes, appraised her face and checked out her body the way men often did, while his mother, a bony woman with a hard face and a perfect tan, had a lot of questions about her background. His mother spoke to her as if Maya were interviewing for a job cooking or cleaning house. So she didn't want to go to the game and be judged by his parents. But she decided that if she didn't go, no matter how Shelby explained her absence they would wonder why she hadn't accepted their invitation, and no matter how bad an impression she made in person she would come out worse for not being there.

Not having any alternative, she wore the same outfit she had worn to the fraternity parties, and Shelby told her she looked beautiful, as he had before. He evidently didn't see her clothes, he only saw her, which made her appreciate his compliments.

They were supposed to meet his parents at a reception in the stadium, and after parking in an area reserved for important people they found their way to the room where it was being held. Upon entering, she noticed that the people were mostly older and mostly white. The few blacks, who towered above the other people, were probably former football stars.

They spotted Shelby's parents talking with another couple, and they went over to join them.

"Hey, Shelby," his father said, looking glad to see him. He didn't look glad to see Maya, but he checked her out.

"Is this the golf player?" the other man asked.

"It is," Shelby's father said, though he had been disappointed on learning that Shelby hadn't made the golf team. "Shelby, this is Jim Harwood. We were classmates many years ago, and now he's an important banker in Atlanta."

"I'm not important," the man said. "There are no important bankers left in the private sector."

The two men laughed bleakly.

"Mr. Harwood, this is Maya," Shelby said, introducing her.

"Maya? What an exotic name." The man looked her over as if he didn't know what to make of her. "Are you an international student?"

"Ah'm from Alabama," Maya said, for Shelby's sake putting on an accent.

"You're from Alabama? I don't believe it," Harwood said. "Except for our wives, I never saw such a pretty girl from Alabama."

"Her parents are Spanish," Shelby's mother said.

Since she understood what his mother was doing, Maya didn't correct her. It was all right to have parents who were Spanish.

Harwood introduced her and Shelby to his wife, who was happily drinking champagne.

A black man in a white jacket stopped and asked what Maya and Shelby would like to drink. They both ordered cokes.

"Maya plays soccer," Shelby told the Harwoods. "She's on the women's team."

"I really don't know much about soccer," Harwood said. "I only know we lost to the Japs in the finals of the Women's World Cup."

"You mean the Japanese," his wife said.

"Whatever you call them, we lost to them. How's your team doing?"

"We're doing all raht," Maya said, keeping the accent.

"Well, keep the Tide rolling," Harwood said, patting her on the shoulder.

Her muscles tensed, but she smiled and said: "Ah will, sir."

They had seats for the game that people would die for, Shelby told her. She tried to look appreciative, and she tried to follow the action as the teams marched back and forth on the field like troops of soldiers. They wore so much protective equipment that you couldn't see their faces, you could only see their numbers. But after a while she was able to distinguish some of the players, especially the guys who ran out and caught passes. And when Marquis Maze returned a punt, reversing field and changing speed to elude tacklers for an eighty-three-yard touchdown, she jumped to her feet and cheered with the rest of the excited fans.

"Thanks for coming to the game," Shelby said when he let her off at Tutwiler.

"Thanks for taking me," Maya said.

"I noticed you didn't correct my mother when she said your parents were Spanish."

"I knew what she was doing. That's okay."

"I hope she doesn't still say that after we're married."

"Right now we have more important things to worry about."

"I guess we do," Shelby said.

They kissed goodnight.

The next afternoon they played Kentucky, and Judson brought her father to see the match. They played well in the first period, outshooting their opponents, but they failed to score. Only two minutes into the second period Kentucky scored on a long shot by a midfielder, and Alabama played hard, trying to catch up. About halfway through the period things got out of control, and they began to draw fouls and then yellow cards and finally a red card, which left them one player short. Five minutes later their goalkeeper drew a red card, and Kentucky scored another goal. From then on it was an uphill battle. Alabama scored a goal on a penalty kick, but Kentucky scored two more goals and won the match 4-1.

The coach upbraided them for the five yellow cards and the two red cards, saying: "That's not the kind of soccer I expect you to play. I expect you to play hard, but I also expect you to play fair. You can see what happens when you don't play fair."

They were all silent, and no one even suggested they had gotten bad calls from the referees. Though Maya hadn't drawn a foul, she believed that if she had scored or enabled Erin to score, their teammates wouldn't have been under so much pressure, so she felt as if she had gotten one of the red cards.

"Okay," the coach said. "Let's put that one behind us and move ahead. We have two matches in Mississippi next weekend."

When Maya came out of the building with Erin she saw her father, Judson, and Shelby waiting for them. She could tell from the look on Judson's face that he would have said the same thing the coach had said, but he must have assumed that the coach had said it so there was no need for him to repeat it. He simply asked: "Where would you guys like to eat?"

"I don't know," Maya said, not caring where they ate.

"How about the Cypress Inn?"

No one objected, so they headed there, with Maya and her father and Erin in Judson's car and Shelby in his car.

After they had ordered, Judson turned to Shelby and asked: "What are you up to?"

"Nothing much," Shelby said. "I didn't make the golf team."

"You didn't? I'm surprised. You must have had a lot of competition."

"I did. There were guys who already play on the tours."

"You're still playing, aren't you?"

"Yeah. But I'm not playing as much as I would have if I'd made the team."

"Why not? To play golf, you don't have to be on a team."

"I know, but I don't feel like playing as much."

"Shelby's trying to organize a team for intramural soccer," Maya said, not wanting him to leave a bad impression.

"That sounds like a good idea," Judson said.

"I'm working on it," Shelby said gamely, "but I don't have a team yet."

"Well, in the meantime keep playing golf. It's a game you can play your whole life."

"That's what my father says."

As they approached Judson's car after leaving the restaurant they saw that it was damaged on the left rear. A car must have smashed into it while the driver was carelessly backing up to get out of the parking lot.

"Thanks for letting me know about this," Judson muttered to the absent driver. He got into the car and started the engine and tried the lights, with his door open.

"The left tail-light doesn't work," her father told him. "Try the turn signal."

When Judson tried it the signal made a rapid clicking sound.

"That doesn't work either."

"Great," Judson said, getting out of the car. "Well, it's too late to have it fixed tonight. We'll have it fixed tomorrow morning."

"Can you drive without the tail-light?" Maya asked. She was conscious of Shelby examining his own car to make sure it wasn't damaged.

"Yeah," Judson told her. "I just have to be extra careful."

While Shelby went his own way Judson drove her and Erin back to their dormitory, and then he headed back to Harperville.

Lying in bed, Maya prayed that her father and Judson would get home safely. She knew that Judson would be extra careful, but she still worried that something would happen, so she left her phone on just in case.

Before the alarm went off the next morning she heard her phone. She rolled over and reached toward her bedside table to get it, hoping it was Shelby.

"Maya?"

"Yeah. Judson?"

"I'm sorry to wake you," Judson said, "but you need to know what happened. I would have called you last night, but I didn't want you to lose sleep worrying."

"What happened" she asked, suddenly awake and alert.

"About halfway home we were stopped by a cop. He cited me for a tail-light infraction. That should have been all, but then he shined his flashlight on your father's face, and he asked your father for identification."

She knew what was coming.

"When your father couldn't produce it, he made us go with him to the police station."

"Are you still there?"

"Yeah. But they finally let me make some phone calls. Before I called you, I called Trevor, and he's on his way here."

"Where are you?"

"In Miletus. It's about forty minutes from Tuscaloosa."

"I'll ask Shelby to drive me there."

"Don't you have classes?"

"I can cut them."

"I expect that Trevor will make them release us," Judson said calmly, "so it's not necessary for you to be here. There's nothing you can do to help us."

"I still want to be there."

"All right. They're telling me my time is up. I'll call you after they release us."

She immediately called Shelby.

"I'm sorry to wake you," she told him, "but I need a favor."

"Sure," he said, sounding groggy. "What is it?"

"I have to go to Miletus. It's about forty minutes from here."

"I'll find it on my GPS. When do you have to be there?"

"As soon as possible."

"I'll pick you up in fifteen minutes."

As she got dressed she told Erin what had happened. Erin was supportive and offered to help in any way she could.

Maya was standing in front of Tutwiler when Shelby arrived. She hopped into his car, and as they left town she explained why she had to go Miletus.

Shelby told her not to worry since even his father, who didn't like Trevor, admitted that he was a brilliant lawyer.

Miletus was smaller than Harperville, and they had no trouble finding the police station. When they entered the building they saw Trevor in the waiting area.

"What's happening?" Maya asked him.

"Let's go outside," Trevor said, getting up. "We'll have some privacy there."

They went out into the parking lot, where there were idle police cars. Two birds were fighting fiercely over a crust of pizza that lay on the asphalt.

After looking around to make sure that no one was listening, Maya asked: "Are they in jail?"

"They're in a holding area," Trevor said after sweeping hair off his forehead.

"Why haven't they been released?"

"They have to be released by the judge, and he hasn't come to work yet."

"When does he come to work?"

"At ten. So we have to wait at least an hour. If you want to have breakfast, there's a diner down the street."

The idea of eating anything made her feel sick, but out of consideration for Shelby she asked him: "Do you want to have breakfast?"

"It would kill some time," Shelby said.

"Okay." She turned back to Trevor. "Why are they holding Judson and my father?"

"They're holding Judson for not having the required lighting on the rear of his vehicle, and they're holding your father for not having a document that shows his immigration status."

"I thought that part of the state law was stopped by a federal judge."

"It was. But they can claim they weren't acting under that law. They can claim they were making a routine check."

She fumed for a while, and then she asked: "What could they do to my father?"

"They could turn him over to the immigration department."

"And what would happen then?"

"There would be a hearing to decide if your father should be deported."

"Would they let you present a case for not deporting him?"

"Of course they would," Trevor said. "Your father has the right to be represented by counsel. And I could present a strong case for not deporting him."

"Could you get him released in the meantime?"

"I'll try, but they could hold him until they verify his status."

"How long would that take?"

"It shouldn't take more than a few hours. In fact, they should have begun that process."

"So my father won't have to spend another night in jail?"

"He shouldn't have to," Trevor said.

"Does my mother know what's happening?"

"They let your father call her last night to tell her he wouldn't be coming home. I talked with her this morning, and I told her what I'd learned from Judson."

"What did she say?"

Trevor grimaced. "She said your family should have gone back to Mexico as soon as they passed that immigration law."

"It sounds like she blames you."

"She does, but she blames your father more."

As usual Maya could see her mother's side of things as well as her father's side, and she realized that while Trevor handled the legal aspects of the situation she had to try to reconcile the conflict between her parents.

SIX

TREVOR STAYED AT the police station hoping to meet with her father and Judson while Maya and Shelby went to the diner, where they killed some time. Shelby had a full breakfast with eggs, bacon, potatoes, and toast, and Maya had a piece of his toast, which she nibbled anxiously. Shelby kept trying to assure her that everything would be all right, and she appreciated his efforts, but she didn't believe him. She had a feeling that her whole world was about to collapse. It didn't help when she looked around the diner and saw that except for her and a bus boy, everyone was white.

They got back to the police station a few minutes before ten, and they waited another half hour for the judge to arrive. They were finally admitted to the courtroom, where they took seats in a middle row and waited again.

At eleven fifteen her father and Judson were escorted into the courtroom by a police officer. Maya caught her father's eye, and she clasped her hands at the level of her chin in a gesture of prayer. He nodded in acknowledgment, telling her with his expression not to worry, everything would be all right. The two men were then seated in the front row with Trevor.

A few minutes later the judge ambled in, preceded by a man in uniform who said: "All rise."

The judge was a tubby man with slicked-back gray hair and heavy jowls. He called the court to order in a deep voice with a thick accent, as if he had cotton in his mouth.

There were several cases ahead of them, and Maya watched as the judge meted out fines for traffic violations. He talked familiarly with the offenders, who were evidently local people. They all pleaded guilty and acted very grateful for the judge's leniency.

Finally, they called Judson's case, and with Trevor at his side he approached the judge.

"Which of you is Judson McBride?" the judge asked.

"I am, sir," Judson said quietly.

"And I'm his attorney, Trevor Wilcox."

The judge squinted at Trevor, asking: "Do I know you?"

"I don't believe we ever met," Trevor said.

The judge frowned as if he was trying to recall something, and then after clearing his throat he proceeded. "Mr. McBride, you're charged with operating a vehicle without the required lighting on the rear. How do you plead?"

"I plead guilty," Judson said.

"Since this is your first offense, I'm fining you one hundred dollars."

Unlike the local people, Judson didn't look grateful for the judge's leniency, but he made no comment. He inclined his head and stepped away.

They called her father's case next.

"Are you Ramiro Méndez?" the judge asked her father in a tone of voice that people used when they were speaking to inferiors.

"Yes, sir," her father said respectfully.

"Mr. Méndez, you're charged with not carrying a document that shows your immigration status. How do you plead?"

Trevor intervened, saying: "My client doesn't have to plead anything. In accordance with the federal law, I move that his case be transferred to an immigration judge."

"I'll take your motion under consideration," the judge said with narrowed eyes. "But we're going to hold your client until we verify his status."

"Have you begun the process?"

"We began it this morning."

"Then you should know his status within a few hours."

"We're dealing with the federal government," the judge said with contempt. "We probably won't hear from them until tomorrow."

"In the meantime you don't have to hold my client."

"We're going to hold your client until we verify his status," the judge repeated doggedly.

"You have no reason to hold him."

"We do. There's a risk of flight."

"Why would he flee? He has a family in Harperville."

The judge scowled. "These people always flee when the law catches up with them."

"Well, for the record," Trevor said, "I object to your decision to hold my client. Your court has no jurisdiction over him."

"You can object all you want. This is my court, and my decision stands." The judge banged his gavel as if he were killing a noxious insect. "Next case."

As her father was taken away by a police officer he made a soothing gesture to Maya with both hands meaning there was nothing to worry about.

Outside, she had more questions for Trevor, who joined her and Shelby in the parking lot. She began by asking: "Do you think they'll deport my father?"

"They've been deporting a lot of people. But last month they initiated a policy that suspends deportation proceedings against illegal immigrants who pose no threat to national security or public safety. They review the cases to identity those who should be deported and those who should be granted relief."

"Do you think he has a good chance of being granted relief?"

"I think he has a very good chance. He's lived in this country for fifteen years, and there's no indication whatsoever that he poses a threat to national security or public safety."

"How long will it take to review his case?"

"They have about three hundred thousand cases to review, so it could take months."

"And what will happen to him in the meantime?"

"He'll be released. As soon as I get him out of the hands of this judge and into the hands of a federal judge, there shouldn't be a problem."

"Do you know that judge?" Shelby asked. "He acted like he knew you."

"He must have remembered me," Trevor said. "I remember him. Before he was a judge he was a lawyer, as most judges were, and he defended a white supremacist, a member of the Ku Klux Klan. I was working for the district attorney at the time, and we won our case against him. We sent his client to prison, where he belonged."

"Then he's a racist," Maya said.

"You can't always judge lawyers by their clients, but in this case I think you can. So I want to get your father out of his hands as soon as possible."

"Can I talk with my father?"

"I think they'll let you. I'll ask them now."

Trevor was about to go inside when Judson came out looking as if he wanted to deliver a *mawashi geri* to the legal system.

"Are you all right?" Trevor asked.

"Yeah, I am," Judson muttered. "I'm sorry, Maya. This is my fault. We should have spent the night in Tuscaloosa and had the tail-light fixed in the morning."

"You didn't know you'd be driving through a county of fascists," Trevor said.

"I should have guessed that something would happen."

"It's not your fault," Maya said. "It's the fault of that law and the people who passed it. We never had any problems before."

"She's right," Trevor said. "That law changed everything."

"It didn't change anything," Judson said. "It only brought out the worst in people."

"I was going to ask them if Maya can talk with her father. Are you heading back home?"

"As soon as I get that tail-light fixed."

"Can I go with you?" Maya asked.

"Shouldn't you go back to Tuscaloosa?"

"I have to see my mother."

"Okay. You can go with me."

"I'll take you," Shelby offered.

"You already did enough by bringing me here. I'll see you back on campus."

While Trevor went inside to ask if she could talk with her father, Maya walked with Shelby to his car and gave him a loving kiss of thanks.

She was escorted by a police officer into a room that had a table and two chairs. Behind her was an opaque window that must have enabled the police to observe the people in the room.

The police officer invited her to sit down, and then he left her. A few minutes later he brought her father into the room. Her father looked as if he hadn't slept all night, but other than that she didn't see any signs of mistreatment.

"Stay on your side of the table," the police officer told her as she moved to go and hug her father. He evidently wanted to keep the table between them in order to prevent her from slipping a weapon to the prisoner.

Maya and her father sat down at the table across from each other, and they waited until the police officer had left the room before speaking.

"*Cómo estás, papá?*" she asked him.

"*Estoy bien. Y tú, hijita?*"

"*No estoy bien.* I'm worrying about what these people might do to you."

"Don't worry. Trevor will get me out of here. Did he explain what he's trying to do?"

She nodded. "Yes. And I have confidence in Trevor. But I don't trust the government."

"I don't trust the state government, but I trust the federal government. They're on our side."

"If they are, then why didn't they pass a law that would give us legal status?"

"They had other priorities. But their new policy will help us."

"Well, I'm not going to stop worrying until Trevor gets you out of here."

"He told me it should happen this afternoon. They only have to verify my status."

After a pause Maya said: "I'm going home to be with mom. I'm going with Judson after he gets that tail-light fixed."

"*Qué mala suerte,*" her father said, shaking his head. "I told Judson it wasn't his fault, but he blames himself for our getting stopped."

"It would have happened sooner or later."

"That's what I told him, but he still blames himself—after all he's done for our family."

"I wish there were more people like Judson."

"There're enough people like Judson. It doesn't take that many. And when you talk with your mother, try to make her see the positive side."

"What's the positive side?"

"The positive side," her father said, "is that there are people like Judson and Trevor."

"But aren't they outnumbered by people like that judge?"

"I don't believe they are. I still believe that most people in this country are good."

"And you still want to stay here?"

"Of course I want to stay here. Don't you?"

"In my heart I do," Maya said honestly, "but in my head I sometimes wonder if we'd have a better life in Mexico."

"Do you know what's happening there?"

"No." She hadn't been following the situation in Mexico.

"The country has been taken over by drug lords, who are not only killing each other but are also killing innocent people. They're killing people every day."

"That sounds bad."

"It *is* bad. And it's getting worse. So I don't want my children to live there."

"What if mom wants to go back there anyway?"

Her father sighed. "If your mother insists, I'll go back with her. But try to make her see that we'll have a better life here."

"Okay. I will," Maya said, feeling the heavy weight of that responsibility.

"And whatever happens," her father told her, "promise you won't give up the dream."

Maya hesitated, but sensing that her father needed her support to get through this ordeal, she said: "I promise."

Judson and Trevor were waiting outside when she emerged from the police station.

"My lights are working now," Judson said. "They only had to replace the bulbs. I can have the damage repaired later, so I'm heading back to Harperville."

"I'm going to stay here," Trevor said, "until they release Ramiro. And then I'll bring him home."

"Should I stay here too?" Maya asked.

"No, you should go home and be with your mother."

"When do you think they'll release my father?"

"This afternoon. He should be home in time for supper."

Reassured, she thanked Trevor and went with Judson, whose car was parked out on the street.

"Your father doesn't seem to have been discouraged by this experience," Judson said when they were in his car.

"He hasn't been. He still wants to stay in America."

"So he hasn't given up his dream."

"He made me promise not to give it up."

"How do you feel about that?"

She paused to reflect while they headed down the main street. "I feel I'm in the middle, being pulled in opposite directions."

"I understand. And your parents both have valid positions. Your mother sees how things have changed from the time when America welcomed immigrants, while your father still sees a land of opportunity where his children can have better lives than they'd have in Mexico."

"Do you think America still is a land of opportunity?"

"Well, look at your own case," Judson said, accelerating. "If your family was still in Mexico, would you be going to the university?"

"No. But if we went back, we'd be in a better position than we were before."

"You would be, so your mother has a point. But your father would argue that your family can still benefit from staying in America."

"My sister and brother can still benefit from staying here."

"Your mother can too. She's speaking much better English now, so she can get an education and a better job."

"They say there aren't any jobs now."

"There are jobs," Judson said, "but there aren't enough of them, so we need to create more of them. We just have to understand that this recession is the worst we've had since the 1930s, and that we'll take longer than usual to recover."

"When we do recover," Maya asked, "do you think people will feel differently about immigrants?"

"Some people will. But some people will take a long time to accept immigrants as equals. Some people still haven't accepted blacks as equals."

"Is there racism in Mexico?"

"There's racism everywhere. When I lived in New York I knew a guy who did business in Mexico. He said that more than ninety percent of Mexicans have Indian blood, but in all his years of traveling there he saw only white people in the top positions of organizations. And that included the government."

"Now that I think about it," Maya said, "the recent presidents have all been white."

"So you can't get away from racism."

"You can in sports. There's no racism on our soccer team."

"You're right," Judson said. "So stick with soccer, and you'll be fine. Don't worry about the politicians, who only bring out the worst in people."

It was almost two when Judson let her off in front of her house. On the way she had called and let her mother know she was coming, and her mother was sitting on the porch, waiting for her.

She thanked Judson and rushed to her mother, who rose and hugged her protectively.

"Estás bien?" her mother asked her, examining her.

"Yeah, I'm okay. And papa's okay."

"They let him make a phone call last night," her mother said, "so at least I knew he wasn't in an accident."

"I'll be right back," Maya said, having to go to the bathroom. "Can I bring you anything?"

"Sí, por favor. There's a pitcher of lemonade in the refrigerator." Drinking lemonade was a custom her mother had acquired from her neighbors.

She returned with the pitcher and two glasses, which she set on the table between them and filled. She sat down and took a sip of lemonade, which tasted good. Her mother struck the right balance between the degrees of sweetness that the kids wanted and her father wanted.

Maya related what had happened in the courtroom, and then she explained the process of verifying her father's immigration status. "So papa should be released this afternoon, and he should be home in time for supper."

"What happens then?"

"The federal government will review his case."

"And how long will that take?"

"Trevor said it could take months."

"Then the kids can finish this semester before he's deported."

"Trevor thinks he has a very good chance of being granted relief under a new policy."

"I heard about that policy," her mother said, as usual having her own sources of information. "No one knows how it's going work, or what's going to happen."

"Well, I have confidence in Trevor's judgment."

"I do too. But I don't trust the government."

Hearing her own words spoken by her mother, she realized that their positions weren't far apart, but remembering how her father had asked her to try to make her mother see the positive side, she quoted him, saying: "I don't trust the state government, but I trust the federal government. They're on our side."

"I don't think they are. They haven't done anything for us."

"They've initiated this new policy."

Her mother looked doubtful. "I think we should plan to go back to Mexico after the end of this semester. I mean, your father and I and the kids. You haven't had any problems at the university, have you?"

"No. I don't think they care about my status."

"Then don't get into trouble.".

"I won't," she said, remembering what she had done to that guy at the fraternity party. At the time it hadn't occurred to her that laying him low with a *teisho uchi* might have triggered an investigation into her background, but in the future she would have to consider that risk before acting.

"Except for you, we'll be better off in Mexico."

"You really think Selina and Victor will be better off?"

"I think they will. If they do well in high school there, they can go to college and get good jobs."

"Papa said the country has been taken over by drug lords."

"I heard it's a problem only in the north, along the border. We'll be in Puebla, where it's not a problem."

Not having information to use against her mother's sources, Maya couldn't argue. She could only say: "Papa said he doesn't want his children to live there."

"If we had a choice, I'd stay here. But I don't think we'll have a choice. And I don't want to live in a country where I always have to worry about being deported."

"Well, if papa's granted relief under the new policy, then we won't have to worry about being deported. We'll have a way of becoming legal."

"I'll believe that when it happens," her mother said, staring resolutely into the distance. "But in the meantime I'll prepare for the worst."

Around three in the afternoon she called Trevor to find out if her father had been released yet.

"I checked with the clerk five minutes ago," Trevor told her, "and he said they still hadn't heard from immigration."

"What if they don't hear by the end of the day?"

"If they don't, then I'll talk with the judge, and I'll find a way to get your father out of here."

While she waited to hear back from Trevor she killed a half hour checking her text messages and sending replies to Erin and Shelby. Then she walked over to Main Street and headed toward to the old pool, almost hoping she would run into the three guys who had blocked her way last summer. She imagined the satisfaction of breaking their bones with kicks and punches.

But they weren't around, and turning back, she felt bad about her violent feelings. Instead of going toward the pool, she should have gone toward the church.

As she passed the familiar stores, Maya realized that she was beyond feeling she didn't belong here. She felt like an alien.

She had left Main Street and was entering her neighborhood when her phone vibrated. It was Trevor.

"I'm sorry," he said. "I couldn't get your father released. I went to see the judge around four, but he'd left for the day. He must have slipped out the back since I didn't see him go. He dumped the problem onto his clerk, as judges often do, but the clerk has no power to do anything."

"Can you find the judge at home?"

"He's not listed, and the clerk won't tell me where the judge lives. If he did, he'd probably lose his job."

"So my father has to spend another night in jail?"

"I'm afraid so," Trevor said. "But I'm going to spend the night here, and I'm going to waylay the judge in the morning. I'm also going to make some calls to the immigration department."

"Have you talked with my father?"

"Not since this morning. They wouldn't let me talk with him."

"This isn't right," Maya said, her anger rising.

"It sure isn't," Trevor said. "If I didn't know where we were, I'd think we were in a police state."

"Should I go to Miletus tomorrow morning?"

"I think you should go back to Tuscaloosa. You have classes, and you have soccer practice. And there's nothing you can do here to help your father."

"Okay. I'll go back to Tuscaloosa."

When she got home she reported the latest development to her mother, who didn't seem surprised. Her mother only said: "We should have gone back to Mexico last summer."

That evening, as she ate the home-cooked Mexican food, Maya realized how much she had missed it. Her mother had told Selina and Victor that their father was staying with Judson to help him get the orchards ready for the winter, so they didn't talk about his situation. Instead, they let the kids talk about what had happened at school that day and what their friends were doing. When the kids asked Maya why she was home, she told them it was because she missed them, which was partly true. If it weren't for her real reason for being there, she would have been happy to be home with her family.

Before going to bed she exchanged text messages with Erin and Shelby. To explain Maya's absence at soccer practice, Erin had told the coach she wasn't feeling well, which could have meant a number of things. She thanked Erin and told her she would be back tomorrow. Shelby asked her how she was doing, and she told him she was doing all right. And she thanked him again for driving her to Miletus.

Lying awake in bed that night she applied her conversations with her parents to the different scenarios she imagined. If her father was granted relief by the end of the semester, there would be no problem. If he wasn't, he would be deported, and her mother would follow with the two kids. But if his case was still being reviewed by her mother's deadline, there would be a conflict between her parents, with her father unwilling to give up his dream and her mother wanting to end the uncertainty about their future. That would be the worst scenario since it had the potential to break up their family, and Maya would have to decide whether to keep her promise to her father or fulfill her responsibility to her mother. She could avoid taking sides by staying at the university since both her parents wanted her to get a degree, but she would still feel that by staying in America she was taking her father's side.

After praying that her father would be granted relief and that everything would be resolved in a way that would make both her parents happy, she finally went to sleep.

The next morning she took an early bus to Tuscaloosa, arriving in time to make her history class. She left her phone on during the class since she would have gladly paid the penalty for violating the professor's ban on phones if only it was a call from Trevor telling her the judge had released her father.

On the way back to her dorm after class she called Trevor. It was after eleven, and by now he should have had a chance to talk with the judge.

"The judge didn't come in today," Trevor told her. "The clerk said it's his day off, though he didn't mention that yesterday. But I found a judge in immigration who says he'll give them an order to release your father."

"Will that happen today?" Maya asked.

"He says it will. He also says they verified your father's status yesterday."

"They did? Then that judge had no reason to hold my father."

"No legal reason. I suspect he had another reason."

"Well, I hope you can have him disrobed."

"I probably can. But that's not my primary goal. My primary goal is to get your father out of here."

She asked him to call her as soon as her father was released.

Returning to her room, she found Erin there, and they got sandwiches from Julia's Market, which they ate in the room so they could talk in private.

After hearing the details of her father's situation Erin said: "So they're going to release your father today."

"They're supposed to," Maya said, "but I'm still worried."

"Are you worried that it won't happen?"

"Yeah. I am. So I'm praying that it *will* happen."

"I'll pray with you. When my mother got sick, I prayed that she would get well."

"Do you think it helped?"

"I don't know if it helped my mother, but it helped me."

They ate their sandwiches in silence for a while, and then Maya asked: "If you were in my situation, and your mother wanted to go back to Mexico but your father wanted to stay in America, what would you do?"

"I'd stay at the university and let them work it out."

"You wouldn't take a side in their conflict?"

"If I took a side, I'd be trying to influence their decision. And they have to make their own decision."

Conscious of sounding like her father, Maya said: "Well, maybe they won't have to make a decision. Maybe the federal government will grant my father relief under its new policy, and then my mother won't have to worry about our status."

"I'll pray for that to happen," Erin said. "I'll go to the noon mass tomorrow."

"Don't you have a class at that time?"

"I do, but the professor sucks. I'd rather be in church than in his classroom."

Maya laughed—for the first time since the phone call from Judson yesterday morning. And silently she thanked God for giving her Erin as a roommate.

When she went to soccer practice that afternoon the coach looked at her with concern and asked: "How are you feeling?"

"I'm feeling fine," Maya said, remembering what Erin had told him and avoiding specifics.

"Do you want to take it easy today?"

She shook her head. "I want to have a real workout."

"You wouldn't be hiding something, would you?" the coach asked as if he had detected a shadow in her eyes.

"Oh, no," she said, not ready to share her problem with him but realizing that sooner or later she might have to. At least she felt he would be on her side.

They had a good practice, and Maya didn't think about her problem again until she stepped under the shower, which washed away only the sweat and the dirt.

At her locker Maya checked her phone for messages and saw there had been a call from Trevor.

Expecting to hear that her father had been released, she returned the call with a thumping heart.

It took Trevor a while to answer.

"Did they release him?" she asked excitedly.

"No. They didn't," Trevor said. "They took your father out of his cell last night, and they drove him to Laredo."

"What?" She felt as if she had been kicked in the stomach.

"At quarter after three I got the order from immigration to release your father, and I presented it to the clerk. That's when he told me what they'd done."

"They deported my father?"

"They did. I'm sorry."

"But how could they *deport* him?"

"That's a good question. They don't have the power to deport people. So they're wide open for legal action."

"Well, what are you going to do now?"

"I'm going to work with immigration to bring your father back to America."

"Do you think you can?"

"I know I can," Trevor said. "I talked with the immigration judge who gave the order to release your father, and he said he'll rescind your father's deportation."

"How long do you think that'll take?"

"It shouldn't take more than a week or so."

"But meanwhile we don't know where my father is."

"I assume he's just across the border in Nuevo Laredo."

"Does my mother know what happened?"

"Yes. I called her after I called you."

Maya didn't have to ask how her mother had reacted. But she would have to ask Shelby to drive her to Miletus the next morning so she could join Trevor in confronting the judge. She still had confidence in Trevor, but she no longer believed what they had taught her in school—that America had rule of law, not rule of man.

SEVEN

THEY ARRIVED IN Miletus at ten the next morning, and they parked in the lot that served the police station, the courthouse, and the town hall. They found Trevor in the waiting area outside of the judge's chambers, pacing the floor.

"He hasn't come in yet," Trevor told them.

"I hope he's not playing golf today," Shelby said.

The three of them sat down, and they waited for the judge, who didn't arrive until one thirty. By then Trevor had learned about the federal judge's rulings on the state immigration law, which she had issued at twelve thirty. The judge had upheld most of the law, including the part that required law enforcement officers to determine the immigration status of people they stopped, detained, or arrested. The judge had also upheld the part that required public schools to report the status of students. Pending final judgment in the case, the judge had stopped the state from enforcing the part that made it a crime for illegal immigrants to work, the part that made it a crime to harbor or transport illegal immigrants, and the part that prohibited illegal immigrants from attending public universities.

"So they can't prohibit Maya from attending the university?" Shelby asked hopefully.

"They can't for the time being," Trevor said. "But I must tell you, the judge stopped that part of the law due to a technicality. There was faulty, contradictory language that made it look as if the state was classifying aliens, which it doesn't have the power to do. The judge found nothing wrong with the principle of prohibiting illegal immigrants from attending public universities. So a final judgment might uphold that part of the law."

"If that happens, could they apply the law to Maya?"

"If they try to apply the law to her, we'll argue that she was admitted to the university before the law was passed."

"Would you have a strong case in her favor?"

"Yes. But you never know what a judge will do, so we don't want her status to come to the attention of the university."

"What about my father?" Maya asked. "Do the rulings allow the state to deport him?"

"They clearly don't," Trevor said. "The state still has to follow the existing federal process."

"Then what made this judge think he could deport her father?" Shelby asked.

"He must have thought he could get away with it."

At that point the judge arrived.

"We need to talk," Trevor said, rising.

"You may need to talk," the judge said, walking by them, "but I don't need to. If you want to appeal, go ahead."

"I'll do more appeal. I'll have you indicted."

The judge stopped. "Indicted for what?"

"For violating the federal law."

"I followed the state law," the judge said, "which was upheld today by a federal judge."

"You didn't follow the state law," Trevor argued. "That law requires you to follow the federal process for deporting aliens, which is set forth in 8 USC Section 1229A. As a county judge you had no jurisdiction over this case, and you had no power to deport my client."

The judge glanced over at the clerk, who was sitting at the reception desk, doing something on his computer, and then he said: "If you want to talk, come into my chambers."

They all started to follow him.

"I didn't invite all of you," the judge said, stopping.

"This young woman is my client's daughter."

"Who's the boy?"

"He's my boyfriend," Maya said. For this purpose she wished

she had said that Shelby was her fiancé, but the truth had come out automatically.

"I'll let her come in, but not the boyfriend."

"Okay," Shelby said, taking the rejection with good grace.

When they were in his chambers the judge closed the door behind them and went around his desk and sat down, saying: "We followed the federal process. We contacted the immigration department to determine the status of your client, and we got a response."

"When did you get a response?"

"Yesterday."

"I was here all afternoon yesterday, and at least every half hour I asked your clerk if he'd gotten a response. I asked him just before he left for the day, and he told me he still hadn't gotten a response."

"Well, he was mistaken. He doesn't always focus on things," the judge explained. "He spends too much time playing games on that damned computer."

"If you got a response, then what did they tell you?"

With a look of vindication the judge said: "They told us your client was not lawfully present in this country."

"If they did," Trevor said, "then they must have also told you they had jurisdiction over his case."

"We didn't talk with anyone. My clerk got the information electronically."

"But you know that the federal government has jurisdiction over such cases, and that only the federal government has the power to deport people."

"The purpose of the Alabama law," the judge retorted with his jowls shaking, "is to protect the people of this sovereign state from the evils of illegal immigration. As a judge invested by this county I have a duty to enforce that law. If I'd turned your client over to the federal government, they would have granted him relief under their new policy, and he would have stayed in Alabama, taking a job away from an American."

"The state still doesn't have the power to deport people."

"The state *does* have the power to deport people. It has that power under the Tenth Amendment to the Constitution, which provides that powers not granted to the federal government are reserved to the states."

"With respect to immigration, that issue was resolved by the Supreme Court in 1976."

"It wasn't resolved to our satisfaction."

"Well, you know what happened the last time this state challenged the federal government."

"You mean on the issue of slavery?"

"No. I mean on the issue of civil rights."

"We lost on that one," the judge said bitterly. "But we're not going to lose on this issue. We have a lot of support on it."

"I don't think you do. I think you should look beyond the borders of Ratliff County."

"I don't care what you think," the judge said, scowling at Trevor. "You know, I remembered you from the time when you worked for the district attorney in Birmingham, and I had my clerk check your background. You got your law degree at Harvard, so you think you're better than people like us. But you're not better, and you know what? You don't belong in Alabama any more than the man we deported."

"So are you going to deport me?"

"I would if I could. But I can deport people who are living in this state illegally."

"They'll stop you," Trevor said with certainty. "And they'll disrobe you."

"They can't do anything to me for following the state law."

"Maybe they can't. But they can do a lot to you for knowingly violating the federal law."

"We'll see about that," the judge said. "And now, if you don't mind, I have to get to work. I have a busy calendar."

Outside, they regrouped in the parking lot.

Maya listened patiently while Trevor told Shelby what had

happened in the judge's chambers, and then she asked: "What are you going to do now?"

"I'm going to bring your father back to America," Trevor said with determination.

"How are you going to do that?" Shelby asked.

"He talked with an immigration judge yesterday," Maya said, "who said he'll rescind my father's deportation."

"What will happen when he comes back?"

"They'll review his case," Trevor said. "Her father will be in the same position as he would have been if that judge had followed the federal process."

"At least that creepy judge said one thing that gives me hope," Maya said. "He said they would have granted my father relief under their new policy."

"He knew what he was doing. And in my case I can use that against him. I can argue that he was trying to subvert the federal immigration policy."

"What if they don't rescind the deportation?" Shelby asked.

"They will rescind it," Trevor said. "They can't let states deport people. They'd lose control over immigration."

Assured that her father would come back to America, Maya began to worry about his present situation. "I wish he'd call and let us know where he is."

"Without a cell phone," Shelby said, "it's hard to make a call in a foreign country."

"He'll find a way," Trevor said. "If he's staying in a hotel, they'll have a phone there."

They stood for a while in silence, and then Shelby said: "I'm going back to Tuscaloosa. Are you coming with me?"

"I have to go home and be with my mother."

"You can go with me," Trevor said.

"Will you be back on campus tomorrow?" Shelby asked.

"Yeah, I'll be back tomorrow. I can't keep cutting classes and missing soccer practice."

She thanked Shelby for driving her to Miletus again, and then she followed Trevor to his car.

When they were a few miles out of town Trevor said: "Even knowing that judge's background, I never expected him to do what he did."

"If you had, could you have stopped him?"

"Sure. I could have been waiting outside the jail last night with a federal agent."

She caught the irony in this statement, but she still had the feeling that Trevor was blaming himself. "When you asked the clerk if they'd gotten a response, you had no reason to suspect that he was lying."

"The judge said that the clerk was mistaken. If he was, then it suited the judge's purpose. It gave him an opportunity to deport your father."

"Maybe the judge told the clerk to lie to you."

"That's what I'm thinking. And if I can prove that, I can nail them for conspiring to subvert the federal process."

"How could you prove it?"

"The judge said the clerk got the information electronically, which would have left a trail in the system."

"Couldn't they erase the trail?"

"They could erase it at their end, but not at the other end."

"Could the clerk say he hadn't seen the response?"

"Every time I asked him if he'd gotten a response he checked his computer, right in front of me. So he saw the response, and he lied about it."

"If you could prove he lied about it," Maya said, following a line of argument, "would that speed up the process of rescinding my father's deportation?"

"I think it might," Trevor said. "For one thing, it would piss off the immigration judge I'm working with, and that could make him expedite things."

When Maya got home she found her mother in the kitchen making tortillas, kneading the *masa harina* with one hand while she held the bowl with her other hand.

"Has hablado con papá?" she asked her mother.

"I talked with him an hour ago. He's in Nuevo Laredo. He said he's fine."

"Is he going to stay there?"

Her mother straightened up and took a handful of the dough and rolled it between her hands, making a ball. "I told him he should go to Puebla and stay with your Uncle Benito."

In the living room there was a photograph of Uncle Benito holding her when she was two, but she didn't remember that far back. "Is he going to Puebla?"

Her mother put the ball of dough on the wax paper that lay on the bottom of the tortilla press. "He's going to stay in Nuevo Laredo until he talks with Trevor."

Taking her father's side, Maya said: "Trevor says he can bring papa back in a week or so."

After laying a piece wax paper on top of the ball her mother pulled down on the press and flattened the dough. It looked as if she had used more force than usual. "I know Trevor's a good man, and I believe he's a good lawyer. But there's a limit to what he can do for us."

"He says the judge violated federal law, and that he can get the immigration department to rescind the deportation."

"Even if he can," her mother said, carefully removing the tortilla from the press, "it's not going to happen in a week or so. And I don't want your father to stay in Nuevo Laredo waiting for it to happen."

She watched her mother lay the tortilla in the blackened skillet that was on the stove. "Where is he staying?"

"In a cheap hotel. He asked me to send him some money." Her mother would do that through Western Union, which had an office at the Winn-Dixie. Both her parents regularly sent money to their families in Mexico.

"I guess it'll save money if he stays with Uncle Benito," Maya acknowledged.

"It'll give him a chance to look around for a place to live."

"So you're still planning to go back to Mexico?"

"More than ever," her mother said, deftly taking an edge of the tortilla with her fingers and turning it over. "I don't want to live in a country that doesn't want us."

"You shouldn't judge the country by the action of one man."

"It took more than one man to pass that law."

"Well, then maybe we could move to another state."

Her mother removed the tortilla from the skillet and set it on a damp towel. "Why should we move to a place where we don't know anyone when we have family in Mexico?"

"We have more opportunity in America."

"That's what your father believes, but he's wrong. The world has changed," her mother said, rolling another ball of dough, "and your father's living in the past. The future isn't in America, the future is in countries like Mexico."

Maya assumed that her mother had gotten this idea from her usual sources, and she wished she had her own sources. As she watched her mother put the ball on the wax paper she could only ask: "Do you really believe that?"

"Yes. I do," her mother said, pulling emphatically down on the press.

"So even if Trevor brings papa back and gets the immigration department to grant him relief, you don't want to stay here?"

Her mother sighed. "If that happens, I'll reconsider. But I don't believe it's going to happen."

"Well, let's wait and see," Maya said, relieved that her mother's mind wasn't closed. "Do the kids know what happened to papa?"

"I told them he went to Mexico to look for opportunities there."

"You didn't tell them he was deported?"

"No. I didn't want them to worry."

"But you talked with them about the possibility of going back to Mexico?"

"Yes. I have to prepare them for the idea. And of course they don't like it," her mother added.

"I can understand why they wouldn't like it. They were born here, they grew up here, and they have friends here."

"They're young enough to make new friends in Mexico."

"But they don't even speak Spanish well."

"Their Spanish will improve when they live among people who always speak it."

Watching her mother remove another tortilla from the skillet, Maya reflected that four out of five members of their family were against the idea of going back to Mexico, and out of sympathy for the underdog she moved a little toward her mother's side, which left her in the middle.

The next morning she took a bus back to Tuscaloosa, and she arrived in time to make one of her classes. She didn't see Erin until soccer practice, and in the presence of their teammates they couldn't talk about what had happened.

Erin had covered for her again, but the coach evidently hadn't bought the excuse that Maya wasn't feeling well since at the end of practice he asked her to come to his office after she had showered and changed.

His door was open, and he asked her to close it behind her.

"Please sit down," he told her, indicating the chair in front of his desk.

Maya sat down, not knowing how she was going to answer the questions she expected him to ask. She couldn't lie to him, but she could hold back information.

"You missed two practices," he said, looking at her directly. "Your roommate said you weren't feeling well."

Maya said nothing, lowering her eyes.

"I have a feeling that something's wrong. Can you tell me about it?"

"I can't," she said, shaking her head. "It's personal."

"Whatever you tell me, it won't go anywhere."

She decided to trust him, feeling that she owed him the truth because he had invested so much in her. "It's a family problem."

"A problem between your parents?"

"Yeah, but that's not the main thing. The main thing is, my family is here illegally, and yesterday a county judge deported my father."

"What?" The coach frowned. "I don't know much about the immigration law in this country, but that doesn't sound right."

"It's not right, but it happened."

"Can you give me some background?"

"My parents came here illegally when I was three. My father picked peaches, and my mother cleaned houses. They worked for people who didn't care if they were illegal. But last summer the state passed a law that changed things for us."

"How do you mean?"

"The law made it a crime for us to work, and for people to hire us, and for people to rent a house to us. The day before the law was supposed to go into effect, a federal judge stopped it for a month so she could review it. But people acted as if the law was in effect, and last Sunday the man my father works for was stopped by a cop while he was driving home from the match. He wasn't speeding, but someone had smashed into his car in the parking lot of the Cypress Inn and broken a tail-light."

"The cop stopped him for a broken tail-light?"

"Yeah. My father was with him, and the cop asked them for identification. The law requires cops to do that if they have a reasonable suspicion that a person is here illegally. And when my father couldn't prove he was here legally, the cop arrested them."

"Where did this happen?"

"In Ratliff County. It's between here and Maynard County, where we live. If it had happened in Maynard County there wouldn't have been a problem."

"Why wouldn't there have been a problem?"

"Judson, the man my father works for, is an important member of the community."

The coach nodded as if he understood. "So they were arrested. What happened then?"

"They were held overnight," Maya said. "They went before a county judge the next day, and Judson was fined. Trevor, our lawyer, made a motion for my father's case to be transferred to an immigration judge, but the county judge overruled Trevor and held my father for another night. The judge was supposed to release my father after verifying his status with the immigration department, but that night he had my father driven to Laredo and taken across the border to Mexico."

"Where's your father now?"

"He's in Nuevo Laredo, waiting for our lawyer to bring him back to America."

"Is there a good chance it will happen?"

"Trevor's confident it will. He's dealing with the immigration department, and he thinks it'll take a week or two."

"Then what?"

"If all goes well," Maya said, "my father will be granted relief under a new policy of the federal government, and he'll be able to stay in this country."

"But in the meantime he's in Mexico, and you're worried about him."

"I am. And the reason I missed practice was I had to go home and be with my mother."

"How does she feel about the situation?"

"She doesn't like it. She doesn't want to live in a country where she always has to worry about being deported. She wants to go back to Mexico. But my father wants to stay in America."

"I understand what your father wants and what your mother wants, but what do *you* want?"

"I want what's best for my family."

"Even if it's not the best thing for you?"

"I can't imagine it not being the best thing for me. I mean, the worst thing would be if this conflict breaks up my family."

The coach studied her. "I assume you realize that whatever your parents decide to do, you could stay at the university."

"I could, except there's another problem. I'm illegal, and the state law prohibits illegal immigrants from attending public universities. Yesterday a federal judge stopped that part of the law, but she stopped it due to a technicality, so a final judgment could let the state implement it."

"I don't understand. If there was a law that prohibits illegal immigrants from attending public universities, how did you get admitted here?"

"I was admitted before the law was passed. I guess as long as they had my transcripts and my SATs and my recommendations, they didn't care about my status. But if they found out that I'm illegal, they could kick me out."

"I wouldn't let them. You and Erin are the best pair of forwards I've ever coached, including both men and women."

Maya didn't know what to say.

"So don't worry about the bloody law."

"Well, I don't worry about it when I'm playing soccer."

"Then we'll have you playing around the clock."

"I wish I could. It would take my mind off this whole thing."

The coach studied her for a while, and then he said: "I understand your situation, and I know it's hard, but I'm not going to be soft on you."

"I don't want you to be soft on me. I want you to bring out the best in me."

"I'll do that. I promise," the coach said, looking at her with obvious respect. "Now, run along and have a good evening."

Instead of taking the bus back to her dormitory, Maya decided to walk since she needed time by herself to think about what the coach had said. It made her feel better, and it made her believe that if the university ever found out that she was illegal, he wouldn't let them kick her out. But he couldn't help the other members of her family, and she wasn't convinced that it would be best for her family if she stayed at the university while they went back to Mexico. Still, he had raised some important questions. What did *she* want? And would what was best for her family be the best thing for her?

She wasn't used to dealing with such questions, and they made her wonder. Had she done well in school only because her parents wanted her to, and did she play well at soccer only because her coaches wanted her to? Had she earned her brown belt at karate only because her *sensei* wanted her to? She must have wanted to do those things since they gave her a lot of satisfaction. But would she have done them on her own? If her family went back to Mexico, could she stay at the university and survive on her own? Did she want to do what was best for her family only because she needed them?

She was walking toward University Boulevard struggling with these questions when her phone vibrated. She assumed it was Shelby, but when she took it out she saw a number on the screen that she didn't recognize.

Thinking the call might be important, she answered it.

"*Hola, hijita,*" said a distant voice.

It was her father. "*Hola, papá. Dónde estás?*"

"I'm in Nuevo Laredo. Is this a good time for you to talk?"

"*No hay problema.* I'm walking back to my dormitory from soccer practice."

"I'm sorry I won't be at your match this Sunday."

"I'll miss you," she said sadly.

"It's all right," he said. "I'll be at your match next Sunday."

"You think you'll be back by then?"

"Without a doubt. Trevor told me it would take only a week."

"He told me a week or so."

"That's what he told me. But he always allows more time than he thinks he'll need."

"Well, I hope it does take only a week," Maya said, finding herself in the usual position between her father and her mother. "Are you going to stay in Nuevo Laredo?"

"If I'll be back in a week or so," her father said, "it wouldn't make sense to go to Puebla. That's a long way from here."

"You'd have a free place to stay."

"It would cost me as much to travel to Puebla roundtrip as it costs for a week in this hotel."

"What's the hotel like?"

"It's not bad. The bathroom's down the hall, but there are

only five rooms on my floor. So it's no worse than being at home with one bathroom for five people."

"Is Nuevo Laredo a big city?"

"It's a very big city, and it's very busy. It exports a lot of Mexican goods to America. In fact, there are several truck drivers staying on my floor."

"Would you want to live there?"

"Oh, no. There's a lot of crime, related to drugs. They say the drug lords run this city."

"Then maybe you shouldn't stay there," Maya said, conscious of sounding like her mother.

"Don't worry. I'm in a safe area. And I don't go out at night."

"Where do you eat?"

"The hotel has a restaurant, and there are other restaurants around here. I go where the truck drivers go. They know where to get a good meal."

She arrived at University Boulevard, where she stopped and watched for a chance to cross. As usual there was a lot of traffic. "Who drove you to Laredo?"

"Two police officers."

"How did they treat you?"

"Like a prisoner."

"And you still want to come back to this country?"

"They're not like most Americans."

"Are you sure?"

"I'm sure. Most Americans are good people like Judson and Trevor and Father Philip."

Inclined to believe this, she moved a little toward her father's side as she crossed the street and continued walking toward Bryant Drive.

"How are they treating you at the university?"

"They're treating me well. When I'm sitting in classrooms, or eating meals, or playing soccer they don't make me feel like a Mexican."

"They make you feel like an American?"

"I guess they do," Maya said. "At least they make me feel like I belong here."

"You do belong in America."

"I assume you know that whatever happens, mom's planning to go back to Mexico."

"I know she is. But when they give us a way of becoming legal, I believe she'll change her mind. Your mother wants to know where she stands," her father explained. "She doesn't want to always worry about her status."

"Well, I don't blame her," Maya said, veering back toward her mother's side.

"I don't blame her either. The truth is, I blame myself for not finding a solution earlier."

"You had no control over the situation."

"But I got us into the situation."

"Do you have regrets about going to America?"

"No matter what you do," her father said after a pause, "you have regrets. But being back in Mexico now and seeing what it's like, I know I would have had more regrets if I'd stayed in this country. So I feel like I made the right decision."

"I feel like you did for me," she said. By now she had come to Bryant Drive, where she turned and headed west toward her dormitory. "I just had a talk with the soccer coach. He wanted to know why I missed practice, and I told him about your situation. I also told him about my own situation. And he said he wouldn't let them kick me out."

"So there's another good American."

"Actually, he's Irish. He said that Erin and I are the best pair of forwards he ever coached."

"He did? Well, I'm sure he meant it. Take it to heart."

"I wish I could see you this Sunday, but maybe I'll see you the following Sunday."

"You will. Don't worry. I have faith in Trevor."

"Te amo, papá. Que Dios te proteja."

"Te amo, hijita. No te preocupes."

When Maya returned to their room she found Erin lying on her bed sending a text message. That was how Erin stayed in touch with her boyfriend. She seemed happy to keep her boyfriend at a distance and exchange text messages with him.

Maya did a back flop onto her bed and waited for Erin to finish her message.

"So how did things go with the coach?" Erin asked.

"I told him about my father's situation," Maya said. "I also told him about my own situation. And he said he wouldn't let them kick me out."

"Does that make you feel better?"

"Yeah. He said that you and I were the best pair of forwards he ever coached, including both men and women."

"He did? Wow." Erin was silent, and then she said: "That gives us something to live up to."

"It does. Along with some other things he said, it also raises questions in my mind."

"Questions? Like what?"

"Like what do I want? Like who am I playing for?"

"I know who I'm playing for. I'm playing for my teammates, I'm playing for the coach, I'm playing for my parents, and I'm playing for myself."

"I noticed you put yourself last."

"They're not in order of priority. They're all important."

"You mean you couldn't just play for other people or just for yourself."

"I could, but I wouldn't have my whole heart in it."

"Well, I know I'm playing for other people," Maya said, "but I never really thought about whether I'm playing for myself."

"You like playing soccer, don't you?"

"Oh, yeah. I love playing soccer."

"Then you're playing for yourself. But at the same time you want to live up to other people's expectations, so you're also playing for other people."

"I don't have any question about that. When my father and

Judson come to the match, I feel like I have more to play for."

"If your father doesn't come this Sunday, I think you'll feel the same way."

"Because he's in my head?"

"And in your heart."

"So if my family goes back to Mexico and I stay in America," Maya reasoned, "maybe I'll still feel like I'm doing it for them as well as for myself."

"I think you will," Erin said confidently. "But why would your family go back to Mexico? I thought your lawyer was going to bring your father back."

"I believe it'll happen," Maya said. "But my mother has doubts. She always has doubts."

"She sounds like my mother. Maybe having doubts is an occupational hazard for mothers."

"Maybe it is. But why would it be?"

"Mothers are the last line of defense for the family."

"So they're like goalkeepers?"

Erin laughed. "I wasn't thinking about soccer, but they really are like goalkeepers. As long as nothing gets by them, people believe they're doing fine. But if one ball gets by them, people wonder why they didn't stop it."

"I'm glad I'm not a goalkeeper."

"I am too. But someday we'll be mothers."

"I'm not ready to think about that yet. But I guess I should keep it in mind whenever I feel like judging my mother."

"I should too. I should think of my mother as a goalkeeper."

Lying on her bed, Maya checked her phone for text messages. There were two from Shelby, who wanted to see her. She was tired from the bus trip and from soccer practice, but she felt she owed him for driving her to Miletus twice, so she suggested he pick her up at six thirty that evening, which gave her an hour or so to rest before going out again.

As usual Shelby didn't keep her waiting, and she appreciated how considerate he was. On the way to Sonic she told him what was happening. She even told him about the conflict between her parents. And he listened attentively.

When they had placed their order he said: "So Trevor thinks your father has a good chance of being granted relief under the new immigration policy."

"Yeah. He does. And I trust his judgment."

"But you're still worried."

"Well, it's a new policy, and no one knows how it's going to work. And my mother doesn't want to wait to see how it's going to work. In fact, she says that if nothing happens by the end of the semester, she's going back to Mexico."

"Will your father go with her?"

"I don't know. If he does, he won't be happy. Why go now when he has a chance of being granted relief?"

"I guess he'd go to make your mother happy."

"Would you do that if you were in my father's position?"

"I'd do anything to make you happy."

Maya wondered if she would do anything to make Shelby happy. She wanted to believe she would, but she wasn't sure.

"If your family goes back to Mexico," Shelby asked, "would you go with them?"

"My parents both want me to stay here and get a degree."

"But that'll take four years. Would you be able to go to Mexico during that time?"

"If I left this country, I couldn't come back."

"So you wouldn't see your family for four years."

Depressed by the thought, Maya said: "I don't think I could go that long without seeing my family."

"I understand," Shelby said.

At that moment their food arrived, and they ate in silence for a while, munching on burgers and picking at French fries.

Then Shelby said: "Remember the fallback I suggested last summer after they passed the immigration law?"

She did remember. "Getting married?"

"Just listen. If we got married, you could go to Mexico and see your family."

"I guess I could. But I still have doubts about getting married to solve the problem."

"We wouldn't get married to solve the problem. We'd get married because we love each other and want to spend our lives together. But it would also solve the problem of your not being able to see your family, which I assume would make you happy."

"It *would* make me happy."

"So if your family goes back to Mexico, we have a fallback."

Thinking about it, Maya could see how her staying at the university and getting her degree would make her parents happy, and how her being able to see them in Mexico would make her happy. But she couldn't see how her marrying Shelby would make his parents happy, and at least for that reason she hoped they wouldn't need a fallback.

During that week Maya talked with Trevor every day to find out how her father's case was going. Trevor always took her calls, and after giving her an update on her father he told her what was happening with the Alabama immigration law. The coalition of civil rights groups, which along with the federal government and the church coalition had sued the state, asked the federal judge for an order to suspend implementation of those parts of the law that she had upheld while they pursued an appeal. They also asked a federal appeals court in Atlanta to review the judge's decision. Meanwhile, the federal government was also reviewing the decision. So it looked as if the case would go to a higher court and eventually to the Supreme Court, where the case against the Arizona immigration law was heading.

Maya was heartened by this news, but her immediate concern was bringing her father back to America, and though she tried to put this concern out of her mind while she was studying, it kept disrupting her concentration. It even intruded while she was taking an exam in history, and as a result she felt she hadn't done as well as she should have.

On Friday they traveled by bus to Starkville, Mississippi to play Mississippi State. It was a long, boring trip, and while her teammates chatted and listened to music and dozed, Maya stared out the window, wondering if her father was all right.

The match was in the evening, and though they had time to recover from the trip, they had to play without their starting goalkeeper since she had drawn a red card in the previous match and without their coach since the team as a whole had drawn a red card. But they went out there fired up and determined to play better than they had in the previous match.

The other team scored only three minutes into the match, but halfway through the period Dana scored on a pass from Maya. Alabama went ahead on a rebound from a shot by Maya that hit the crossbeam, but a few minutes later Mississippi State tied the score. Alabama played well in the second period but failed to score, and after two scoreless overtime periods the match ended at 2-2. Though it would have helped the team to have its starting goalkeeper, Maya blamed herself for not scoring, especially since she had hit the frame five times. If only one of those shots had been a fraction of an inch closer, they would have won.

On Sunday they played Mississippi in Oxford. Mississippi, which had lost six of their last seven matches, was up for the match whereas Alabama didn't have their usual energy. Maya and Erin both had bad days, and neither of them had a shot on goal. Mississippi scored early in the first period on a header by a girl from Brazil, and later off a corner kick. In the second period the girl from Brazil scored unassisted, and the final score was 0-3. After the match the coach was relatively kind when he said: "This wasn't a good day for us."

Judson came to the match, and Maya was glad to see him there. She spotted him in the stands a few minutes before the match began, and reckoning how far he had driven to get there—she later learned it was two hundred and thirty miles—she appreciated his being there for her. Mindful of her conversation with Erin, she played for him, but she also played as if her father were there with him. But for some reason she just couldn't get herself going.

After the match she talked with Judson before she had to get on the bus back to Tuscaloosa. Showered and changed, she met him on the sidewalk in front of the building where the locker rooms were.

"You had a bad day," he said as if he understood that those things happened.

"Yeah," she said. "I don't know why."

"Maybe you were worrying about your father."

"I pretended he was here, but I guess it didn't work."

They moved from the sidewalk into an area shaded by trees.

"I talked with him early this morning," Judson told her. "He's in good spirits. He's expecting to come home next week."

"Is that what Trevor told him?"

"I'm sure Trevor told him it would take longer, but you know your father."

She smiled. "Yeah. But I hope he's right."

"You never know. I also talked with your mother. She's not in good spirits. She's getting ready to go back to Mexico."

"I know she is. But she could change her mind."

"She could. And if they give your father a way of becoming legal, I think she will."

"You know, at times I'm on my mother's side, and at other times I'm on my father's side."

"I understand," Judson said. "But you don't have to be on one side or the other."

"How can I avoid it?"

"By being on both sides."

"Doesn't that leave me in the middle?"

"It does. But that's all right," Judson assured her. "If we had more people in the middle that damn law wouldn't have been passed, and that damn judge wouldn't have been able to deport your father."

"So it's good to have people in the middle?"

"I think it is. The more people we have in the middle, the fewer people we have at the extremes."

"But why do we have people at the extremes?"

"If you asked Father Philip that question, what would he tell you?"

"He'd tell me it's God's plan."

"He would. But I don't know what God's plan is, so I have to work with what I know. And what I know is that when people don't feel good about themselves they blame other people."

"Why wouldn't that judge feel good about himself?"

"I can only imagine," Judson said. "But he evidently doesn't, so he blames other people for how he feels."

"Why would he blame my father?"

"He doesn't blame your father personally. He blames what your father represents."

"You mean illegal immigrants?"

"Yeah. It used to be blacks, but now it's illegal immigrants."

"But we're at the bottom of society. Why doesn't he blame people at the top?"

"People who don't feel good about themselves never blame people above them. They always blame people below them."

"Well, it's not our fault they don't feel good about themselves."

"It's their own fault how they feel. But they can get away with blaming people below them."

Maya understood. "So that's why I took it out on my sister when I didn't feel good about myself."

"That's why husbands take it out on their wives, and why mothers take it out on their kids."

"Then I should feel sorry for that judge?"

"No. You should try to understand him, and you should make sure that people like him never get into positions of power."

"How can I do that?"

"By staying in the middle."

After reflecting Maya said: "My father believes that most people in this country are good. Do you believe that?"

"Yes, I believe it, though at times I wonder. This morning I got an email from a guy I used to spar with in New York. It attached a video of Obama admitting he wasn't born in this country. Of course the video was a fabrication, but the guy who sent the email actually believed it."

"Why did he believe it?"

"Six months ago his business went under. But instead of accepting responsibility for his failure, he blames Obama. At the end of his email he said, in all capital letters, that our country is being run by an illegal alien."

"Would he have said that if Obama was white?"

"That's a good question," Judson said. "I think you know the answer. But most people aren't like that guy, and most people aren't like that judge."

As they were talking her teammates had been heading for the bus, which stood in the parking lot with its engine running, and it looked like she would be the last one on. Not wanting to hold them up, she said: "Well, I better go. Thank you for coming."

"I hope to bring your father to the next one."

She went into his open arms and hugged him, pressing her face against his chest, and then she scampered to the bus.

On Wednesday she learned from the television news that the federal judge had refused to stop the Alabama immigration law while the federal government appealed her ruling of the previous week. So the parts of the law that the judge had upheld, including the part that allowed police to ask for immigration papers during routine traffic stops and the part that required schools to report the immigration status of students, would go into effect. Maya was discouraged by this news. The way things were going, it looked as if her mother was right in believing they should go back to Mexico.

On Thursday they traveled to Columbia for their match with South Carolina, and that evening in their motel room they watched the Yankees play the Tigers in the fifth game of the playoffs. Erin had explained that the Yankees had to win this game or they would be eliminated, and she was tense as the Tigers took an early lead and held it. She went absolutely crazy when Alex Rodriguez struck out in the seventh inning with the bases loaded and only one out.

"You bum!" Erin yelled at him. And her language got worse when he struck out again in the ninth inning to end the game and end the season for the Yankees. After several expletives she said: "I hate that guy. We could get five good players for the money we pay him."

"Why don't they get rid of him?" Maya asked.

"They signed a ten-year contract with the bum. They're stuck with him."

"I guess I don't understand baseball."

"You're lucky. The more I understand it, the less I like it. I think I'm going to cheer for the Tigers now."

"Who will they play next?"

"Texas. And I hate the Texas team. It's owned by Bush."

"You mean the former president?"

"Yeah. The guy who got us into those wars."

"Does his team make money?"

"I don't know. It doesn't have to. He has all that oil money."

They could have talked all night, but they had a big match the next day, so they went to bed, and exhausted from the trip, they had no trouble sleeping.

The match didn't go well for them. South Carolina scored three goals in the first period, the first within ten minutes of play and the third about midway through the period. Alabama made a comeback in the second period, outshooting the other team, and they finally scored on a penalty kick by Erin. But ten minutes later South Carolina added a goal, and the final score was 1-4. Though Maya led her team in shots on goal, she failed to score, and she walked off the field at the end of the game unhappy with her performance.

They played Florida on Sunday afternoon. Florida was ranked eleventh in the nation, but Alabama scored first on a goal by Jackie. They maintained their lead until almost the end of the first period when Florida scored on a perfect play. Alabama extended the tie until late in the second period, defending and attacking with everything they had, but Florida eventually broke the match open with three quick goals, and the final score was 1-4. Maya and Erin had each taken only one shot on goal, and neither had scored, but they didn't feel as bad as they had after the South Carolina match because they thought Florida had a better team.

"I know you all would have felt better," the coach told them, "if you'd pulled off an upset. But you played well, and I'm proud of you."

His words held Maya above the surface of despair on the long trip back to Tuscaloosa, as her father's arms had held her above the surface of the water when he was teaching her to swim, but it wasn't enough to lift her spirits. They had lost four of their last five matches, and all she had to look forward to in the coming week was three midterm exams.

On Wednesday she was alone in her room after taking an exam, feeling she hadn't done well on it, when her phone vibrated. It was Trevor.

She answered, saying: "Hi, what's happening?"

"I have good news," Trevor told her. "The federal government has rescinded your father's deportation. He should be home in a few days."

"Does my mother know?"

"I just told her. She sounded happy."

"Thank you," she said as her heart filled with gratitude.

EIGHT

SHE TRIED TO call her mother, but no one answered. She assumed that her mother was out shopping or cleaning someone's house, so she went down to Julia's Market and got a sandwich to bring back to her room. While she was eating she checked her phone for messages. There was one from Shelby, asking her to call him.

She called him back and shared the news about her father.

"Thank God," he said as if he understood how much she had been worrying. "Do you know when he'll be back?"

"No. But it should be soon."

"I think we should celebrate tonight."

"I can't tonight. I have my last exam tomorrow. But I could go out tomorrow night."

"Then we have a date. I saw on the news," Shelby continued, "that Latinos went on strike today to show how much the state needs them."

"Really?" She was heartened. "Did it have much impact?"

"Some poultry plants in Albertville had to shut down, and some Mexican grocery stores and restaurants were closed today."

"Well, at least someone is taking action."

After ending the call she tried her mother again and got her.

"Did you call a half hour ago?" her mother asked.

"Yeah. Where were you?"

"I was down in the basement doing the laundry."

The basement was like a dungeon, and until recently neither Selina nor Victor would venture there alone. She hoped her mother hadn't run up the stairs to answer. "Trevor called me and told me the good news."

"It's only a step," her mother reminded her.

"It's a major step," Maya said, resisting the pull of her mother away from a positive view. "And the next step is for papa to be granted relief."

"The next step is for him to get home."

"Did you talk with him today?"

"Yes. He called me after Trevor called him."

"Did he tell you when he's coming?"

"They have to complete some paperwork, but he thinks it'll be in a few days."

"That's what Trevor told me. So maybe he'll be home by this weekend."

"I wouldn't count on it," her mother said. "He'll be lucky to be home by next week."

At least her mother was allowing that much. "We have soccer matches on Friday and Sunday. I hope he can come to the match this Sunday."

"If not, he could come the following Sunday."

"We're playing Georgia that Sunday. The match is in Athens. But we have a match at home that Thursday."

"I thought you played on Fridays."

"We usually do. I guess we're playing that match on Thursday because of the travel."

"Well, let's not speculate," her mother said. "Let's just pray that he'll get home safely."

When Erin came back to their room after her lab exam Maya told her the good news, and Erin gave her a hug, saying: "I'm so happy for you."

"I hope he'll be back for the next soccer match."

"I do too. We could use his support. You know, since we both have our last exam tomorrow, we should go out tomorrow and celebrate."

"I told Shelby I'd go out with him tomorrow, but we should all go out together."

"Would that be okay with him?"

"I'm sure it would be."

While they were on the bus going to soccer practice she

texted Shelby and asked if it would be okay if Erin joined them tomorrow night. A few minutes later he texted back saying it would be fine. He would pick them up at six thirty.

Soccer practice went well, and after showering and changing she stopped at the coach's office to tell him the good news. He made a gesture with his fists as if his team had scored a goal, and then he said: "Thanks for sharing that with me."

The next day she took her last exam, and she felt she did better. She also felt she did better at soccer practice. As they rode back to the dormitory she and Erin mostly talked about what they would wear that night. She finally decided to go with the outfit she had worn to the fraternity parties, and Erin came up with a skirt and top from the back of her wardrobe. Looking at each other in the bathroom mirror, they had a mutual feeling which Erin expressed: "For a pair of battered soccer players, we don't look bad."

When they went down to meet Shelby instead of seeing his Corvette she saw a black Lincoln Town Car.

"Where did you get this car?" Maya asked.

"I rented it for the occasion. If we'd taken the Corvette, one of you would have had to sit in the other's lap."

"Duh, I should have realized that."

Treating Maya and Erin equally, Shelby insisted that they both ride in the back seat while he played the role of chauffeur.

As they settled into the plush seats Erin said: "I feel like we're going to the prom."

"Actually we're going to the Cypress Inn," Shelby told them over his shoulder. "I thought it would be appropriate."

"It would be," Maya said, "since our trouble started there."

"Well, don't let anyone smash into this car," Erin said.

"I sure won't," Shelby said. "I don't want them to raise my insurance premium."

He parked the car well out of the way.

To begin the celebration they ordered a bottle of non-alcoholic sparkling wine, which the waiter showily poured into champagne glasses.

"To Maya's father," Shelby said, raising his glass in a toast.

"To you and Erin and Trevor and Judson and all the people who helped us," Maya said. *"Que Dios los bendiga."*

"To Maya," Erin said, *"mi mejor amiga."*

When they got back to their room she called her father at the hotel. The man who answered told her to wait, and it took a while for her father to get on.

"Hola, hijita!" he said happily.

"Hola, papá. I got the good news from Trevor."

"Thank God for Trevor. I don't know what I would have done without him."

"He told me you'd be back in a few days."

"I hope to be back in time to see you play this Sunday."

"We're playing LSU."

"Are they good?"

"Yeah. It'll be a good match."

"How are you doing in your courses?"

"I think I'm doing fine. I just took my last midterm."

"Well, I hope you're studying hard."

"I am." She glanced at Erin, who was bent over a textbook. "My roommate's setting a good example for me. She's taking all these killer courses in biology and chemistry."

"I like that girl. I'm glad you have her as a roommate."

"Mom said you have to complete some paperwork."

"Trevor's helping me," her father said. "The American consul's helping me too."

"She thinks you'll be lucky to be home by next week."

"She always prepares herself for the worst."

"But if that's the worst, it's not so bad."

Her father laughed happily. "No, it's not. On that point your parents aren't too far apart."

"Eso me hace feliz, papá."

"Nos vemos este domingo, hijita."

When she got up on Friday she discovered that her phone wasn't working. Neither she nor Erin knew anything about phones, so she needed to find a phone shop. She asked people at breakfast, and someone recommended a shop on 15th Street. It was within walking distance, so after her last class that morning she headed there.

She found the shop with no trouble, and a guy who looked no older than she was, an Asian guy, solved the problem. She gladly paid him the ten dollars he charged her, and she left the shop feeling she had been reconnected with the world. Luckily, she hadn't missed any calls. She hadn't even missed a text message.

She wasn't familiar with 15th Street, having been there only to go to a diner, so she walked along it to see what was there. In the next block she came to a Mexican restaurant called Flor de Puebla. Since it obviously wasn't part of a chain, she wondered if it might have real Mexican food. It was quarter after twelve, she was hungry, and the name suggested that the owners could be from her family's home town, so she went in.

On the right was a bar, and on the left were wooden tables without cloths. Not wanting to sit alone at a table, she approached the bar.

"You'll need to show me identification," the guy behind the bar said. With his deep black eyes and his glossy black hair and his brown skin, he had to be Mexican.

"I don't want to drink," she told him. "I just want to eat."

"Then you can sit down. I'll get you a menu." His muscular body was tightly clothed in a black tee-shirt and black jeans, and as she watched him move she was fascinated by the *machismo* that he projected.

He handed her the menu, which she perused. It didn't have the things they usually served in so-called Mexican restaurants. It had things that Mexicans ate, including chicken and pork dishes that her mother made.

"Do you need any help?" the guy asked.

"No, thanks. I'm fine. I'm impressed by this menu."

"Debes ser mexicana, chica."

"*Soy americana. Mis padres son de México.*"

"You don't look American. You look Mexican."

"You can't tell about people from their looks."

The guy smiled, flashing bright white teeth. "I can tell a lot. And I can tell from the way people talk if they're students at the university."

"Are you saying students aren't welcome at this place?"

"Of course they're welcome. Without students we wouldn't have a business."

"Then what are you saying?"

"I'm saying I can tell you're a student."

"Well, you're right. I *am* a student."

"And I'm a bartender," he said, offering his hand. "My name is Diego."

She hesitated but she finally took his hand, saying: "*Encantada*. My name is Maya."

"Maya," he repeated, nodding in approval. "Now, that's a real Mexican name."

She decided not to tell him her full first name and what it meant. He might have gotten the wrong idea. "Are you from Puebla?"

"How did you guess?"

"From the name of the restaurant."

"The owners are from Puebla, and since I'm from Puebla they gave me a job."

"When did you come here from Mexico?"

"Seven years ago. I didn't come here to be a bartender," he added. "I came here to be a student at the university."

"By now you must have graduated."

"I didn't graduate. I dropped out."

"Why did you drop out?"

"To help our people."

"By tending bar?"

"I do this job to support myself," Diego said. "It's not my main occupation."

"What's your main occupation?"

"It would take a while to explain it to you. Can you meet me this evening?"

As inexperienced as she was, Maya could see that this guy was probably feeding her a line in order to lure her into going out with him. "No, I can't."

"How about tomorrow?"

"No, thanks. I have a boyfriend."

"Then you're not interested in what I do."

She hadn't meant to turn him off completely, so she looked for a way to redirect their conversation. Remembering what Shelby had told her about Latinos going on strike, she asked: "Was this restaurant closed yesterday?"

"Why would we have been closed?" he asked blandly. "It wasn't a Mexican holiday."

"I heard that Latinos went on strike yesterday to protest against the state immigration law."

"As a matter of fact, we *were* closed. The owner gave us a day off and paid us."

"He sounds like a good man to work for."

"He is. He supports our people."

Reluctant to pursue this subject, Maya looked down at the menu and studied it. *"Cómo son las chuletas de puerco adobadas?"*

"Son excelentes."

"Then I'll have that. Does it come with tortillas?"

"It comes with fresh tortillas, made here."

Luckily, people started coming to the bar and demanding Diego's attention. They looked like students, but they were trying to act like Mexicans. They spoke to Diego in high school Spanish as they ordered *margueritas* and *nachos*.

They didn't bother her, and she enjoyed the food. It wasn't as good as her mother's cooking, but it was the best Mexican food that she had eaten outside of her home, and she decided to come back with Erin when soccer season was over. They could sit at a table where she could avoid talking with Diego.

"You liked it," he said, taking her plate, which she had wiped clean with tortillas.

"Yeah. It was good." She asked for the check and paid it,

leaving him a generous tip. She got off the barstool and said: "*Adios.*"

"*Adios, chica,*" Diego said smoothly. "If you ever need me, you know where to find me."

She walked out puzzled by that remark. Within a few minutes she decided that it must have been an extension of his line.

That evening while they were eating at Baker Dining Hall she told Erin about the Mexican restaurant she had found on 15th Street. "It's not another Taco Bell. It serves real Mexican food. We can go there after soccer season."

"Why not before?" Erin asked.

"We won't have time."

"Okay. We'll go there after soccer season."

Maya took a bite of pasta, chewed, and then swallowed. "Well, actually there's another reason."

"There is?"

"Yeah. It's the bartender."

"What about him?"

"He's Mexican."

"Is there something wrong with that?"

"No. But there's something about him that unsettles me."

"You mean he's sexy?"

"I guess he is. He has a great body, which he shows off in a tight tee-shirt and tight jeans."

"Then why don't you want to see him again until after soccer season?"

"I don't know. I guess I already have enough on my mind."

"Did he try to pick you up?"

"Yeah." She recounted what Diego had told her leading up to his statement that tending bar wasn't his main occupation. "So when I asked him what his main occupation was, he asked me if I could meet him this evening."

"That sounds like a line."

"I thought it did. When he persisted I told him I had a boyfriend, and that turned him off."

"Do you have any idea what he does?"

"He said he dropped out of the university 'to help our people,' whatever that means."

"It probably means he's an activist."

"That's what I figured. So I asked him if the restaurant was closed yesterday."

"Why should they have been closed yesterday?"

"I heard that Latinos went on strike yesterday to protest against the immigration law. He said they *had* been closed, but he said it was his boss's idea."

"So maybe he's not an activist."

"Then what does he do to help our people?"

"If you really want to know, you can ask him."

"Yeah. But I'm not in a hurry to find out," Maya said.

"Then we'll go there after soccer season," Erin said.

On Friday evening they played Arkansas. They were up for the match, and they established ball possession right away. They scored about halfway through the first period on a play that started with Erin, who passed to Maya, who put it right on the foot of Jackie in front of the goal. And Maya scored about fifteen minutes later on a rebound from a shot by Dana. They scored again early in the second period on a long shot by Jackie, and the final score was 3-0.

"This was your best effort so far," the coach told them. "You started fast and you didn't let up. You played ninety minutes of good soccer."

It really felt great to win after all those losses. Maya only wished her father could have been at the match, and she hoped he would be at the next one.

Back in her room, she called Trevor to see if there was any news. There was no news about her father, but Trevor informed her that a federal appeals court in Atlanta had temporarily blocked two more parts of the immigration law: the part that required schools to report the status of students, and the part that allowed local authorities to file misdemeanor charges against immigrants who were caught without documents to prove their legal status.

"So we're making progress," Trevor said.

"But if those parts of the law were blocked only temporarily," Maya said, conscious of sounding like her mother, "they could still go into effect eventually."

"They could. But now the other side has to prove its case. And the further we go with the process, the further we get away from Montgomery."

On Saturday afternoon, unable to concentrate on her history reading, she called the hotel in Nuevo Laredo and asked to speak with her father.

"He checked out this morning," the man told her.

"Are you sure?" she asked him, not daring to believe it.

"We're talking about Ramiro Méndez, right?"

"Right. What time did he check out?"

"Before eleven, so he wouldn't have to pay for another night. He told me he was going home."

After ending the call she shared her joy with Erin, who was at her desk studying.

Erin interrupted her work to help Maya calculate how long it would take her father to get home. They assumed he would cross the border around noon and catch a bus in Laredo. With information on bus schedules that they got from the internet they figured it would take him about twenty-four hours to arrive in Montgomery, so he wouldn't make it to the match against LSU the next day. But he would be home by that evening.

On Sunday she and Erin went to the nine o'clock mass, where they prayed for her father's safe return.

They were warming up for the soccer match when she spotted Judson in the stands alone. She hadn't expected to see her father, so she could accept his absence, believing she would see him at the next match.

They were wearing pink uniforms to promote breast cancer awareness, and they felt good about what they were doing, but they couldn't get their offense going. In the first period Maya had the only shot on goal for her team, which was stopped by the goalkeeper, while LSU had ten shots, one of which scored late in the period.

At half-time Maya wondered if her play was being affected by her disappointment over not seeing her father in the stands, and while the coach was giving them a pep talk she summoned the will not to think about herself but to think about the team.

They played more aggressively in the second period, and Maya had three shots on goal, the first of which hit the crossbeam. But that was as close as they got to scoring since her other two shots were both a little wide of the net, and late in the period LSU added an insurance goal, so the final score was 0-2.

As she left the field after the match she caught Judson's eye, and he clapped his hands for her performance. He then made a gesture that meant he would wait for her, and he was there when she and Erin came out of the building.

"Hey, Mr. McBride," Erin said.

"Hey, Erin. You played well."

"I could have played better."

"I guess my father didn't get home in time," Maya said.

"I called your mother before I left," Judson said, "and he wasn't there yet. It's a long way from Laredo to Harperville."

"I wish he had a cell phone so I could call him."

"We all wish he had a cell phone. But you know your father."

"He thinks cell phones damage your brain."

"He could be right."

"So we just have to wait?"

"That's all we can do. Are you hungry?"

"We're starved," Maya said, speaking for both Erin and her. At that moment she saw Shelby approaching them. "Can Shelby join us?"

"He's always welcome. Where would you like to eat?"

"Anywhere." She thought of suggesting Flor de Puebla, but she quickly dismissed the idea.

"How about the Cypress Inn?" Judson said. "You all like that, don't you?"

"Yeah. We don't eat enough fish."

"If fish is brain food," Erin said, "then we need to eat more fish to repair the damage from our cell phones."

"Who said cell phones damage our brains?" Shelby asked.

"My father thinks they do," Maya told him.

"Did he get home?"

"Not yet. But he's on his way."

When they got back to their room that night she wanted to call her mother and ask if her father had gotten home, but she knew that if she did and her father hadn't gotten home, it would make her mother worry. It would also make her worry.

So she waited to hear from her father.

The next morning she diligently practiced her *kata* on the patch of lawn at the end of the parking lot, hoping it would take her mind off her father, but she couldn't stop worrying about him, so after her psychology class she called Trevor to find out what was happening.

"As far as I know," Trevor told her, "he's on his way home."

"Do you know if he crossed the border?"

"No. But I know he checked out of the hotel before eleven on Saturday. I talked with him just before he left."

"Then he must have crossed the border on Saturday."

"I think we can assume he did. His papers were in order."

"Do you know which bus line he was using?"

"Greyhound," Trevor said. "He was hoping to make the two-thirty bus to Houston, but he could have missed that. The next one was at five fifteen. And that would have put him behind for the rest of the trip."

"If he took the later bus to Houston, when would he have gotten home?"

"I worked that out as far as Montgomery. If he took the later bus to Houston, he would have arrived in Montgomery at two fifty-five this morning."

"Then he should have gotten home by now."

"Not necessarily. There isn't a bus from Montgomery to Harperville, so your father was planning to use a livery service.

Judson offered to pick him up in Montgomery, but your father refused since he didn't want Judson to go to all that trouble, and he didn't know when he'd arrive in Montgomery."

"But he'll be home by tonight, won't he?"

"He will if he made all his connections and if all the buses ran on time."

"Okay. Thanks. I won't call my mother until later."

"Wait until this evening," Trevor advised her.

She waited until ten to call her mother, who picked up after the first ring.

"Hola?" her mother said as if she were expecting the caller to be Spanish speaking.

"Hola, mamá. Ya ha llegado papá?

"No. I thought he might be calling."

"Have you heard from him?"

"No. And I'm worried. He should have gotten home by now."

"Well, something must have happened to delay him."

"Then why hasn't he called me?"

"I don't know," Maya said. "Maybe for some reason he can't. I mean, if he's still on a bus he can't call you."

"I guess he can't."

"I think we should find out if he got on the bus in Laredo."

"I don't know how we could do that."

"Trevor would know."

"Would they have a record?"

"They collect tickets. They must do something with them."

"Could you call Trevor? Your English is better."

"Okay. I'll call him."

"I'll let you know if I hear from your father," her mother said. *Que Dios lo proteja."*

"Que Dios lo proteja. Te amo, mamá."

It was late to call Trevor, and there was nothing he could do at this hour, so she waited until morning to call him.

"Have you heard from my father?" she asked him, sitting on the edge of her bed.

"No. I haven't," Trevor said tautly.

"Could you find out if he crossed the border?"

"Yes, I can start the process, and I can contact the police in Laredo."

"Why Laredo? He was in Nuevo Laredo."

"My Spanish isn't good. And the police in Laredo will know how to contact their colleagues across the border. Presumably, they work together."

"I'm worried," Maya said, looking for some reassurance. "I'm afraid something happened to him."

"Well, he could have been delayed by a number of things."

"If he'd been delayed, he would have called us."

"I'll get on it right away," Trevor told her.

That evening he reported back to her and told her he was still waiting to find out if her father had crossed the border or if he had gotten on the bus. Meanwhile the police in Laredo and Nuevo Laredo were keeping an eye out for him but weren't looking for him because they hadn't classified him as a missing person.

The next day, as she was going back to her room after a class, she got a message from Shelby saying he didn't feel well, so he couldn't see her that evening. She replied saying she was sorry and she hoped he would get better soon.

Before she went to soccer practice Shelby texted her again saying he thought he had the flu. She told him to stay in bed and drink plenty of liquids.

She was back in her room after soccer practice when Trevor called her and reported that her father hadn't entered the country, so something must have prevented him from getting to the border. As requested by the police in Laredo, the police in Nuevo Laredo were looking for her father, who was now officially classified as missing.

Before suiting up for the match with Tennessee on the next evening she called Trevor to see if there had been any developments, and Trevor said there hadn't been any.

"Are you all right?" the coach asked her.

"Yeah. I'm fine." She hadn't told him that her father was missing, and there wasn't time to tell him now.

"Well, try to focus," he told her, patting her on the shoulder.

While they were warming up she spotted Judson in the stands. Though she hadn't expected to see her father, she felt a letdown at not seeing him as if she had been hoping that somehow he had managed to cross the border without being detected, as he did when he first came to America.

It was more than ten years since they had beaten Tennessee, which was highly ranked, so they all knew what they were up against. But they went out and challenged their opponents from the very beginning. Early in the first period Maya pounced on a loose ball in front of the net and drove it into the upper left corner. In the rest of the match she had three more shots on goal, and though she didn't score again, they didn't need another goal to win since they kept Tennessee from scoring.

"This was our best performance of the year," the coach told them. "And it kept us in the running for the tournament."

Maya was on a high when she came out of the building with Erin, and at first she was glad to see Judson waiting for her, but then she noticed the expression on his face, and she knew he had bad news for her.

"I'm so sorry," Judson said with tears in his eyes.

"Oh, my God. What happened?"

"They killed your father."

"No," she cried. "No!"

"On his way to the border," Judson said slowly, "he was caught in a cross-fire between drug gangs. They killed him and two other bystanders."

Screaming, she went into Judson's arms.

She soon became conscious of other arms around her and sounds of grief from another person. She knew without looking that it was Erin, and she held on to her *sensei* and her roommate for dear life.

NINE

JUDSON DROVE THEM back to the dormitory and waited outside for Maya to pack a bag. As she staggered around the room in a daze, with tears blurring her vision, Erin stood by her and helped her find things. At one point she stopped, and clinging to Erin she burst into sobs, and Erin held her, silently supporting her.

Erin accompanied her down to where Judson was waiting for her and gave her a long loving hug before she got into the car. Through the window she saw Erin clasp her hands in a gesture of supplication, and she waved to Erin, thanking her.

After they had ridden in silence for a while she asked Judson: "How's mom?"

"She's angry."

"I can understand, but I don't feel angry. I feel—" Unable to express how she felt, she started crying again. "I just can't believe they killed papa. He was coming home, and he was going to have a way of becoming legal."

"I know," Judson said.

"He was going to realize his dream."

"After all that happened your father never lost his faith in America. He worked hard, and he took care of his family. He was a good man."

"Then why did God let them kill him?"

Judson didn't say: "If you asked Father Philip that question, what would he tell you?"

"If it was part of God's plan," she said, trying to answer her own question, "then I don't accept the way He does things. It wasn't just for Him to let them kill my father."

"I don't think it was just either, but God may have a different idea of justice."

Staring ahead into the tunnel made by the headlights, Maya resolved to put her question to Father Philip, even though it seemed hypothetical since she couldn't believe they had killed her father. "Do you think the police in Nuevo Laredo could have made a mistake in identifying him?"

"They could have, but it's not likely. Police are careful in indentifying victims."

"Maybe they're not careful in Nuevo Laredo."

"Why wouldn't they be?"

"Police in Mexico are corrupt, especially in the border towns that are run by drug lords."

"Who told you that?"

"My father did. And my mother agreed. She didn't want my father to stay in Nuevo Laredo. She wanted him to go to Puebla. But he didn't want to travel that far since he expected to be home in a week."

"If he'd gone to Puebla," Judson pointed out, "he still would have had to come through Nuevo Laredo to cross the border."

"I know. I was thinking what my mother's going to say."

"You should let her say it. She needs to get it out. But you can tell her what I just told you. It wasn't his decision to stay in Nuevo Laredo that got him killed."

"It was that law, wasn't it."

"Yes. And that judge."

"Then I blame the people who passed that law, and I blame that judge."

"If you need to blame someone, blame them. But after a while you should stop blaming them. If you don't, then you'll end up like that judge."

"You said he was like that because he blamed other people for how he felt about himself."

"It has the same result when you blame other people for things that happen."

"Well, I do blame the people who passed that law, and I do blame that judge, but I don't blame my father. And I don't want my mother to blame him."

"She needs to get it out," Judson repeated.

They rode in silence for a while, and then Maya said: "So you don't think the police in Nuevo Laredo made a mistake?"

"I don't think they did. They may be corrupt, but I don't see what reason they would have to misidentify a victim."

"Maybe they wanted to cover up the fact that the victim was a member of a drug gang."

"Maybe. But I wouldn't pin my hopes on that theory."

"I won't," she said. But she started looking for another theory since she couldn't believe they had killed her father.

Judson went into her house with her, carrying her bag. They found her mother in the kitchen sitting at the table. Her mother thanked Judson for bringing Maya home, and then Judson left them alone together.

Maya stood in front of her mother feeling unsteady, as if she just regained her feet after being knocked down on the soccer field. *"Dónde están los niños?"*

"They're upstairs."

"How are they?"

"They don't understand what happened."

"Oh, mama," she cried, going to her mother and kneeling down and putting her arms around her mother's solid body and laying her head in her mother's lap, where almost choking on her intakes of breath she cried her heart out.

"Está bien," her mother repeated, stroking her head.

"No creo que mataron a papá."

"Yo no lo creo tampoco, pero lo hicieron."

Maya finally raised her head and looked up at her mother's face, which was ravaged by grief. She realized that as great as her own loss was, her mother's loss was greater. "I'm sorry, mama. I'm so sorry."

"You're a comfort to me," her mother told her, gazing at her tenderly.

They remained in that position for a while, and then Maya got up and sat in the chair next to her mother. "Do you know where papa is?"

Her mother nodded. "The police in Nuevo Laredo have him. They're waiting for us to make arrangements for the funeral."

"Can we bring him back here?"

"Trevor's going to find out if we can. I know he'd want to be buried here," her mother said with an edge in her voice.

"If we can't bring him back, then we have to go to Mexico."

"I'm going to Mexico anyway. I don't want to live in the country that killed your father."

"But they killed him in Mexico."

"The drug lords killed him. And who can we thank for the drug lords? Americans who buy drugs from them. So America killed him."

"Papa wouldn't say that."

"I know he wouldn't. But I'm saying it. That's how I feel."

She remembered what Judson had said about letting her mother get it out, so she tried to facilitate the process by saying: "Well, I blame some Americans. I blame the people who passed that law, and I blame that judge who deported papa."

"I blame them," her mother said. "But I also blame your father. If he hadn't stayed in Nuevo Laredo, he wouldn't have been killed."

"But he still would have had to come through Nuevo Laredo to cross the border."

Her mother dismissed this argument by saying: "If we'd gone back to Mexico after the state passed that law, he wouldn't have had to cross the border."

"He wanted what was best for our family."

"I know he did. We both did. We just had different ideas about what was best."

"I don't think either of you was wrong."

"Well, if one of us was wrong," her mother said with tears beginning to run down her cheeks, "I wish it was me."

She took her mother's hand and said gently: "You were both right, mama."

Carrying her bag, she went upstairs to see how the kids were. She found them together in the room she shared with Selina. They were in their pajamas, slumped on Selina's bed with their backs against the wall like teddy bears that had lost stuffing.

"How are you guys doing?" Maya asked.

"Is papa coming home?" Victor asked.

"He's going home," Maya said.

"What do you mean?"

"He's going home to God."

"Will we see him again?"

"We will, but not in this life. We'll see him in heaven."

"Do you really believe in heaven?" Selina asked, challenging her.

"I really do," Maya said for the sake of the kids. She wasn't sure if heaven existed, but if it did she was sure their father would be there.

"According to mama," Selina said, "we're going to Mexico."

"It looks that way," Maya said.

"I don't want to live in Mexico. I want to live here."

"You don't have a choice."

"Our friends are here."

"You can make friends there."

"I don't want to have Mexican friends," Selina said. "I want to have American friends."

"You have Mexican friends here, don't you?"

"No. I don't. The Mexican kids in my class are all losers."

"So are the Mexican kids in my class," Victor said.

"Are *you* going to live in Mexico?" Selina asked.

"I'm going to stay at the university until I graduate," Maya said. "And then I'll have to see what happens."

"That's not fair," Selina said. "If you get to stay here, we should get to stay here."

"If you were in college, you could stay here. But at your age you have to be with your mother, and she's going to live in Mexico."

"This whole thing sucks," Selina said.

"Yeah, it sucks," Victor said.

She didn't tell them: "Look, guys. Your father is dead. That's what you should be sad about instead of about leaving your friends."

Before going to bed she checked her phone, purely out of habit, and she found a message from Shelby that said: "I feel better. How was the match?"

She replied: "We won. I'll call you in the morning."

She turned off her phone and put it on the table next to her bed and switched off the light. If she hadn't been tired from the soccer match and the trip home and the ordeal of what had happened, she couldn't have slept, but she finally got a few hours of respite.

Her first thought after opening her eyes the next morning was that it had been a nightmare, they hadn't killed her father, and he would come home.

Then she faced the brutal reality: her father wasn't coming home, except as a dead body to be buried if Trevor was able to bring it back.

She lay in bed for a while having no reason to get up. But then she heard her mother going downstairs to make breakfast, and that gave her the motivation to raise herself. After getting dressed she got her phone and turned it on. There were no new messages, and it was too early to call Shelby, so she slid the phone into a pocket of her jeans and headed downstairs, leaving her sister in the oblivion of sleep.

In the kitchen her mother had already made a pot of coffee and was slicing *chorizo*. At the sight of food Maya realized that she hadn't eaten anything since lunch yesterday.

"*Cómo estás, hijita?*" her mother asked her.

"*Estoy bien. Y tú, mamá?*"

"I'm okay. Are you hungry?"

"*Sí.* How can I help you?"

"You can warm up some tortillas."

She went to the other side of stove, on which there were three cast-iron skillets. There was one that was just the right size for tortillas, and she turned on the burner under it. She waited until the pan was hot, and then she took a tortilla off the pile on a plate and carefully laid it into the pan, using a motion she had learned from her mother.

They worked together in silence, not needing to talk. She felt the comfort of being with her mother, and she hoped her mother felt the same way.

Since they didn't expect the kids to get up for a while, they made breakfast for themselves: chorizo, beans, and eggs on a tortilla, topped with salsa. If her father had been there, her mother would have spiked his food with fresh *jalapeño*.

They ate in silence taking comfort from the food, and she helped her mother prepare for the next round of cooking, which would come when the kids got up.

Before that happened, she went out onto the front porch and called Shelby.

"How are you feeling?" she asked him.

"Better," he said in a hoarse voice.

"I'm at home now."

"What are you doing there?"

"Judson brought me here last night after the match." She didn't know how to say it but she made the plunge. "They killed my father."

"What?" Shelby's voice cracked. "What did you say?"

"They killed my father. He was on his way to the border crossing in Nuevo Laredo, and he got caught in a battle between two drug gangs."

"Oh, Jesus," Shelby said.

"I don't believe it happened, but it did."

"I'm so sorry." It sounded like he was crying. "I'll come there right away."

"You don't need to come here. You need to take care of yourself."

"But I want to be there for you."

"You're there for me."

He cleared his throat, and then he asked: "Are you bringing him back?"

"We're hoping we can, but we don't know. We're waiting to hear from Trevor."

"So you don't know how long you'll stay there."

"I'll probably stay here through the weekend."

"What about the match on Sunday?"

They were playing Georgia in Athens, and the team would leave on Saturday since the match was at noon. "I really haven't thought about it, but I'll probably miss it."

"Then I'll drive down tomorrow morning."

"Shelby, you don't need to come here," she repeated, hoping he would understand. "It's enough for me to know you're there for me."

"Okay," he finally said. "But I want you to know I love you."

"I love you too. I'll talk with you later."

They spent the day waiting to hear from Trevor, unable to make any decisions until they knew where the funeral would be.

Around four, while she was lying on her bed resting, the coach called her.

"Erin told me what happened to your father," the coach said. "How are you doing?"

"I don't know. I still can't believe it."

"How's your family doing?"

"My mother's okay. My sister and brother don't understand what happened."

"Well, you should stay there as long as you're needed."

"What about the match on Sunday?"

"Don't even think about it. We'll miss you, but your family comes first."

"Okay," she said with mixed feelings. She knew the coach was right, but at the same time she didn't want to let down her team.

It was after six when they heard from Trevor. They were sitting on the porch, and her mother asked her to talk with Trevor since her English was better.

"What's happening?" she asked him.

"We're getting nowhere. They've raised a lot of obstacles."

"The Mexicans?"

"The Americans. Or I should say both. The police in Nuevo Laredo aren't cooperating, and our state department isn't being helpful. They don't want to deal with it."

"But they were letting my father come back."

"He was alive then. It's a different situation now."

"Well, what did they tell you?"

"They told me it would take a while, and if you want my honest opinion, I think they'll drag it out until you have no choice but to bury your father in Mexico."

"If we did, would they let us bring him back someday?"

"I don't know. But if you bury him in Mexico, you should let your father rest in peace."

"I have another question," Maya said, thinking ahead. "If we go to Mexico for the funeral, will they let us come back?"

"They might, but you'll have to start a process, and that'll take a long time."

"Mom doesn't want to come back, but I do."

"You're in the same position as the rest of your family, so if you're not planning to stay in Mexico you shouldn't go there."

"Okay, thanks. I'll let you know what we decide."

After turning off the phone she reported the conversation to her mother.

"It's what I expected," her mother said. "At least now we know what to do."

"Well, I don't know what to do."

"Your father would understand if you didn't go to his funeral. He'd want you to stay at the university."

"You think he would?"

"I know he would."

"But I'd feel bad about not going to his funeral."

"He wouldn't want you to feel bad," her mother told her. "He'd want you to feel good because you'd be fulfilling his dream."

"I guess he would," Maya said, though she wondered if anything could justify not going to her father's funeral.

The next day after helping her mother clean up after breakfast she walked to Immaculate Conception, where she found Father Philip in his office.

"Maya," he said, rising from the chair behind his desk. From the expression in his voice and on his face, it was evident that he knew what had happened. Ignoring the taboo against touching young people, the priest came around his desk and hugged her. "I'm so sorry."

"Thank you, father."

"How are you all doing?"

"We're trying to deal with it."

"Please sit down and tell me about it."

She sat down in front of his desk and Father Philip sat down behind it.

"I think you know what I'm going to ask you."

"Why did God let them kill your father?"

"Why did He? My father was a good man."

"The standard answer to that question is, it was God's plan. And I believe it was. But I know you're looking for a more satisfying answer."

"I am. I mean, I don't see how it could serve God's plan to have a good person killed."

"It served His plan to have our Savior killed."

"My father wasn't our Savior."

"Still, his sacrifice could serve a purpose."

"What purpose?"

"Helping your people achieve equal status in America. Unfortunately, it takes sacrifices to achieve such purposes."

Maya shook her head. "But that wasn't my father's mission. His mission was his family."

"Then maybe it could be your mission."

"I don't want a mission. I want my father."

"I know," Father Philip said gently. "It's too soon."

"I have another question," Maya said after a pause. "They won't let us bring my father back, so the funeral will have to be in Mexico."

"We can have a memorial service here."

"That would be nice. But I might not be here for the service. If I go to the funeral in Mexico, they won't let me back into the country."

"I assume you talked with Trevor about that."

"I did. He said that if I wasn't planning to stay in Mexico, I shouldn't go there."

"Have you decided what to do?"

"I haven't yet. My mother said I should stay at the university because it would fulfill my father's dream. But if I don't go to my father's funeral, I'll feel bad."

"I agree with your mother. Your father would want you to stay at the university, and if you want to honor him, you can do it that way instead of going to his funeral."

"Are you saying it wouldn't be wrong if I didn't go?"

"I'm saying it would honor your father if you stayed at the university. It's not a question of right or wrong."

"Well, what about my family?"

"What about them?"

"If I stay, I'll feel like I abandoned them."

"Did you feel like you abandoned them when you left home to go to the university?"

"No. But it's different now. And I want what's best for my family."

"Your mother's a competent woman," Father Philip said. "If she said you should stay at the university, she thinks it's best for your family."

"Then I should stay at the university?"

"You should do what your heart tells you to do. So listen to your heart."

As she walked home she listened to her heart, and one thing it told her was not to miss the soccer match, so when she got home she called the coach.

"I want to play in the match on Sunday," she told him.

"Are you sure?" he asked doubtfully.

"Yeah. I'm sure. I know it's what my father would have wanted."

"Well, we're leaving in an hour, so there's no way you can make the bus."

She thought for a moment, and then she said: "I'll ask Erin to bring my uniform and shoes, and I'll find a way to get to Athens."

"Okay." He told her where the team was staying. "I'll see you there."

After ending that call she called Erin, who answered right away.

"How are you doing?" Erin asked her.

"I'm doing better. At least I made one decision. I'm going to play on Sunday."

"You are? That's great."

"I won't make the bus, so I'll get to Athens on my own."

"I'll bring your uniform and shoes," Erin told her.

"That's what I was going to ask you."

"And a sports bra."

"Yeah. There should be a clean one in my top drawer."

"I'll find it." There was a pause. "I went to the evening mass yesterday, and I prayed for you and your family."

"Thanks. You're my best friend."

"You're mine too. I'll see you in Athens."

She thought of asking Shelby to drive her to Athens, but she dismissed the idea since he had the flu and even if he didn't he would have to drive from Tuscaloosa to Harperville and then to Athens, which a search told her was about two hundred fifty miles from Harperville. The only person she could ask was Judson.

She was sure he would do it, which actually made her hesitate because he had done so much for her family and she didn't want to take advantage of him. But having no choice, she finally called Judson.

"I need a big favor," she told him.

"Sure," he said. "What is it?"

"I need to get to Athens for our match tomorrow."

"Are you going to play?" He sounded as if he was all in favor of the idea.

"I don't want to let down the team. And it would be good for me," she added. "I'm having a hard time dealing with this."

"When do you want me to pick you up?"

"Whenever you can."

"It's about a five-hour drive from here, so if we leave at one o'clock we can get there by six. Since it's Saturday, the traffic shouldn't be too bad."

"Okay. I'll be ready at one."

On the way she told him about her family's situation. When she had finished he asked: "Have you decided what to do?"

"Yes. I'm going to stay at the university."

"Have you told your mother?"

"Not yet. I'll tell her when I get home from Athens."

"I think she'll support your decision."

"I know she will," Maya said. "But I'll still feel bad about not going with them."

"I understand. But I think you can do more for your family by staying at the university."

"That's what Father Philip said. But I don't see what I can do for them."

"You can set an example for your sister and your brother."

"I never thought of myself as an example."

"I know you didn't," Judson said. "But you were an example for the kids in karate. They all looked up to you."

"They did?"

"Remember Jenny? At the *shiai* last week she earned her yellow belt."

"Wow. That's great."

"And you were the one who gave her what she needed."
"Well, I tried to help her."
"You not only tried, you succeeded."
After reflecting Maya asked: "If I want to set an example for my sister and my brother, couldn't I do that better in Mexico?"
"You said they wanted to stay in America."
"They do. They don't want to leave their friends."
"So by staying in America," Judson said, "you'll encourage them to come back."
"You mean as international students?"
"If they do well in school, they'll be admitted to a university."
"What about the money?"
"Don't worry about the money. Your mother will have it."
From this comment and from what Father Philip had told her, Maya was gaining a different perspective on her mother. "So you think my mother will be all right without me?"
"She'll be all right economically."
"But what about my sister and my brother? Wouldn't they be more influenced by my example if I was living with them?"
"No, I don't think they would be," Judson said. "I think we're always more influenced by members of our family when they're not living with us."
Maya fell into a silence having a lot to think about.

Judson let her off at the motel where the team was staying, and she quickly found Erin in their room. She called the coach to let him know she had arrived, and then she had dinner with Erin, Dana, and Jackie.
For the first time in weeks she slept well, and she was ready for the match with Georgia.
Again they were the underdog. Georgia had a winning record in the conference and was certain to make the tournament, while Alabama had a losing record and desperately needed a win or a draw to stay in the running. They outshot Georgia in the first period, but about halfway through the period Georgia scored on a penalty kick and took the lead. In the second period

Alabama tied the match on a header by Dana off a corner kick, but less than a minute later Georgia went ahead again on a penalty kick. Within the next minute Alabama tied the match again on a penalty kick by Erin. They played out the regular time and two periods of overtime without another score, so the match ended at 2-2.

"You showed how tough you are," the coach told them afterward, "by coming back from behind twice. You played a good match against a strong opponent. And you earned a point toward qualifying for the tournament."

Maya had taken seven shots, three of which had hit the frame, and she wished that at least one of them had been a little closer.

As she left the building the coach stopped her and put his arm around her shoulder. "I know how hard it must have been for you to come and play today. But I want you to know that without you, we would have lost. You kept us in the match."

"Thanks," she said. "I just wish I'd scored a goal."

"I know, I know. But by coming that close you kept them on the defensive."

She appreciated his comment since she hadn't looked at it that way. And when Judson told her essentially the same thing in the car, she felt better about the match. But nothing could relieve the pain in her heart.

When she got home it was after eight, and she found her mother in the bedroom that her parents had shared, already packing.

"How was the match?" her mother asked, folding a top she wore often.

"It ended in a draw," Maya said.

"Did you have dinner?"

"Yeah. We stopped on the way." She watched her mother carefully lay the top in the suitcase which lay on the bed. "When are you leaving?"

"This Wednesday."

"Does that give you enough time?"

"I think it does. We're taking our clothes and our personal

things in suitcases, and we're shipping the furniture to Puebla."

"What about the lease?"

"Trevor handled it. There was no problem with the landlord."

"Are you traveling by bus?"

"No. By plane. I didn't want to make the kids sit on a bus for two days."

"What does it cost to fly to Puebla?"

"About fifteen hundred dollars for the three of us."

"That's a lot of money."

"Judson paid for it."

Maya wasn't surprised by that.

"He also gave us a pension for your father."

With that information Maya understood why Judson had said her mother would be all right economically. "Where will you leave from?"

"Birmingham. We stop in Houston, and from there we go directly to Puebla. We get there in less than eight hours."

"That beats the bus. How will you get to Birmingham?"

"By car service. Judson arranged it."

"I'll go with you to Birmingham. I can take a bus from there to Tuscaloosa."

"What about your classes?"

"I'm doing fine. I want to stay with you as long as possible. I may not see you for a few years."

Her mother continued packing in silence.

Before going to bed she texted Erin and Shelby saying she would be back on Wednesday. She asked Erin to pass the message on to the coach.

She was lying in bed in a swirl of emotion when Selina, who she thought was sleeping, came over and crawled into bed with her. Selina snuggled up against her, with an arm around her waist. It didn't take long for her to feel Selina's tears through her tee-shirt.

"Don't worry. Everything's going to be all right," she told her sister, conscious of sounding like her father. "Everything's going to be all right."

The car service picked them up at eight on Wednesday morning since they needed to be at the airport two hours before their flight, which was at twelve ten, and it took a little more than an hour to drive from Harperville to the Birmingham international airport. Her mother's Mexican passport had been renewed, and the kids had gotten American passports, so they didn't expect to have any problem checking in, but they allowed some extra time just in case.

With their eyes fixated on their phones in a last binge of texting, the kids said nothing the whole way. When they arrived at the airport they dragged themselves out of the car as if they were being taken away to be executed. Maya stayed with her family until they were cleared through security, and she stood there watching them move toward the gate until they were lost in the stream of people following them. At that moment she was convinced that instead of staying in America she should have gone with them to Mexico.

It was almost two when she got back to the dormitory. She was glad to find Erin in their room, and they hugged each other for a while in silence.

Then Erin said: "I was afraid you might go with your family."

"I felt like I should have. I still do. But even my mother said I should stay."

"Your mother wants what's best for you."

"I know she does. I just hope it's best for my family."

"She must believe it is," Erin said.

"But she doesn't know," Maya said. "And I wonder if I'll ever stop feeling I should have gone to my father's funeral."

"Think about what your father would have wanted. That should help."

It did help, at least enough so she could focus on their last soccer match of the season. It was against Auburn, their archrival, which had a better record both overall and in the conference. If they lost to Auburn the season would be over, but if they won they had a chance of qualifying for the SEC tournament. They also needed a win to achieve their goal of having a winning season. So there was a lot of pressure on them.

The match was at home on Friday evening, and when she spotted Judson in the stands she imagined her father sitting next to him, waving to her. She believed that whatever happened, her father would always be there for her.

They started strong and fired nine shots within the first twenty minutes, keeping Auburn on the defensive. They continued to dominate ball possession until they finally scored with less than five minutes left in the period on a penalty kick by Erin. In the second period, despite the efforts of Auburn to make a comeback, Alabama increased their lead on a goal by Dana. But with less than fifteen minutes remaining Auburn scored on a perfect play, and with less than six minutes Auburn tied the match on a penalty kick.

With victory apparently eluding them and time running out, Maya got the ball on a sloppy clearance and quickly drilled it into the net to put her team ahead 3-2.

They had to untangle themselves from a heap to play out the few remaining minutes, and then they celebrated, drawing the coach into their jumble. They were going to the tournament for the first time in three years, they had beaten Auburn for the first time in six years, and they had a winning season for the first time in eight years.

"I wondered what you'd do after they tied it," the coach told them. "I should have known. You're a great team."

In the coach's words Maya heard her father, who she knew was celebrating somewhere, and at least for a moment she didn't feel the pain in her heart.

TEN

THE TOURNAMENT, which began on Wednesday, November 2, was being held at Orange Beach, Alabama. As the team was boarding the bus they learned that their goalkeeper had been named to the all-conference second team, and that Erin and Maya had been named to the freshmen team. Those accolades helped to propel them mentally on the long ride down to the Gulf, which took more than five hours.

Maya had never seen the ocean, and as the driver gave them a tour along Perdido Beach Boulevard she marveled at the pure white sand, which looked like powdered sugar. She and Erin shared a room, and after being confined in the bus for so long they couldn't wait to go out and stretch their legs walking on the beach.

"I love the smell of the ocean," Erin said, breathing in deeply through her nose. "It reminds me of going to the beach when I was a kid."

"Did you live near a beach?"

"We weren't far from a beach on the Sound. But the best beaches were on the ocean, out on Long Island. We rented a house at Bellport for a week every August."

"It must have been fun."

"It was. But my parents knew that one week was enough. When we left we always wished we could stay longer."

Maya smiled, thinking how the same principle applied to her sister and her brother at the old pool in Harperville. With a pang, she missed them.

Since Alabama had just squeaked into the tournament they were seeded last of the eight teams, and they were scheduled to play South Carolina, which had won the conference title in the regular season and was seeded first. Alabama's chances of winning the match were so slight that they felt as if they had nothing to lose.

The match was in the Orange Beach Sportsplex, which had hosted the tournament before. The stadium was almost filled, and it took Maya a while to spot Judson. He was wearing the usual black polo shirt, which stood out from the mostly light shirts of the crowd. From the cheers for the respective teams, it seemed like there were more fans of South Carolina than of Alabama, though they had to travel farther to get there.

The two teams played even, trading shots on goal, until almost thirty minutes into the first period when Dana scored on a pass from Maya with a low shot inside the far post. South Carolina tried very hard to make a comeback, relentlessly controlling the ball in the second period, but Alabama stopped them with a tough defense and a great performance by their goalkeeper, who got her seventh shutout of the season. The final score was 1-0, and Alabama defeated the team that had been favored to win the tournament.

"That was a great team performance," the coach told them. "You took the lead, and you stopped the other team from scoring. And they weren't an easy team to stop, as you know from our previous encounter with them."

Judson took her and Erin to dinner at a seafood restaurant, where they replenished the energy they had burned in the match. Though they didn't talk about her father, Maya was conscious of the empty chair at the table where he would have been sitting.

When Judson let them off at their motel he put an arm around her shoulder and said: "Your father's proud of you. I hope you can feel it."

"I can," she said, appreciating his validation.

On Thursday they practiced lightly and rested, and on Friday evening they played Florida, which had beaten Georgia in the first round. Florida was seeded fourth and had beaten them in their previous encounter, so again they went out with low expectations.

The match was even until Maya scored about thirty minutes into the period on a pass from Erin, but they lost their lead within a minute, and the score was 1-1 at the end of the first period. In the second period Florida outshot them almost three to one, and they were on the defensive most of the time. They held out until the eighty-first minute when Florida scored the decisive goal. The final score was 1-2.

"You played a great match," the coach told them. "And in case you don't know it, this is farther than we've gotten in the tournament in a long time."

They didn't feel too bad about losing to Florida, and they felt even less bad when Auburn beat Florida on Sunday to win the tournament. They had beaten Auburn, so on that occasion they had proven they were as good as any team in the conference.

On Monday they learned that they had made it into the NCAA Women's Soccer Tournament for the first time in thirteen years. They had earned the spot by beating South Carolina, the SEC Conference champions, and Auburn, the SEC Tournament champions, as well as by beating highly ranked Tennessee and San Diego State. They would play the University of Miami on Saturday. Since Miami was ranked ahead of Alabama, the match would be held at Cobb Stadium in Coral Gables.

They traveled by plane from the Birmingham airport, leaving on Thursday, which hardly gave them enough time to catch up on their studies. They went to bed early in Miami, and after their practice the next day they took a little time to see Coral Gables and Coconut Grove and South Beach. They had dinner at a Cuban restaurant and again went to bed early, wanting to be rested for the match the next day.

The match was at one in the afternoon, and there weren't many spectators, implying that soccer wasn't important to Miami students. The two teams played even in the first period, with Alabama going out ahead in the twentieth minute on a goal by Dana, but ten minutes later Miami tied it up. Alabama played aggressively in the second period, outshooting Miami by almost two to one, and they took the lead again in the seventy-first minute on a goal by Erin, whom Maya had set up with a pass. But five minutes later Miami tied the match again, and for the next fifteen minutes the two teams battled, trying to make the winning goal. At the end of regular time the score was still 2-2, so they went into overtime. During that period neither team was able to penetrate the other team's defense, so they went into a second overtime. Only two minutes into that period Miami scored, and that was it. The tournament was over for Alabama, and Miami advanced to the next round.

"That was a hard way to end the season," the coach told them, "but I want you to know how proud of you I am. You fought hard, you never gave up. You kept getting better, and you moved soccer at Alabama to a higher level."

Back in their room, Maya had a meltdown. With the season over she didn't have soccer to focus her mind on and put her heart into. She was faced with the undeniable fact that she would never see her father again. And seated on the edge of her bed, she started crying.

Erin immediately came to her and sat next to her and put an arm around her.

"I'm sorry," Maya said. "I can't help it."

"It's all right," Erin said soothingly.

She found a haven on her friend's shoulder, where she cried her heart out. She cried because she had lost her father, she cried because she missed her mother, and she cried because she didn't know who she was, or where she belonged, or what would become of her.

"It's all right," Erin murmured, stroking her back.

She knew these words of comfort didn't mean that what distressed her was all right but that it was all right to cry. And she cried until she had no more tears.

On the following Saturday Shelby drove her to Harperville for the memorial service that Father Philip had scheduled for eleven o'clock.

A lot of people were there. They were mostly Latinos, but other members of the congregation were there, including Judson, and nonmembers, including Trevor and Mr. Otis. It was gratifying for Maya to see how many people came to pay their respects to her father.

Maya sat in the front pew, with Shelby next to her. Father Philip had asked her to select a reading from the epistles. After leafing through her Bible she decided to read a passage from Corinthians 1 that she felt reflected the spirit of her father. Since there were people in the church who understood only Spanish or only English, she was prepared to read it in both languages.

Shortly before the service began she happened to glance around and see Erin with Dana and Jackie and the coach enter the church, and she was deeply touched.

When the time came for the epistle she went up to the pulpit and found her place and began reading: "Love is patient and kind. Love is not jealous or boastful. It is not arrogant or rude. Love does not insist on its own way. It is not irritable or resentful. It does not rejoice at wrong but rejoices in the right. Love bears all things, believes all things, hopes all things, endures all things. Love never fails."

She paused and then began again: *"El amor es paciente, es bondadoso—"*

After the gospel Father Philip stepped down from the pulpit and gave a eulogy, saying: "Ramiro Méndez was a member of our community, a neighbor, and a friend. He came here fifteen years ago driven by the dream of living in America. He was achieving that dream when something happened. The state of Alabama passed a law whose purpose was to deny that dream to Ramiro and people like him. And as a result of actions incited by that law Ramiro was deported to Mexico, where he was killed in a battle between drug gangs. His death seems senseless, but we know that nothing happens in this world without a purpose. And if only his death reminds people that hatred has consequences, and if his sacrifice turns that hatred into love, then Ramiro won't have died in vain. You heard the message of the reading that his daughter Maya selected. I hope that message reaches everyone in Alabama, everyone in America, and everyone in the world."

Several members of the community got up and gave eulogies in Spanish, and then Father Philip continued with the service. When she got up to receive communion she urged Shelby to go with her, and he finally did.

Afterward there was a reception in the meeting room of the parish house, where women from the community had brought pans of Mexican food.

"I see what you mean," Shelby said after tasting it. "That's not at all like Taco Bell."

She talked with Judson and Trevor and Mr. Otis and people who approached her to express condolences and wish her well. She repeated many times that her family was living with her mother's brother in Puebla while they looked for a house, and that her mother was planning to start a business, most likely a restaurant.

She thanked Erin and Dana and Jackie and the coach for coming. She hugged them all one by one, including the coach, who held her gingerly.

On their way back to Tuscaloosa they passed through Melitus, and Maya had a strong urge to find that judge and confront him with the consequences of what he had done. But the urge was overcome by the spirit of the service, and anyway it was Saturday, so she wouldn't know where to find him.

On Monday morning, as she was returning to the dormitory from her history class, she felt her phone vibrate. She didn't recognize the number of the caller, but she thought it might be someone with a message from her mother, so she answered it.

"Is this Maya Méndez?" a woman's voice asked.

"Yes," she said cautiously.

"This is Heather, the secretary of Dean Carter. He would like to see you, and I wonder if you're free anytime between now and twelve thirty."

"I'm free now."

"Oh, that's perfect." Heather gave her the location of the dean's office.

Maya walked there feeling anxious since she believed that deans didn't want to see students unless there was a problem.

When she got there Heather, a maternal woman, greeted her with a friendly smile and told her she could go right in.

The dean rose from his desk stiffly. In his dark blue suit and white shirt and plain tie he could have been a funeral director. His face was gaunt and his faded blue eyes were shielded by thick silver-rimmed glasses. In a thin, high voice he said: "Maya?"

"Yes, sir."

"I'm Dean Carter. Please sit down."

She sat in the chair in front of his desk while he sat down behind it. There were pictures on the desk, but she couldn't see who was in them since they faced away from her.

"I hear you're a very good soccer player."

"I do my best," she said humbly.

"I also know you're a good student."

She waited for him to continue, hoping he would get to the point soon.

"So I'm sorry I have to tell you—" He cleared his throat. "Your admission to this university wasn't valid."

"Why wasn't it valid?"

"You don't have legal status in this country."

"But a judge stopped that part of the law. And I was admitted before the law was passed."

"It's not the law, it's our policy."

"If it's your policy, someone should have told me before."

"The admissions people should have told you. I guess they were eager to recruit you."

"It's not fair. If they'd told me before, I could have gone to another university."

"Maybe you still can, but you can't remain here."

She remembered what Erin had told her. "Does my coach know about this?"

"Not yet. I wanted you to know first."

"Well, I'm going to tell him," Maya said, rising. "And you're going to hear from him."

"I'll listen to what he has to say," the dean said, still sitting, "but I can't change our policy. I wish I could because I don't want to lose you."

"If you really mean that, you'll find a way around the policy."

"There isn't any way around it."

She searched his face, and what she saw was a weak bureaucrat carrying out orders. She turned and left without another word.

As soon as she had left the building she called the coach, who luckily was in his office.

"I need to talk with you," she told him.

"Come right over," he responded immediately.

She found him at his desk, wearing sweats and looking as if he had just worked out. There were drops on his forehead.

Unable to sit down, she started telling him about her conversation with the dean. When she got to the part about her admission not being valid and the reason why not, the coach banged his fist on the desk and roared: "That sounds like bullshit. They may have such a policy, but as far as I know they never applied it to anyone."

"Then why are they applying it to me?"

"I don't know. But I'm going to find out." He got the number of the dean's office and called it. He talked with Heather, and when he ended the call he said: "I have an appointment in a half hour. I better take a shower and look presentable."

"I'll go back to my room and wait to hear from you."

"I'll come and see you after the meeting."

As she walked to Tutwiler she tried to see the situation as her father would have. The coach would make the dean realize how important she was to the soccer team, and the dean would find a way around the policy. But then she saw the situation as her mother would have. The dean would tell the coach there was no way around the policy, and she would be expelled from the university. If that happened, she would have no choice but to go to Mexico and join her family. She had nowhere else to live.

When she entered their room she was glad to see Erin, who was at her desk studying.

Erin turned and seeing Maya's face asked: "What happened?"

"I was summoned to the dean's office," Maya said. "He told me my admission wasn't valid because I don't have legal status."

"But you were admitted before that law was passed."

"I told him that, and I told him a judge stopped that part of the law, but he said it wasn't the law, it was their policy."

"Their policy? That sounds like bullshit."

"That's what the coach said."

"He knows about it?"

"I told him. He should be meeting with the dean now."

"He'll fix it," Erin said confidently.

"What if he doesn't have the power to fix it?"

"He must have the power. Athletics are important to them."

"Maybe something else is more important to them."

"Something else? What do you mean?"

"The coach said that as far as he knew they never applied such a policy to anyone, so why are they applying it to me?"

Erin frowned. "Do you think they have a particular reason for applying it to you?"

"I don't know what to think," Maya said. "But I wonder if they're applying it to me because I'm not white."

"You do? Well, maybe they are."

"I don't want to believe they're racist. This is a university."

"It's a public university," Erin pointed out, "which is ultimately controlled by politicians."

Maya followed this line of reasoning. "And if it's controlled by the politicians who passed that law, then it's racist."

"Yeah. If we could find out if they've applied that policy to other students in your situation, we'd know what they're doing."

"Well, I don't know any other students in my situation."

"I don't either. People don't post that information on their Facebook."

"The coach said he'd find out why they're applying the policy to me. He said he'd come here after his meeting."

"I have a lab, but I can stay here."

"No, don't miss your lab. I can tell you later what he says."

Before leaving, Erin hugged her and said: "Don't worry. We're not going to let them break us up. We're going to find a way to stay together."

An hour later the coach called her and told her he was in front of her dormitory in his car. She hurried down, and responding to his gesture she got right in.

"You have a boyfriend," he said. "You must know a place where we can park and talk."

"There's a place by the river."

"Just tell me how to get there."

He followed her directions, and within ten minutes they were parked there.

It felt strange being with the coach at the place where she made out with Shelby, and it altered their positions in the relationship. Instead of having a desk between them, they were side by side looking at the river.

"It's a nice place," the coach said. "I should come here with my wife."

She knew he didn't expect a response, so she remained silent.

"I found out why they're applying the policy to you. An important alumnus, a major donor, went to the president and complained about their admitting illegal aliens. The president asked him for an example, and he gave your name."

"Did the dean tell you who the alumnus was?"

"No, he wouldn't tell me. I guess he doesn't want to risk a lawsuit. Anyway, the alumnus told the president that if they continued to let illegal aliens attend the university he wouldn't give them any more money. He said that if the university didn't expel you immediately, he'd cut off his funding. So the president told the dean to expel you."

"Can you get them to rescind my expulsion?"

The coach shook his head. "I don't have the power of the football coach. But I have a solution. If you leave the university and go to Mexico, I can bring you back as an international student. I already checked with the person who administers scholarships, and she told me your scholarship was allocated to me, and that I can use it however I want as long as I comply with the university's policies. And there's no policy that would stop you from attending as an international student."

It sounded too good to be true. "Are you sure you can do it?"

"If I had any doubts, I wouldn't raise your hopes."

"But what about the important alumnus?"

"He can't stop them from admitting international students. I'm sure they make more money on those students than he could ever donate."

Beginning to believe it would happen, she asked: "When would I be able to come back?"

"In the spring semester," the coach said. "I assume you have a Mexican passport."

"Yeah, and it's up to date. My mother wanted us all to be ready to go back to Mexico."

"Then go quietly, and I'll start working with admissions."

"Should I go and see the dean again?"

"I think you should. You should leave a good impression on him," the coach added.

"You mean I didn't?"

"He said from the way you looked at him before you left his office, he had the feeling you wanted to kill him."

"I did want to kill him. But I could see how weak he was, so I had pity on him."

"You're not only a good soccer player," the coach told her, gazing at her with admiration, "you're also a good person."

"You're a good person," Maya said, kissing him on the cheek.

As soon as the coach let her off at the dormitory she called Shelby. She had guessed who the important alumnus was and why he had gone to the president.

"Hey, what's happening?" Shelby asked.

"I need to see you," she told him. "Can you pick me up in front of my dorm?"

"I'll be there in five minutes. Is anything wrong?"

"I'll explain when I see you."

He was there in only a little more than five minutes. She got into his car, wondering where they could go and talk. She didn't want to go back to the place by the river since she had come away from there with such a positive feeling, so she tried to think of someplace else.

"You want to go to the place by the river?"

"I want to go to a Mexican restaurant."

"I thought you didn't like Mexican restaurants."

"I don't like fake Mexican restaurants," Maya said, "but I discovered a real one."

"You did? Where is it?"

"On 15th Street."

She told him how to get there, and he found a parking place not far away. When they walked in she saw Diego behind the bar, and he gave her a look as if to say: "So you really do have a boyfriend."

A waiter who also looked Mexican led them to a booth, where they sat down. They ordered cokes, and as soon as the waiter had left them Shelby asked: "What is it?"

She started relating her conversation with the dean. She paused when the waiter brought their drinks along with menus, and then she resumed.

When she got to the part about her admission not being valid, Shelby said: "That sounds like bullshit."

"That's what the coach said, and that's what Erin said."

"Well, if that's what all three of us said, we must be right."

"I think you are. But there's more to it." She went on to how an important alumnus went to the president.

"Oh, my God," Shelby moaned, bringing his palms up against his mouth as if to say no evil.

"You know who the alumnus was?"

"I don't know, but I can guess. God damn him!"

"If it was your father, why did he do it?"

"To make you go back to Mexico."

"Because I'm an illegal alien?"

"No. Because you're my girlfriend, and he doesn't want me to marry you."

"Where did he get the idea that you might marry me?"

Shelby paused to think, and then his face clouded. "He got it from me. The weekend of the Arkansas game I had breakfast with my parents on Sunday morning at their hotel. And my mother asked if I was serious about you."

"You mean the girl with the Spanish parents?"

Shelby grimaced. "I said I *was* serious about you. I said I was hoping to marry you."

"Well, that's why your father wanted to get rid of me."

"It's my fault," Shelby said with tears forming in his eyes.

"It's not your fault. It's your father's fault for not being able to accept a girl who isn't white."

"But if I hadn't said I was hoping to marry you—"

"Hush," she said gently, feeling his pain. "Your mother asked you a question, and you gave her an honest answer. What else could you have done in that situation?"

"I could have lied."

"You couldn't have lied. And even if you had, your mother would have known you were lying."

After a silence Shelby said: "So you're leaving the university?"

"They haven't given me any choice."

"Where are you going?"

"I'm going back to Mexico." She had decided not to tell him about the coach's plan, afraid that it would get to his father, who might somehow be able to prevent her from getting a student visa. And it was true: she *was* going back to Mexico.

"If we got married, you could stay here."

"That really wouldn't solve my problem. Before I marry you or anyone, I have to know who I am and where I belong."

"You belong with me."

"Maybe I do," Maya said, "but we haven't been together long enough for me to know that."

"We would have been together four years here. That would have been long enough."

"Maybe. And maybe we'll be together again. But now isn't the right time for us to get married."

Staring at the table, Shelby said: "I hate my father."

"Don't hate him. You're lucky you still have a father."

"I'm sorry. I didn't mean to be insensitive."

"I know. It's all right." She reached out and ran her fingers through his soft hair. "For what it's worth I still love you."

"It's worth a lot. And I still love you."

Back in their room she gave Erin the latest developments, sharing her conversations with the coach and with Shelby.

"So the coach doesn't have the power to stop them," Erin said, sitting on the edge of her bed, "but he has the brains to get around them."

"I feel it's too good to be true," Maya said. "But that's how my mother would feel. My father would feel it's what should happen."

"It should happen. So let the coach make it happen."

Maya decided to follow that advice. "I hope I wasn't too hard on Shelby. I mean about his offer to marry me."

"He's not ready to get married. He's eighteen, and since boys are two or three years younger than girls emotionally, you could say he's fifteen or sixteen."

"Still, he was nice to make the offer."

"He's a nice boy. But it sounds like his father isn't very nice."

"I understand why his father did it. He was trying to protect his family. But I don't forgive him," Maya added.

"You know," Erin said after a silence, "it could turn out better this way. I mean, if you're an international student you won't have to worry about being deported."

"I thought of that. And it *will* be better in that sense. But I'll also lose something."

"What will you lose?"

"The hope of being an American, at least in the near future. If my father had made it back across the border, we would have had a way of becoming legal. This way I'll be a Mexican girl attending an American university."

"After what they did to your family, I don't know why you still want to be an American."

"Because it's what my father wanted."

"Not because it's what *you* want?"

"I don't know what I want," Maya said. "I told Shelby that before I marry him or anyone, I have to know who I am and where I belong."

"What did he say?"

"He said I belong with him."

"I knew it. Boyfriends are so predictable. They think they can give us identities."

"Well, at least having a boyfriend made me feel I belonged here. It made me feel like an American girl, instead of like an illegal alien."

"But if you're no longer an illegal alien," Erin said, "you'll see things differently."

Maya understood. "You mean I'll have a different perspective as an international student."

"Yeah. And maybe that'll help you find out who you are."

"Well, at least it'll change the way I appear on the team roster. Instead of Maya Méndez from Harperville, Alabama, I'll be Maya Méndez from Puebla, Mexico."

The next morning, seeking his advice, she called Trevor and told him what had happened.

He waited until he had heard it all, and then he said: "We can fight the university, but I don't think we have a strong case. I mean, even if they were applying the state law, I still think the part that doesn't allow illegal immigrants to attend public universities is the least open to challenge. But since they're saying it's not the law, it's their policy, we'd have to prove they're applying that policy in a way that violates federal law, and maybe we could do that, but if we lost then they probably wouldn't admit you even as an international student. Organizations don't welcome people who sue them."

"So you think I should go with the coach's solution?"

"I think you should. It's a good solution. And luckily your papers are in order on the Mexican side. When would you go back there?"

"I don't know. I guess as soon as possible."

"Have you told your mother?"

"No, not yet. I'm going to tell her when I know what I'm doing."

"She'll be happy to have you at home for a while."

His comment made her realize that as much as she had resisted the idea, home was where her mother was, and she began to think of Puebla as her home.

She called the dean's office, and his secretary told her she could come right over.

When she entered his office she noticed that he acted wary of her, and for a moment she imagined giving him a *mei geri* right in the groin. But then she remembered what the coach had said about leaving a good impression on him, so she sat down in front of his desk with her hands in her lap like a good girl.

"I really can't tell you how sorry I am," the dean began.

"It's all right. I understand. I only wanted to talk about the timing."

The dean looked relieved. "Well, you can have whatever time you need to wind up your affairs. Of course, within reason."

Maya had planned to go with Shelby to Harperville the next day and spend the Thanksgiving break with Judson. Not wanting to linger, she said: "I'll leave tomorrow."

"You can take longer if you need more time."

"I don't need more time, thanks."

"From what the coach told me, I know the soccer team will miss you."

"I'll miss the soccer team."

"Well, I'm sorry this happened," the dean said as if he meant it. "If I had my way—"

She raised her hand to stop him from saying any more. "I understand. And I don't blame you. I mean, you're only doing your job."

She spent the next several hours going around and telling her professors she was leaving the university—for family reasons. They were nice to her, and they told her they hoped she would come back soon. They didn't ask for a specific reason why she was leaving, though one of them surreptitiously glanced at her belly to see if she looked pregnant.

It was now the middle of the afternoon, and since Erin was in a lab now, instead of heading back to the dorm Maya walked to Flor de Puebla for the ostensible purpose of having some Mexican comfort food.

Diego was standing behind the bar, and though there was no one sitting at it, Maya took a stool at the far end, away from the entrance.

"Cómo estás?" Diego asked familiarly.

"Bien. Y tú?" She could feel his dark eyes assessing her.

"I can't complain. A pretty girl just came in and sat down at my bar."

She knew this was only a *piropo*, but she didn't know how to respond to it. "Could you get me a coke, please?"

"Sí, señorita. Would you like a menu?"

"Yes, please." She watched him fetch the coke, impressed as before by what his tee-shirt and jeans revealed about his body.

"How's your boyfriend?" Diego asked, setting the drink on the bar in front of her.

"He's fine." She reached for the glass and took a sip.

"He looked like a real high-class *gringo*."

"I don't like that word."

"Gringo? It's not pejorative."

"It can be pejorative."

"Well, I didn't mean it that way. I only meant he looked like a high-class American."

"He's rich," she said, not knowing why.

"That's good. You don't want to marry a guy who's poor."

"Who said anything about getting married?"

"Isn't that what happens at the university? People from the same social class meet each other, and they get married."

"I'm not one of them."

"I can see you're not. You don't look like any of them."

Instead of asking him what she looked like, Maya said: "You said you came here as an international student."

"Yeah. I came here to study engineering."

"Why here? Why not a university in Mexico?"

"I thought I'd get a better education in America."

"Did you plan to stay here?"

"I planned to go back to Mexico, where I could get a good job with an American degree."

"Why did you drop out?"

"I told you," he said as if she hadn't listened. "I dropped out to help our people."

"But you didn't tell me what you do."

"I would have told you, but you said you couldn't meet me that evening."

She still wondered if he was feeding her a line, and she decided to test him by saying: "What if I told you I'm leaving the university and going home?"

"Where's home?"

"Puebla."

"Why are you leaving?"

"They kicked me out."

"They did? What happened?"

"They found out that I'm illegal."

"How did they find out?"

"An important alumnus told them."

Diego smiled wryly. "Your boyfriend's father?"

"How did you guess?"

"You said he's rich, and I'm sure his father doesn't want some greasy little spic to get her hands on all that money."

By herself she wouldn't have gone so far, but his observation pushed her there, and she didn't try to justify what Shelby's father had done.

"So they applied that law to you," Diego muttered.

"They said it wasn't the law, it was their policy."

"Law or policy, it doesn't matter. What matters is the racism that underlies their laws and their policies, the racism that governs their behavior."

"Well, I have a way around it," she said. "I'm coming back as an international student."

"That won't help us. It only lets them get away with what they do to us."

"So what do you expect me to do? Kill the dean?"

Diego shook his head. "We don't kill people. We try to convince them to do what's right."

"And how do you convince them?"

"By making them see it's in their interest to do what's right."

"I'd like to hear more about what you do, but I don't have time. I'm leaving tomorrow."

"Do you have to leave then?"

"I have to be out of the dormitory by then. I'm going to Harperville to spend Thanksgiving with my *sensei*."

"Your *sensei*?"

"My karate teacher. I have a brown belt."

"You do? I have a black belt."

She thought he was trying to top her, but then he pointed to the black belt he wore with his outfit, making her laugh. "I thought you were serious."

"I do have a sense of humor," he said, flashing his teeth.

"When I'm back as an international student, I'll come and hear about what you do."

"You won't want to. You'll be legal then."

"But you were an international student. That didn't stop you."

"It did stop me. It stopped me from seeing what they were doing to us."

"What opened your eyes?" she asked.

"It would take a while to explain it to you," he said, repeating what he had said before. "Can you meet me this evening?"

She wanted to hear more about what he did, but she had only one more night in Tuscaloosa, and she wanted to spend it with Erin. "I'm sorry. I can't."

"Your boyfriend?"

"No. My roommate."

Diego nodded as if he understood. "I would have argued against your boyfriend, but I won't argue against your roommate."

"She's my best friend."

"Then I'll hope to see you when you're back at the university. Will it be this spring?"

"That's the plan."

"Are you going to order any food?"

"Yeah. I'll have what I had the first time I came here."

"Las chuletas de puerco adobadas?"

"That's right." She didn't have to ask if it came with tortillas.

Back in her room, she decided it was time to call her mother. She actually had to call Selina since her mother didn't have a cell phone, and she hoped that her sister's phone was still active.

"Hello? Maya?" Her sister sounded glad to hear from her.

"Hi, Selina. How are you?"

"I'm bored to death, but today I met a cute boy."

"That's good. How's Victor?"

"He's a pain in the butt."

"Is mom around?"

"Yeah, I'll put her on."

She waited for her mother to get on the phone.

"Hola," her mother said anxiously.

"Hi, mom. How're you doing?"

"We're doing fine. How're you doing?"

"Well, something's happened that will make you glad," Maya began. And she told her mother about her situation.

"*Es lo que Dios quería,*" her mother said as if it was the best thing that could have happened. "Do you know when you're coming to Mexico?"

"I haven't booked a flight yet. I have a lot of things to do."

"I understand. But I hope you'll be here soon."

"I'll let you know when I've booked a flight."

"Your Uncle Benito will pick you up at the airport."

"I hope you'll be with him. I won't recognize him, and I'm sure he won't recognize me."

"We'll all be there at the airport to meet you," her mother said. "*Que Dios te bendiga.*"

She and Erin had dinner together at Buffalo Phil's, where they had gone their first night on campus back in August. She had brought Erin up to date on her conversations with the dean and Trevor, so they looked ahead to the spring semester. They talked as if Maya was only leaving for the Christmas break.

Instead of going to class the next morning, Erin helped Maya pack, and she was there in the afternoon when Shelby arrived. Though Maya still didn't have a lot of things, she seemed to have more than when her father had brought her to college in August, and it took them a while to load the car.

She had already said goodbye to the coach and to Dana and Jackie, and now she had to say goodbye to Erin. They hugged each other as if they were afraid they would never see each other again, and maybe they wouldn't.

As the car pulled away from Tutwiler she looked back through the narrow window and saw Erin waving to her, and she waved back with a pang of loss.

They were on the highway before Shelby broke the silence, saying: "I talked with my father."

"You did? When?"

"Last night. I asked him if he went to the president and told him you were illegal. He admitted it, but he tried to justify it by saying he only wanted what was best for me."

Maya said nothing, conscious of having used this justification herself for other things.

"I told him that however he tried to justify it, he had no right to do what he did. He said he did have a right to do it, he had a right to protect his family."

"From what?" she asked, though she knew what it was.

Shelby hesitated. "From an interracial marriage."

"That's the real purpose of the immigration law. It's not to protect jobs, it's to protect the white people of Alabama from interracial marriage."

"We should have gotten over that."

"I think some people have gotten over it," Maya said, "but others haven't."

Shelby was silent for a while, staring at the road ahead of them, and then he said: "I don't want to be like my father."

"You're not like your father."

"But he wants me to be like him. He wants me to graduate from college and come back to Harperville and work in his bank and marry a white woman and have white kids."

"If that's what you want, there's nothing wrong with it."

"It's not what I want. I want to do something with my life."

"Then don't let him make you do what he wants."

"I won't," Shelby said with determination.

"And don't let any woman make you do what she wants."

"I'd do what *you* want. You know what's best for me."

"No, I don't. I don't even know what's best for me."

"You don't? I don't believe it."

"I told you," Maya said softly. "I don't know who I am, or where I belong."

"Well, you don't belong in Puebla."

"Maybe I don't. But I have to go there. I have nowhere else to go now."

Shelby was again silent, and if he believed she had somewhere else to go, he didn't say it. He just said: "I could visit you there during Christmas break."

"Let's see what happens."

"But I don't want to lose you."

"You won't lose me," Maya assured him. "No matter what happens, I'll be there for you."

Without taking his eyes off the road, he reached over and found her hand.

When they had unloaded her things from the car in Judson's driveway, she thanked Shelby with a long kiss.

"I love you," he said.

"I love you too," she said. But afraid he might let it slip to his father in a moment of defiance, she still didn't tell him she hoped to come back in the spring semester.

Judson gave her a bedroom that would have been used by one of his children if he had been blessed with any. It made her feel like his daughter.

That evening, while he grilled a steak, she made a salad, and while they ate in his kitchen they talked about her plans. At one point she asked: "Are people still trying to overturn that law?"

"The churches are active, and so are the other organizations that sued the state."

"Are Latinos active?"

"The Hispanic coalition is active."

"What about other Latino organizations?"

"I haven't heard about any others, but they could be working less visibly."

"You mean underground?"

"It's possible. But when organizations go underground they usually resort to violence."

"Is that why they go underground?"

"There aren't many other reasons for going underground."

"But an organization can be less visible," Maya said, "without being underground."

"Oh, yeah. It can be less visible for lack of money."

As Maya lay in bed that night she remembered what Father Philip had said about how it could be her mission to help her people achieve equal status in America, and before going to sleep she decided not to wait until January to hear more about what Diego was doing.

ELEVEN

THE NEXT MORNING she got up early and helped Judson prepare the Thanksgiving dinner. They were having roast turkey with cornbread and sausage stuffing, collard greens with ham hock, sweet potato casserole, grits spoon bread, and buttermilk biscuits, with pecan pie for dessert.

Maya had always helped her mother prepare dinner for Thanksgiving, which in her family they called *El Día de Acción de Gracias*, but the dishes had been Mexican, so she had to follow Judson's instructions to prepare the Southern dishes. He had made cornbread the day before, and while he prepared the turkey Maya crumbled the cornbread and mixed it in a bowl with sage, thyme, salt, and pepper. She chopped some onion, apple, and celery, which she added to the pan in which she browned the sausage. She stirred that mixture into the cornbread and added some chicken broth to moisten it. And then she put the stuffing into a baking dish.

Meanwhile, the sweet potatoes had been roasting in the oven, and she tested one with a fork and found that it was done. She took the pan with the sweet potatoes out of the oven and let them cool before peeling them. She then cut them into rounds and layered them in a baking dish. She shook some brown sugar over them and stood back while Judson sprinkled them with bourbon. When she had dotted them with butter they were ready for the oven.

Judson put the turkey into the oven and started working on the grits while she washed the greens and cut out the stems. She put them into a pot of boiling water with an onion and the ham hock and turned down the heat and looked for the timer.

"It's in that drawer," Judson said, guessing what she was looking for.

"How long do you cook them?" she asked, finding the timer.

"About an hour." He added a beaten egg to the pot of grits, which he stirred for a while before pouring them into a pan. He set the pan to one side.

"Is there anything else?"

"Yeah. The cranberry sauce." He got a bag of berries out of the freezer compartment. "We could have bought a can of sauce, but this is better."

She watched Judson empty the bag into a pot, add sugar and water, and turn on the heat. She wondered if he took this much trouble cooking for himself, or if there were people he cooked for regularly.

With everything ready they sat down at the kitchen table and rested. Deciding that now would be a good time to let Judson know her plans, she said: "I have to go back to Tuscaloosa."

"Did you forget something?"

"No. I left a loose end."

"Can your roommate handle it?"

"No. It's something I have to handle myself."

"Okay," he said, looking at her with interest. "You've aroused my curiosity. Can you tell me about it?"

She thought for a while about how to explain it, and then she began: "When you brought me home after the Tennessee match, I went the next day to talk with Father Philip. I told him I didn't see how it could serve God's plan to have a good person like my father killed. He said my father's sacrifice could serve a purpose. I asked him what purpose? And he said, helping my people achieve equal status in America. I told him that wasn't my father's mission, his mission was his family. And he said, then maybe it could be *my* mission."

Judson waited for her to continue.

"I must have been thinking about what he said because I went back to a Mexican restaurant where I'd met a guy back in October. He's a bartender. He told me he came here from Mexico to study engineering but he dropped out of college to help our people. I was interested, but I never had a chance to find out what he does."

"And you want to find out?"

"I just want to know, so I can think about it."

"You mean while you're in Mexico?"

"Yeah. It might be something I could do after I come back."

"I understand," Judson said, "and I agree with Father Philip. That could be your mission. But I hope you won't drop out of college to pursue it."

"I won't. I won't give up my father's dream. But right now I don't have a college to drop out of, and I have some time."

"I gather you want to do this tomorrow."

"The sooner I do it," Maya pointed out, "the sooner I can join my mother."

"Okay. I'll drive you to Tuscaloosa tomorrow after breakfast."

"If you drive me to the bus station, that'll be fine."

"Will you come back the same day?"

"I don't know. It depends on when I can talk with the guy."

"Well, in case you have to spend the night, there's a good hotel on Bryant. It's called the Capstone. Here," he said, reaching into his pocket. He pulled out some money and offered it to her. "That should cover things."

She hesitated to take it, feeling he had already done so much for her family.

"Take it. You'll need it."

She finally took it, saying: "Thanks."

They were ready when the guests began to arrive. The first was a young man who had recently arrived from Mexico and was working for Judson, living in the bunkhouse. He was only a few years older than Maya, and he looked relieved to find someone who could talk with him beyond the limits of Judson's Spanish. It made her think how her father had come here at about the same age with his dream of living in America, and she could catch a glimpse of that dream in the young man's eyes.

The next to arrive was a woman who had been Maya's teacher in seventh grade. She was in her fifties and she lived by herself in an apartment in town. She remembered Maya, and she looked delighted to see her.

The next was an old black farmer who lived down the road and eked out a living on his small farm. His son was a captain in the army serving in Afghanistan.

And the last was a black woman in her forties who worked as a teller in the bank owned by Shelby's father, whom Maya recognized as a customer at Otis Pharmacy.

When they had all sat down at the table, with the carved turkey on a platter and the other food in serving dishes, Judson bowed his head and said: "Heavenly Father, Your gifts of love are countless and Your goodness is infinite. On this Thanksgiving Day we come before You with gratitude for Your kindness, and we pray that You will open our hearts to concern for our fellow men and women, so that we may share Your gifts in loving service. We ask for your blessing through our Lord Jesus Christ. Amen."

"Amen," they said together.

As she raised her head Maya realized that the people sitting at the table—black, brown, and white—were all in the same position having no other family to spend this day with but still having much to be thankful for, beginning with the company of each other. And she added aprayer of her own, saying: *"Padre en el cielo, gracias por todo."*

On the bus the next morning Maya began to wonder about her decision. What if she got to Flor de Puebla and Diego wasn't there? Or what if he couldn't see her this evening? She would be alone in Tuscaloosa since everyone she knew had gone home for Thanksgiving. She would probably be the only person staying at the hotel.

So when she walked into Flor de Puebla in the early afternoon she was relieved to see Diego standing behind the bar.

"I thought you left," he said, giving her a puzzled look.

"I did leave. But I came back."

"You already miss the university?"

She sat on the stool in front of him. "I came back to find out what you do to help our people."

"I told you it would take a while to explain."

"You have time now. I'm the only person at the bar." She looked around. "And there're only a few people at the tables."

"Okay," he said. "I'll get you a drink."

She watched him take out a bottle of Modelo Especial and pour it into a frosted glass. She remembered how when she had first come here he had told her she would need to show him identification. Now it didn't seem to matter.

"If you're an illegal immigrant," he said, setting the glass in front of her, "you might as well be an illegal drinker."

"Couldn't you get into trouble for serving me alcohol?"

"Naw. The cops don't care about alcohol. They only care about drugs."

"And you're not involved in drugs?" she asked after taking a small sip of the beer.

"Of course I'm not. What do you think I am?"

"I don't know what you are, but it did cross my mind that you could be involved in drugs."

"I told you I was helping our people," he said forcefully. "And drugs aren't helping our people. Drugs are killing them."

"I know they are."

He looked at her closely as if he had detected something in her eyes. "You mean you know from personal experience?"

"My father was killed by drug gangs."

"*Lo siento mucho*. I hope he wasn't involved in drugs."

"He wasn't. He was caught in a battle between two gangs in Nuevo Laredo. He was an innocent bystander."

"What was he doing in Nuevo Laredo?"

"He was deported, but he was coming back to this country with authorization of the federal government. He was hoping to be granted relief under their new policy."

"*Qué lástima*," Diego murmured, gazing at her with sympathy. "Who deported him?"

"A county judge in Alabama."

"A county judge doesn't have the power to deport people."

"I know, but before we knew it he had my father taken across the border."

"Then your father wasn't killed by drug gangs. He was killed by that judge."

"Well, that's how I feel. And I really want to—" She stopped abruptly.

"Kill that judge? I understand. But killing him wouldn't help your father, and it wouldn't help our people. It would only make things worse for them."

"I know. But what can I do with this feeling?"

"You can channel it into actions that *will* help our people."

She knew about channeling violent feelings since she had been doing that all her life, but she still didn't know what kind of actions he was talking about. "So tell me what you do."

He paused to make margaritas for two customers at a table. She watched his efficient hands as he moistened the rims of two glasses and rolled them in salt and poured the mix and the tequila into a cocktail shaker and dropped in some ice and shook the ingredients and finally emptied the mixed drink into the glasses.

When the waiter had carried the drinks away Diego leaned over the bar and said: "I assume you know what's been happening in the Arab world since last spring."

"I've been following it, but I don't know much about it."

"They organized the protests and the demonstrations through the internet, using Facebook, Twitter, and instant messaging. And they were able to overthrow governments without resorting to violence."

"What does that have to do with our situation?"

"It shows us how to achieve our goal without using violence."

"What's our goal?"

"Our goal is social justice."

"You mean equal status for our people in America?"

"You got it," Diego said.

"Do your actions extend beyond Alabama?"

"We're allied with groups in other states, but right now we're focusing on Alabama. Our immediate objective is to overturn the Alabama immigration law."

"Do you work with churches?"

"We work with all the organizations that are on our side."

She made a decision. "What can I do to help you?"

"If you know how to use a computer," he said, "you can help us reach out to people. You can help us organize protests and demonstrations."

"Could I do that on my own computer?"

"You could, but you could do it better on our computers."

"Where are your computers?"

"They're in my apartment in West Tuscaloosa."

"The problem is," she said, "if I did it there, I wouldn't have any place to stay."

"You could stay at my apartment." Reassuringly, he added: "I have a spare bedroom."

She thought about it. In order to make a contribution she would have to work with him at least a few weeks. Of course when she came back in the spring she could continue working with him, so she didn't have to do it all now. She counted the weeks to Christmas, allowing some extra time, and she came up with three weeks. "If I committed to three weeks, could I stay at your apartment that long?"

"You can stay there as long as you're useful."

Trusting him, she said: "Okay. I'll help you. I just have to let my *sensei* know what I'm doing."

"You make him sound like your father."

"He *is* like my father, especially now. And I don't want him to worry about me."

"He has nothing to worry about. I'll take good care of you."

People were starting to come in for dinner, and Diego was getting busy, so she went out and called Judson and told him she planned to stay in Tuscaloosa until the middle of December. He asked where she would be staying, and she told him she would be sharing an apartment with some other people. As far as she knew, that was the truth since Diego had used the first person plural in describing what he did.

She knew that Judson felt responsible for her, so she agreed to call him from time to time and let him know how things were going.

After ending the call she decided to wait until the next day to call her mother.

Diego was off work at eight, and before coming out from behind the bar he reached down and picked up a pair of helmets. At first she didn't realize what they were for, and he had already handed her a helmet when she asked: "You have a bike?"

"Yeah, how else would I get around?"

She followed him out to the parking lot where she saw a very large motorcycle. She had ridden a few times on a motorcycle but never on such a monster, and she began to wonder what she had gotten herself into. She watched him put on his helmet, still holding hers as if she might yet decline the ride.

"I'll take that," he said, holding out his hand and indicating her shoulder bag.

She gave it to him, and he stored it in a side compartment. She finally put on her helmet after he got on the motorcycle and started it up.

"Come on," he told her, ready to go.

She got on behind him. There was nothing for her to hold on to except him, so she put her arms around him, noticing how hard his body was even in the abdomen. She closed her eyes and braced herself and silently prayed: *"Madre de Dios, protégeme."*

Though she had a good grip on him, she was almost left behind when the motorcycle took off, and she tightened her arms around him.

When she tilted her head to peer around his helmet and see where they were going, she felt the wind on her face, and she was thrilled. She had liked riding around in Shelby's sports car, but that hadn't been anything like this.

They sped along 15th Street under the viaduct and then

turned left into a neighborhood where Shelby would have worried about his car being stolen.

They stopped in front of an old building, and Maya got off.

Diego opened the compartment and took out her bag, and then he hauled out a chain and wound it around a lamppost and secured it to the motorcycle and padlocked it.

"Will that stop people from stealing it?"

"It'll give me time to catch them." He didn't say what he would do when he did catch them, and she didn't ask.

She followed him into the building and up three flights of stairs. He unlocked the door and turned on a light and led her into a living room in which there were two sofas, several chairs, and a table with a lamp on it.

He gave her a tour of the apartment, showing her a room where there were four tables with desktop computers on them as well as other office machines. He then showed her the spare bedroom, the bathroom, and the kitchen.

In the kitchen he reached into a cabinet and took out a bottle of tequila, explaining: "I always have a shot of this before I go to bed. Would you like a shot?"

"I'll have a half shot," she said, figuring she could handle that much liquor.

He filled one shot glass and carefully poured a half into another shot glass, which he handed to her as if it were already a ritual.

They went to the living room, where they sat down in two of the chairs.

She took a tiny sip of tequila, expecting it to taste like the tequila she had once tried at a high school party, and she was surprised by how smooth it was.

"I only drink the best tequila," Diego said as if he had noticed her facial expression.

"I don't drink," she said, "but I could tell it was better than the usual stuff."

"The usual stuff goes into margaritas, where you can't tell the difference."

Feeling comfortable with him, she asked: "How long ago did you drop out of college?"

"I was in my junior year, so it was about four years ago."

"Did something happen that made you decide to drop out?"

For a while he didn't answer her question, and then he said: "Yeah, something happened."

She waited, but he didn't continue, so she prompted him: "What happened?"

He sipped his tequila before saying: "I'd been working at the restaurant since my freshman year. I started as a dish washer, and then I worked as a bus boy, and then as a waiter. When I turned twenty-one I became a bartender. So I'd done every job there, and I knew all the people who worked there."

She listened intently, trying to guess where he was going.

"There was a kid who worked in the kitchen. His name was Miguel. His father came here as a migrant worker and eventually brought his family. There were three kids, and Miguel was the oldest. His father worked construction, and his mother cleaned houses. They were doing well until the accident." Diego paused, staring into his shot glass. "A guy dropped a load of lumber on his father. He was paralyzed from the waist down. He couldn't work, and he couldn't collect disability because he was an illegal immigrant. So Miguel and his mother were supporting the family. Then his mother got a liver disease. It was something that could have been treated with drugs, but his mother didn't have health insurance, and Medicaid wouldn't pay for the drugs because she was an illegal immigrant. So his mother died, leaving Miguel with his father and his brother and his sister to take care of."

"What happened to them?"

"His father committed suicide, not wanting to be a burden to his children, and Miguel sent his brother and his sister back to Mexico, where they're living with an aunt and uncle."

"Where's Miguel?"

"He's still at the restaurant, working as a waiter. Next year," Diego continued, "he'll turn twenty-one, so he can become a bartender and make more money. He sends half of what he makes to his aunt and uncle."

"That's what made you decide to drop out?"

"Yeah. I felt selfish pursuing a degree when things like that were happening to our people. I also felt angry when I heard the politicians talking about how illegal immigrants were consuming public services and costing money for taxpayers. What a load of bullshit. Except for the schools, illegal immigrants don't consume any public services, and the schools in Alabama suck. They do more harm than good to the children."

"There must have been times when you felt like killing the politicians."

"There were, but I learned to channel my violent feelings into productive activities."

"Then you're committed to nonviolence?"

"Yeah, I am. And so are the people who work with me. We're followers of Martin Luther King."

She was greatly reassured by that statement, but she still had a question. "Are you doing things that could get you into trouble with the law?"

"We're doing things that could get us into trouble," he replied directly, "but not with the law."

"What about the immigration authorities?"

"What about them?"

"Couldn't they deport you for what you're doing?"

"I'm not an immigrant. I'm an American citizen. I was born in Los Angeles."

"Then how did you come here as an international student?"

"My father was a baseball player. He was brought here by the Dodgers, and he played on one of their farm teams. He didn't make it to the big leagues, but when he went back to Mexico he had some money, and he started an insurance agency. He wanted me to get a degree from an American university, so he provided the money for me to come here."

It sounded as if his father had a dream for him that was like the dream her father had for her. "Do you ever feel you disappointed your father by dropping out?"

"He used to make me feel that way, but I finally got him to understand that it's my life."

"Well, I hope my father understands."

"I'm sure he does," Diego said.

After finishing her half shot of tequila she said goodnight and went into the spare bedroom, closing the door behind her.

She sat on the bed and took out a notebook and started making a list of things she would need. She had brought an extra pair of panties in her shoulder bag as well as a toothbrush, thinking she might stay one night in Tuscaloosa, but now that she planned to stay three weeks she would need more things, starting with underwear.

With the list done, she got out of her sweatshirt and jeans and rolled into bed in her tee-shirt and panties, expecting to be warm enough with the sheet and blanket.

Her last thought before going to sleep was about her father.

When she got up the next morning she found Diego in the kitchen drinking coffee. It was still dark outside, but he was wearing sweats and he looked as if he had been out jogging. It made her wonder what else he did to stay in shape.

"Would you like some coffee?"

"No, thanks. I don't drink coffee."

"What do you drink in the morning?"

"Orange juice. If you don't have it, I'll buy some today."

"I don't have orange juice, but I have bread. I usually don't eat tortillas in the morning."

"You've become a *gringo*," she teased him.

"Don't knock *gringos*. They have some good qualities. I can't think of any this early in the morning, but I know they have some good qualities."

"They have good hamburgers," Maya said as she found the bread on a cutting board.

"Yeah, they do. And good French fries."

"But aren't French fries French?"

"They're probably as French as the food they serve in their Mexican restaurants is Mexican."

"Probably," she said. She found a knife on the counter and sliced a piece of bread for herself. It was white sourdough, and it smelled fresh.

When she had finished eating he led her into the computer room, where he gave her a lesson in using the internet to organize protests and demonstrations. By eight o'clock she was posting messages, amazed to discover how many "friends" his organization had on Facebook and how many "followers" on Twitter. Urged by a friend, she had created a Facebook page for herself but had rarely found any use for it. Now she could see what Facebook was good for.

Diego had explained that a main strategy of his organization was to enlist support from owners of farms and businesses in construction, food processing, cleaning, and lawn care, which depended heavily on immigrant labor, and to mobilize them into campaigns for laws that were friendlier to immigrants. A main tactic was to collect and disseminate evidence that the state's immigration law was already hurting farms and businesses.

Another main strategy was to enlist support from people who joined demonstrations against any kind of injustice. Maya was gratified to learn that the organization financed its activities mainly with contributions from these people, who could give as little as five or ten dollars using PayPal.

Around nine she was joined by two Mexican girls who worked as order takers at McDonald's. A half hour later they were joined by a blond girl who Maya later learned was a member of an international organization that promoted peace and social justice. They were all volunteers, and they worked steadily, taking breaks only to go to the bathroom.

Diego was working at the computer in his bedroom, and from time to time he came in to see how they were doing, to get their input, and to give them advice. At quarter of twelve he left for work at the restaurant after telling them to help themselves to the food in the refrigerator. Finally taking a break for lunch, they found ham and cheese and lettuce and tomato and bread for making sandwiches.

As they sat around the kitchen table the two Mexican girls spoke in Spanish, and it turned out that the blond girl was fluent in Spanish since she had spent two years in Colombia on a mission there, so they all spoke in Spanish, which Maya enjoyed. She couldn't remember the last time she had hung out with girls her age and chattered in Spanish.

In the middle of the afternoon she took a break to call her mother. She explained that she was working on a project to help their people, and that she would book a flight to Mexico for the week of December 19. She told her mother she was sharing an apartment with two Mexican girls and an American girl, which was partly true, and her mother didn't question it.

That evening she joined Diego at the restaurant, where she had dinner at the bar. And that became her daily routine: breakfast in the kitchen, work in the computer room, lunch in the kitchen, back to the computer room, dinner at the bar, and a ride on the monster back to the apartment.

After a week she broke the routine and called Erin, who came and met her at the restaurant. They sat in a booth so they could have some privacy, and they brought each other up to date. At one point Erin asked: "Have you seen Shelby?"

"No. I haven't," Maya said. "I'm in a different world now."

"You mean you're with Diego?"

"I am with Diego, but our relationship is professional."

"I thought you were attracted to him."

"I am, but I'm happy with our relationship the way it is. I wouldn't want to ruin it."

"I understand. Having sex with him would change things."

"My thrill of the day is riding behind him on his motorcycle back to his apartment. It makes a sports car seem tame."

"I saw the coach yesterday," Erin said, changing the subject. "He told me your process is going well."

"I should call him," Maya said. "It's just that—"

"You're in a different world now."

"Well, I'm not in a different world from you. No matter what happens, we'll always be in the same world."

"No matter what happens," Erin said, taking her hand.

By the end of her second week with Diego she broached the idea of organizing a demonstration against the judge in Miletus. They had just returned to the apartment from Flor de Puebla and were in the living room, sipping tequila.

"That's a good idea," Diego said. "We've demonstrated against the laws, but we haven't demonstrated against the people who enforce them."

"That judge would make a good target."

"I think he would."

"So you want to do it?"

"Yeah. Let's schedule a demonstration for next Wednesday."

He gave her the job of rounding up people to demonstrate. She reached out to people who regularly participated in their demonstrations as well as to people who hadn't been engaged yet, targeting those who lived within seventy-five miles of Miletus since she had learned that people would travel up to an hour and a half to participate in a demonstration.

On Tuesday evening they estimated that as many as two thousand people would be there, based on feedback from potential demonstrators and previous experience.

"You did a great job," Diego told her. "I didn't think we'd get a thousand."

"We haven't got them yet," Maya said, having learned that attendance could be affected by a number of variables, starting with the weather.

Miletus was a forty-minute drive from Tuscaloosa, so they set out at ten the next morning on the motorcycle. Luckily, it was a clear, crisp day with a predicted high of sixty. It also happened to be the seventieth anniversary of the attack on Pearl Harbor.

When they arrived at the courthouse they saw a large crowd

gathered in front of it, holding signs that said: "Impeach Judge Holcomb," "Apply the Laws Fairly," "Love Thy Neighbor," and other messages that reflected the different perspectives of the people in the crowd.

A television crew from Birmingham was there, waiting for some action.

Maya took her sign out of a compartment, unfurled it, and raised it high. With Diego's approval she had written: "Judge Holcomb Killed My Father."

"Here she is," people said as she waded through the crowd, heading to the front. They knew what the judge had done to her father since she told them in her call to action.

With her in front the crowd started chanting: "Impeach Judge Holcomb, impeach Judge Holcomb."

There were already two police officers stationed in front of the building, and now a few more appeared. They looked ready to use force if necessary.

After a while the judge came out wearing his robe and faced the crowd defiantly.

"Is that Judge Holcomb?"

"Yeah," she said, her anger rising at the sight of him.

The crowd raised the volume. "Impeach Judge Holcomb."

He glared at Maya, and then he pointed to her, saying something to a police officer.

The officer came to her and asked: "Are you Maya Méndez?"

"My actual name is Mayahuel Guadalupe Méndez."

"Whatever your name is, you're under arrest."

"On what charge?" Diego demanded, stepping between her and the officer.

"Inciting a riot."

"There's no riot. This is a peaceful demonstration."

"The judge says it's a riot."

"The judge's word is not law."

"Well, he ordered me to arrest her."

"The judge has no authority in this situation. He only has

authority in his courtroom. And we're not in his courtroom, we're in a public place."

The officer turned and looked at the judge for instructions.

The judge motioned for him to go ahead.

"I'm sorry," the officer said, revealing that he wasn't happy with his orders.

"You have no authority to arrest her. And if you don't back off," Diego said, taking out his cell phone, "I'm going to call an FBI agent in Birmingham who investigates civil rights violations. He'll have you fired without pension and health benefits."

The officer paused.

"You want to lose your pension and your health benefits?"

"No. I don't."

"Then back off."

The officer finally backed off, ignoring the judge's imprecations.

"The judge tried to intimidate us," someone said.

"He's a fascist," someone else said.

The crowd started chanting: "Judge Holcomb is a fascist."

The television crew got the action they had been waiting for. They eventually came over and asked Maya for an interview. Without thinking, she agreed, and she told them what the judge had done to her father.

As they rode back to Tuscaloosa, zipping along the highway, Maya was exhilarated by their success. The story of what Judge Holcomb had done to her father would be viewed by millions of people, and that would not only end his career and stop him from hurting other immigrants, it would also raise people's awareness of what was happening.

They were going up the stairs to Diego's apartment when her phone vibrated. It was Judson, and she stopped on a landing to answer it.

"I saw you on television," Judson told her.

"You did? Already?"

"It was on the six o'clock news."

"Well, I haven't seen it," Maya said. "We're just getting home. What do you think?"

"I think you did a great job. Your father would be proud of you. I sure am."

His words meant a lot to her. "Thanks, *sensei*."

She relayed the words to Diego when she caught up with him.

A half hour later, as they were sitting at the kitchen table, her phone vibrated again. This time it was Trevor.

"I must say," Trevor told her, "you did a great job of making people aware of the injustices being done to immigrants. And it could help my action against that judge. But you took a risk."

"I didn't think about that."

"They have your name, and they could make trouble for you with immigration."

Trying not to worry, she said: "I'm planning to go to Mexico the week after next."

"If I were you, I'd go there sooner."

"What could they do to me?"

"They could deport you."

"They could?"

"They could. And if they deport you," Trevor explained with his usual patience, "you'll never get a student visa."

"But they don't know where to find me."

"I reckon they don't. Even I don't know where to find you. But if I were you, I'd go to Mexico sooner than you planned. And I'd avoid being visible."

After turning off her phone she reported the conversation to Diego, who listened attentively and said: "Your lawyer's right. What you're doing now could jeopardize your plan to go back to the university."

"If I avoid being visible," Maya said, "I should be all right."

"You're already visible. And if the university knew you were working with me, they'd never let you back in."

"Why wouldn't they?"

"They don't want troublemakers. So at some point you'll have to decide if you want to get your degree or if you want to help our people."

"I don't see why I can't do both."

"In theory you can. But in reality they won't let you. If you're against the system, then they don't have a place for you."

She thought for a moment and then asked: "So if you wanted to go back to the university, they wouldn't let you back in?"

"If they knew what I've been doing, they wouldn't."

"Did you realize you were taking that risk when you decided to help our people?"

"Yeah. I did. But I made a decision that if I had to choose between getting a degree and helping our people, I'd give up getting the degree."

"Well, I'm not in the same position. I didn't drop out, I was kicked out. And I want to go back to the university and get my degree. I believe that if I have a degree, I can help our people more than if I don't have one."

"In that case, *chica,* you better follow your lawyer's advice."

"You mean to avoid being visible?"

"I mean to go back to Mexico sooner than you planned."

"It sounds like you want to get rid of me," she joked.

"I don't want to get rid of you," he said earnestly. "You've done a lot for the cause. But I don't want you to do anything you'll regret later."

She had a feeling he meant much more than staying with him and working with him, and she realized she wasn't the only one who had rejected the temptation to go beyond a professional relationship. She acknowledged his consideration by saying: "I understand."

TWELVE

OVER THE NEXT few days their number of friends on Facebook and followers on Twitter more than tripled as a result of the publicity from the demonstration in Miletus. Maya was gratified but at the same time she worried about her visibility. By now she was famous, at least among people who worked for the cause. She hoped that the people who worked in admissions at the university and in the immigration department were unaware of what she was doing.

On Sunday night they were sitting at the kitchen table after returning from Flor de Puebla when Diego told her about a new initiative. He explained that they were doing well in gaining support from business people who depended on immigrant labor, but they weren't doing so well with farmers. This failure was hard to understand since if anyone had a vital interest in immigrant labor, farmers did.

"We should have more farmers as friends and followers," Diego said.

"Maybe they don't use the internet a lot," Maya suggested.

"Maybe they don't. Whatever the reason, we haven't recruited as many farmers as we should have, so I've decided to try a different tactic. It's a tactic that César Chávez used in the 1960s. He organized a boycott of table grapes to put pressure on the growers to accept his program for the workers."

She remembered something her father had said about César Chávez. "Didn't he support restrictions on immigrants?"

"He did. The growers were using immigrants to keep wages low and replace workers who made demands. He had a different purpose, but we could use the same tactic for our purpose."

"What would we do?"

"We'd get our friends and followers to boycott peaches."

"Peaches? Why peaches?"

"They're grown in states like Alabama and Georgia that have passed tough immigration laws. They're also grown in California, which hasn't always been friendly to us."

"So how would a boycott recruit farmers?"

"It would get their attention."

"By hurting them economically?"

"It's the only way to get the attention of some people."

"I thought we were committed to nonviolence."

"We are," Diego said. "Boycotts are an acceptable tactic for nonviolent movements. Gandhi used them, and Martin Luther King used them."

She had to accept his word for this since she hadn't learned about such boycotts in her history courses. "And you think a boycott would be effective?"

"Yeah, I do. Thanks to your appearance on television we have enough friends and followers to make it effective."

"So we'd get our friends and followers to boycott peaches," Maya said, beginning to follow the process, "and that would hurt the farmers—"

"They're already being hurt by a labor shortage, so a boycott would tighten the screws on them."

"It might ruin some of them."

"Before it does," Diego said, "they'll get the politicians to change the immigration laws."

"Okay. I can see how a boycott might work. But I don't like it. A boycott of peaches would hurt my *sensei*, who has always been good to my family and other immigrants."

"Your *sensei* is a peach grower?"

"Yeah. When my father came here he picked peaches in my *sensei's* orchards."

"I'm sorry," Diego said, shaking his head, "but we can't tell people not to boycott peaches grown in his orchards. A boycott is a blunt instrument."

"Then we shouldn't use it. We should use other ways to reach farmers."

"We've tried other ways, and they haven't been effective."

"Well, I won't help you organize a boycott of peaches," Maya said. "I won't support an action that would hurt a person who has helped me and my family so much."

"If we want to achieve our mission, we have to be willing to make sacrifices."

"I'm willing to sacrifice myself, but not other people. And even if I didn't know any peach growers," she added, "I wouldn't be willing to sacrifice them."

"Then you have limits as a revolutionary."

"I never said I was a revolutionary."

"I guess you didn't. I guess it was only in my head."

They fell into a silence. Neither of them had to say it was time for her to go back to Mexico.

The next morning when she was done in the bathroom Maya packed her things in the bag she had bought the day after she arrived. She stripped the sheets off her bed and put them into the pillow case, which she left on the mattress. With her bag she went into the kitchen, where she found Diego sitting at the table as if he had spent the night there.

"I'll take you to the bus station," he offered.

"Thanks," she said, "but I can walk there."

He rose from his chair, and gazing at her with a mixture of sadness and admiration he said: "You did a lot for the cause. We'll miss you."

"I liked working with you."

"Well, maybe after you go back to the university we can find a project for you."

"That would be great."

For a while they stood there speechless and motionless, and then he advanced and put his strong arms around her and gave her an *abrazo*, saying: *"Por la justicia social."*

"Por la justicia social," she said, reciprocating his *abrazo*.

She took a last look at him, and hiding her tears she left the apartment.

Outside, she headed for the bus station, taking a route she had used many times on shopping errands. It included a shortcut through a back alley, and she was in the middle of the alley, not paying attention to her surroundings since she was in a turmoil of emotion, when suddenly she saw a guy in front of her blocking her way.

He was a white guy, a big guy with a shaven head and tattoos on his arms.

"Hey, look what I see," he said in a guttural sneer. "A little spic girl."

He could have been speaking only to her, but sensing that he wasn't alone she turned and saw a similar guy to her left.

"I hear they like to fuck," the other guy said.

"You like to fuck?" the first guy asked.

She was about to say no when a guy behind her locked his arm around her throat and began to choke her.

"You hold her, and I'll fuck her."

"We'll all fuck her."

Maya now drew on everything she had learned from her *sensei*, not only in formal fighting situations but also in street fighting. But she had to act quickly because the guy behind her was cutting off her air.

She raised her right knee and with a loud *kiai* brought her heel down on the instep of the guy's right foot. He let her go immediately, howling in pain. She pivoted around, and with a *teicho uchi* she drove the heel of her right palm up at his chin. His head snapped back and he keeled over backward, making a hard landing on the pavement.

The guy to her left came at her now. She faked a punch to his face, and when he raised his hands to protect himself she kicked him in his unguarded groin with a *mae geri*. When he doubled over in agony she struck him in the nose with her elbow, reinforcing the blow with her other hand behind his head. As he went down she made sure he would stay down by giving him a *shuto uchi* in the back of his neck.

The guy who had originally stopped her was approaching her now, brandishing a knife. She remembered how her *sensei* had told her to handle guys with knives, and she let him advance until he was within range, and then she unleashed a *mawashi geri*, swinging her leg around in a kick that connected with his hand and made him drop the knife. When he bent over to retrieve it she put her hands around his neck and brought her knee up into his face. When he straightened up, holding his hands to his battered face, she kicked him in the ribs with a *yoko geri* and as he went down she kicked him in the head for good measure.

A little out of breath, she assessed the scene. The three guys were all down and out, at least one of them with a broken nose and one with broken ribs and maybe one with a skull fracture. She didn't feel bad about hurting them since she had acted in self-defense, but she was sure that these rednecks would hate Latinos even more than they had before, and that they would seek revenge, getting back at people who had never hurt them. Already she could see the consequences of using violence, even if you used it in self-defense.

She picked up her bag and walked quickly to the bus station. She didn't want to be stopped by the police and charged with aggravated assault.

As the bus passed Immaculate Conception on its way into Harperville, Maya saw the notice for a mass in Spanish to celebrate the Feast of Our Lady of Guadalupe, which she suddenly realized was today. She felt a sharp pang of guilt for not remembering the holy day, and feeling that by her negligence she had dishonored her father, she wanted somehow to make amends.

From the bus she had called Judson and let him know when she expected to arrive, and he was waiting for her at the station.

"Thanks for meeting me," she told him. "Can I ask you for another favor?"

"Sure," he said, "as long as you don't ask me to drive you back to Tuscaloosa."

She smiled. "No. I just want you to drive me to church."

"The mass has ended."

"Did you go to it?"

"I took Pablo. I understood most of it. Of course it helps to have known the mass in Latin."

"Well, it's not too late to light a candle."

"Okay. Come on. We can both light candles."

He drove her to the church, which was still open. Judson followed her to the statue of Our Lady of Guadalupe, where she knelt and said a prayer, thanking the Virgin for interceding and saving her life in the alley that morning.

Then she rose and lit a candle and left an offering.

Judson was about to light his own candle when Father Philip appeared.

"I'm sorry I missed the mass," she told him.

"That's all right," he said gently. "You can read the letter from the bishops instead of listening to me read it."

"What letter?"

"The Latino bishops issued a pastoral letter today on the subject of immigration." He reached into the back pocket of his pants and took it out. "I made a copy, not knowing who I might give it to, but I reckon God knew."

"Thank you," Maya said, taking the letter respectfully.

"I hope you'll drop by and see me before you go."

"I will, father. I'll be here for a few days."

Back in the car Judson said: "If I remember correctly, you cut your time short."

"I did," she said. "He wanted me to work on something I couldn't do."

"You mean something you were unable to do?"

"No, something I was unwilling to do."

"Why were you unwilling to do it?"

"Because it would have hurt people."

"I thought his mission was to help people."

"It is," she said, "but he believes that at times you might have to hurt some people in order to help other people."

"And you don't believe that."

"No, I don't," Maya said. "So I told him I wasn't willing to sacrifice other people to achieve our mission, and he said, then I had limits as a revolutionary."

"I think revolutionaries need to have limits," Judson said as they stopped for a traffic light. "If they're willing to do anything to achieve their mission, they're only going to perpetuate the evils they oppose."

"Well, I hope I made him examine his conscience."

"I'm sure you did. It sounds like you didn't have a complete falling out with the guy."

"I didn't. But I did enough with him for now."

The light changed, and Judson made the car go forward.

In silence they passed the sign that invited you to come again to Harperville, and then Sonic, where she had gone so many times with Shelby. She had hardly thought about Shelby since the first time she had climbed on Diego's motorcycle, and she felt bad about it. Shelby had been so nice to her and had done so much for her. And it wasn't his fault that his father had gone to the president of the university and had her expelled. But she had been changed by the events that began with the arrest of her father, and she couldn't go back to being Shelby's girlfriend, sitting beside him in his Corvette with the top down, pretending she was one of those blonds who rode around in convertibles.

They were on the open road when Maya confessed: "I did something before I left Tuscaloosa."

"What did you do?"

"I hurt three guys who tried to rape me."

Judson glanced at her, taking his eyes off the road. "Three guys tried to rape you? Where?"

"In a back alley." She described the encounter, and Judson listened without making a comment. "I didn't kill them, but I hurt them badly."

"You were acting in self-defense."

"I know. But now they'll want to get back at Latinos for what I did to them."

"Whatever they feel about Latinos, it was there already."

"But I made it worse."

"You didn't make it worse. No matter what anyone does to you," Judson explained, "you always have a choice about how you respond. You can get revenge, or you can learn from the experience."

"What can those guys learn from the experience?"

"Not to mess around with girls."

"And what can I learn?"

"Not to take shortcuts through back alleys."

She understood that in both cases his answers were intended only to stimulate her thinking. There was much more she could learn from the experience. "Well, you were a good *sensei*. If you hadn't taught me karate, I would have been dead meat."

"You were a good student. And if you always apply yourself as you did to karate, you'll be good at everything you try to do."

She thought for a moment and then said: "I think my priority now is to be a good daughter. I mean, not only for my father but also for my mother."

"That sounds like the right priority," Judson agreed.

Before she went to sleep that evening she lay in bed and read the pastoral letter, which began: "We the undersigned Hispanic/Latino Bishops of the United States wish to let those of you who lack proper authorization to live and work in our country know that you are not alone, or forgotten. We recognize that every human being, authorized or not, is an image of God and therefore possesses infinite value and dignity. We open our arms and hearts to you."

The letter thanked the immigrants for their contributions to the country, and then it said: "The economic crisis has had an impact on the entire U.S. community. Regretfully, some in reaction to this environment of uncertainty show disdain for immigrants and even blame them for the crisis. We will not find a solution to our problems by sowing hatred. We will find a solution by sowing a sense of solidarity among all workers and co-workers—immigrants and citizens—who live together in the United States."

It went on to say: "We are well aware of the great sacrifices you make for your families' well-being. Many of you perform the most difficult jobs and receive miserable salaries and no health insurance or social security. Despite your contributions to the well-being of our country, instead of receiving our thanks, you are often treated as criminals because you have violated current immigration laws. We are also aware of the pain suffered by those families who have experienced deportation of one of their members."

Maya paused, unable to contain the grievance that rose in her heart. Then she kept reading until she reached the part that said: "We who are citizens and permanent residents of this country cannot forget that almost all of us, we or our ancestors, have come from other lands and together with immigrants from various nations and cultures, have formed a new nation. Now we ought to open our hearts and arms to the recently arrived, just as Jesus asks us to do when he says, 'I was hungry and you gave me to eat; I was thirsty and you gave me to drink; I was an alien and you took me into your house.' "

And finally: "We urge you not to despair. Keep faith in Jesus the migrant who continues to walk beside you. Have faith in Our Lady of Guadalupe who constantly repeats to us the words she spoke to St. Juan Diego, 'Am I, who am your mother, not here?' She never abandons us, nor does St. Joseph who protects us as he did the Holy Family during their emigration to Egypt."

She put the letter down on the bedside table and turned off the light and lay there in the dark feeling the comfort provided by the letter and hearing the voice of her father saying, "You see? Americans are good people." But then she heard her mother asking: "What about those guys in the alley?" And she saw how they could both be right.

The next day she made a reservation to fly to Puebla on Friday. She had to borrow money from Judson to pay for the ticket, but she promised to pay him back.

She called her mother to let her know when she was arriving. Her mother said the timing was good since she could help with the restaurant project.

They were out in one of the orchards tending the trees when she felt her phone vibrate.

It was Trevor, who asked: "Where are you?"

"I'm at Judson's."

"I heard that the police in Tuscaloosa are investigating an incident in which three guys were assaulted by a Mexican girl. They didn't put it quite that way, but you know what I mean. And they contacted the police here."

"Why here?" she asked with her heart in her throat.

"A Mexican girl was seen boarding a bus for Harperville."

"I'm not the only Mexican girl in Alabama."

"I know, but you might be the only one who could do that kind of damage."

"What kind of damage?"

"A broken nose, a cracked skull, and several broken ribs," Trevor said. "According to the Tuscaloosa police, the victims all looked like they'd been hit by a truck."

"Maybe they *were* hit by a truck."

"Yeah, maybe they were. But then why would they admit they were thrashed by a girl?"

"I don't know."

"Well, I called to give you a heads up. The Harperville police are on their way to Judson's now. They figured he might know where you are. And you should be ready with an alibi that proves you weren't in Tuscaloosa when those guys were attacked."

"When were they attacked?"

"Yesterday morning, around eight thirty," Trevor told her, pretending to believe she didn't know when it had happened. "You have a lot at stake. I heard from the immigration department that they're ready to let you come back as an international student.

But if you have a criminal record, they'll change their minds. So don't blow it."

"I won't. Thanks."

She had just finished reporting this conversation to Judson when she saw a big police officer coming toward them. She recognized him, and she was glad she had never gotten into trouble as a kid in high school.

"Hey, Mr. McBride," the officer said.

"Hey, Billy. How're you?"

"I'm fine, sir. You're Maya, aren't you?" Billy said, looking at her with placid blue eyes.

"Yes, sir," she said, projecting innocence.

"I'm just following all leads," Billy explained apologetically to Judson.

"Leads on what?"

"An incident in Tuscaloosa. Yesterday morning three guys were attacked by a girl, who did a lot of damage to them."

"A girl attacked *three* guys and whupped them?"

"She sure enough did. She beat the living shit out of them. They must have been wimps."

"Or else the girl was a guy in disguise," Judson suggested.

"I never thought of that. I mean, I don't see how a girl could whup three guys. And they were big guys."

"I don't either," Judson said. "There must be something wrong with their story."

"Well, I have to ask anyway. Maya, where were you around eight thirty yesterday morning?"

"I was here," she said, as arranged with Judson. "I hadn't gotten up yet."

"You know how teenagers need their sleep," Judson said.

"Yeah, I got two of them," Billy said.

"I can vouch for the fact that Maya was here at that time," Judson told Billy.

"Your word is good enough, sir. I'm sorry I had to bother you."

"I understand. How're the wife and kids?"

"They're fine. The girl can be a problem now and then. I

never expected it. I thought girls were supposed to be easy."

"Boys, girls—they're none of them easy," Judson said. "But they're all worth it."

"I reckon they are," Billy said.

As they watched the police officer leave the orchard and head for his car, Maya asked: "Will that be the end of it?"

"That'll be the end of it. We had to stretch the truth a little, but in this situation we had a good reason. And anyway, you *were* here," Judson said, patting his heart.

"*Gracias.* You saved my life."

"You saved your own life. All I did was cover for you."

She leaned toward him and kissed him on his rough cheek.

The next day when Judson went into town to do errands he left her at Immaculate Conception, where she found Father Philip in his office.

"Hey, Maya," he said, rising from behind his desk. "Did you read the pastoral letter?"

"Yes, father. It gave me hope."

"Well, hope is what we live on. I hear you were on a mission."

"I was. It was a good experience."

"Please sit down and tell me about it."

She sat down in front of his desk and told him how she had joined Diego and how they had organized demonstrations using the internet.

"I wish we'd had the internet in our day," Father Philip said.

"It helps," Maya said. "But you still have to decide how to use it. And Diego wanted to use it for a purpose I didn't agree with."

"What was that?"

"He wanted to organize a boycott of peaches."

"Ah, I see. Like the boycott of table grapes and the boycott of buses in Montgomery. He wanted to apply economic pressure to activate the farmers."

"They're already on our side. They need people to pick the peaches."

"Well, maybe they weren't doing enough for him."

"Maybe they were doing all they could."

"And of course you had a personal reason for not agreeing with that tactic."

"I know I did, but it was also a matter of principle. Whatever your mission, I don't believe you can justify hurting people in order to achieve it."

Father Philip nodded. "You put that well. In fact, I couldn't have put it better."

"So I did the right thing?"

"Do you have any doubts about it?"

"I don't have doubts, but I have feelings."

"What kind of feelings?"

"I feel like I let Diego down."

"You didn't let him down. You took a moral position, which I'm sure he respected."

"I guess he did," she said. "And he left the door open for a future project."

"Then you did well." Father Philip paused, and then he said: "I saw you on television, and you were terrific. You did a lot to make people aware of the situation. I felt like I was back on the road, marching from Selma to Montgomery."

"Thank you, father. I haven't gone to church as often as I should have, and I haven't gone to confession for a while, but I haven't forgotten what you taught me. I never will."

Across the desk he gave her a blessing.

She spent the next two days helping Judson in the orchards and doing errands with him in town. She had just been to the pharmacy, where she had chatted with Mr. Otis for a while, and she was strolling down Main Street when she saw Shelby's father getting out of his Mercedes in front of his bank. There was no way of avoiding him, and as he handed his car keys to a young black man in uniform who would park his car for him, Mr. Harper gave her a look as if he wondered what she was still doing in America.

"Yes, I'm still here," she told him in response to his unasked question.

"You don't belong here," he didn't need to say.

"And in case you're still worrying about it, I have no intention of marrying your son. He's a nice boy, and I'll always appreciate what he did for me, but I have other plans for my life."

Mr. Harper only scowled at her.

"You may think I'm being presumptuous," Maya continued, standing between him and the entrance to the bank, "but I believe you'll be happier if instead of trying to make Shelby do what *you* want, you let him do what *he* wants."

"I don't need your advice," Mr. Harper muttered, trying to get around her.

"Maybe you don't, but I'll give it to you. If I was Shelby's father, I'd be proud of him and I'd accept him the way he is."

Without a backward glance Mr. Harper bolted into his bank.

To allow time to get through security they arrived at the airport in Birmingham two hours early. With Judson accompanying her she checked in and headed for the gate.

When she reached security she stopped, not knowing what to say. She wanted to express her gratitude to Judson, but she couldn't find a way in English or in Spanish. And finally, prompted by her heart, she bowed to her *sensei* and said: *"Arigato gozaimasu.* Thank you for teaching me."

He returned the bow, and then he gave her a big hug.

Acknowledgments

Special acknowledgments to Adam and Judith and Steve and Matt and Reese and Julian and Mark of the San Ken Ryu *dojo* in Hastings-on-Hudson, New York, where I learned what dedicated karate teachers can do for young people—as well as for older people like me.

Arigato gozaimasu.

BOOK CLUB GUIDE TO

The Golden Door

Tom Milton

An introduction to *The Golden Door*

Maya Méndez has lived in Harperville, Alabama since she was three, when her father brought her and her mother there from Mexico to pursue his dream of living in America. Her father works for a major peach grower, and her mother cleans houses. They live in a rented house in a poor area of town, and they are raising two other children, who were born in America. Until now they haven't had to worry much about being illegal immigrants.

Maya has just graduated from high school, where she was the star of the girls' soccer team and the winner of the award for the best all-around student in the senior class. She is planning to attend the University of Alabama, which recruited her for the women's soccer team with a full scholarship. Suddenly her family is threatened and her future is clouded by the passage of a state law that will make it a crime for her parents to work and will prohibit her from attending a public university.

As a brown-skinned girl who has grown up in a predominantly white community, Maya has encountered racism, and her natural inclination is to respond to verbal attacks with physical violence. In order to channel her violent feelings into a disciplined activity, her parents enrolled her at the age of twelve in a karate school that is run by her father's employer. Maya is preparing to earn her brown belt in karate when the anti-immigrant law is passed, and she wishes she could use her karate skills on the people who supported it.

Maya's father still has faith in America and wants to stay there, believing that the people who oppose the law will prevent it from being implemented. But her mother believes that the law sends a clear message to immigrants: they are not wanted in America, and they have no future there. Maya is caught in the middle between her parents, with her heart on her father's side and her head on her mother's side. By the time the law is signed by the governor her mother is ready to go back to Mexico, but her father decides they should stay in America long enough to see how the law will affect them.

Since the law won't be implemented until September 1, and since it's being challenged in court by the federal government, civil liberties organizations, and religious institutions, Maya goes to Tuscaloosa in early August and moves into a dormitory and joins the soccer team for practice. Her roommate, who is from New York, is also a forward on the team, and they play together so well that the coach puts them in the starting lineup.

Now that she is away at college Maya has to learn to balance her time between soccer, classes, studying, and social life. Until now her social life has been dominated by her boyfriend, Shelby, with whom she has been going since junior year in high school. Shelby is attending the university, living in a male dormitory that is very different from the female dormitory she lives in, and he arrived in early August to try out for the golf team, so they really haven't been apart. Maya loves him, and she likes hanging out with him, but with so many other demands on her time she has to dampen his expectation that they will see each other as often as they did when they were at home.

As the weeks pass, some parts of the anti-immigrant law are temporarily blocked by the federal courts, and for a while it looks as if Maya's father was right to stay in America. But then in a series of fateful events that begin with a car being stopped by police for a tail-light violation the spirit of the law catches up with her family, and out of the tragic consequences she struggles to find a mission in life.

A conversation with Tom Milton

Like three of your previous novels, this one deals with the issue of racism. In The Admiral's Daughter *you showed a young white woman fighting against racism in Mississippi during the early 1960s. In* Infamy *you showed a young Latino man encountering various forms of racism at college, at work, and in his social life. In* Sara's Laughter *you showed a white woman coping with her father's racist attitude toward her Latino husband. And in this novel you show a young Latina woman confronting a racist anti-immigrant law that was passed last year by the Alabama state legislature. Since you keep writing about this issue, it's obviously important to you.*

Racism is a monster that lives above or below the surface of society. If it's below the surface, it rears its ugly head at times of economic crisis. And it never seems to lose its power to incite and rationalize social injustice.

In this novel, more than in the others, you show how it feels to be treated unfairly because of race. How did you get into the heart of an eighteen-year-old Latina woman living with her family illegally in east central Alabama?

Over the years as a colleague or friend I've had relationships with Latina women, and as a college professor I've known young Latina women in Maya's situation who have shared their feelings with me, including their fears of being deported.

I know you set this novel in Alabama because of the harsh anti-immigrant law it passed last year, but did you also want to revisit the scene of The Admiral's Daughter, *which you set in Mississippi fifty years ago?*

I did want to revisit that scene to see how things had changed, and the most important change I noticed is that the Deep South isn't so culturally isolated from the rest of the country as it was fifty years ago. But there's still racism. I should quickly add that there's still racism in the rest of the country, though younger people seem less racist than older people, which gives me hope.

You show people in Alabama like Judson and Trevor and Father Philip and Mr. Otis who oppose the anti-immigrant law. Do they reflect a new attitude in the Deep South?

No, not really. There were white people in Alabama fifty years ago who opposed segregation, including Father Philip and Mr. Otis's father. But there weren't enough of them, and there still aren't enough of them, as evidenced by the fact that George Wallace was elected governor back then, and the anti-immigrant law was passed only last year.

Like your other novels, this one also deals with the issue of violence, and you give us yet another perspective by having Maya do karate. Where did that come from?

I recently did karate, long enough to understand it (and earn a green belt), so I knew it was right for Maya, who's inclined by her nature to respond to racial epithets by punching her verbal attackers in the mouth. Karate enables her to channel her violent feelings into a disciplined activity.

Some people would say that Maya has a fine sense of justice, and that people who verbally attack her deserve to be punched in the mouth.

Well, I would say—as a character in *Infamy* said—you cannot achieve peace through war. Acts of violence only lead to further acts of violence.

That's been a theme of all your novels, and I think it's interesting that in this novel the exponent of nonviolence is a karate teacher.

As I was taught it, karate is a system of self-defense. You're not supposed to use it to attack people.

Your view of karate sounds like the Just War Doctrine that was central to your novel All the Flowers.

They both justify violence in self-defense. But I've been wondering if violence is ever justified, even in self-defense.

I'd like to hear your thoughts on that later, but now I'd like to talk about Maya's mentors. She has three adults outside her family who give her guidance: her karate teacher, the parish priest, and the family lawyer.

Don't forget her soccer coach.

So she has four mentors. In that sense, she's blessed. So why did you give her all those mentors?

In her situation, with her natural inclination to respond to injustice with violent actions, she probably wouldn't have had a chance without the guidance of her mentors, and even then she gets into trouble.

All your heroines get into trouble. All have their values tested by events. And all have something important in common—they define themselves by what they believe in, not by their relationships with men. Does that make you a feminist?

It makes me an advocate. I belong to a generation that fought for civil rights, for peace, for women's liberation, and for the environment. We're still a long way from achieving our goals in these areas, including social and economic justice for women, so I'm still an advocate on all those issues.

I like the way you show Maya playing on a women's soccer team, living in a female dormitory, and trying to find an identity that's independent of her relationship with her boyfriend.

She's trying to find her place in the world, moving from outcast tomboy to girlfriend of the town prince to brown belt in karate to member of a women's soccer team to immigrant rights activist, while veering back and forth between the positions of her father and her mother on the American dream.

Listening to you, I realize that with all the issues this novel addresses—racism, violence, and gender identity—it's a universal story of a young person trying to find herself in a hostile world.

For most young people the world is hostile, and like Maya they feel they don't belong wherever they are. In her situation the hostility is explicit, but it's there for most of them at some level, to some extent. So my heart is with them.

Discussion questions

1. Discuss this novel's treatment of racism, violence, and gender identity.

2. Discuss the statement by Trevor that the people who support anti-immigrant laws like the one in Alabama want to turn America into a gated community.

3. Maya's father believes that the words engraved at the base of the Statue of Liberty are still true, whereas her mother insists they are no longer true. What do you think?

4. Explain how Maya is affected by the conflict between her father and her mother.

5. How does Maya's relationship with Shelby help her or hinder her in finding her identity?

6. What role does Judson play in Maya's development?

7. What roles do Father Philip and Trevor play in Maya's development?

8. What new perspectives does Maya gain from Erin?

9. What role does the coach play in Maya's development?

10. How are Maya's values tested by her relationship with Diego?

11. Explain how the plot is driven by the hopes, dreams, beliefs, or values of the characters. Which character has the most effect on what happens?

12. Describe the three situations where Maya uses her karate skills. Was she justified in using those skills?

13. Does Maya resolve the conflict between her parents? Explain.

14. Given the events of the story, is the ending inevitable? Explain.

15. How would you project Maya's future?

www.ingramcontent.com/pod-product-compliance
Lightning Source LLC
LaVergne TN
LVHW040735250326
834688LV00031B/308